W9-BTZ-914

JUN 8

SEEING DARKNESS

Also by *New York Times* bestselling author HEATHER GRAHAM

THE STALKING
THE SEEKERS
THE SUMMONING
A LETHAL LEGACY
ECHOES OF EVIL
PALE AS DEATH
FADE TO BLACK
A DANGEROUS GAME
WICKED DEEDS
DARK RITES
DYING BREATH
A PERFECT OBSESSION
DARKEST JOURNEY
DEADLY FATE
HAUNTED DESTINY
FLAWLESS
THE HIDDEN
THE FORGOTTEN
THE SILENCED
THE DEAD PLAY ON
THE BETRAYED
THE HEXED
THE CURSED
WAKING THE DEAD
THE NIGHT IS FOREVER
THE NIGHT IS ALIVE
THE NIGHT IS WATCHING
LET THE DEAD SLEEP
THE UNINVITED
THE UNSPOKEN
THE UNHOLY
THE UNSEEN

THE EVIL INSIDE
SACRED EVIL
HEART OF EVIL
PHANTOM EVIL
NIGHT OF THE VAMPIRES
THE KEEPERS
GHOST MOON
GHOST NIGHT
GHOST SHADOW
THE KILLING EDGE
NIGHT OF THE WOLVES
UNHALLOWED GROUND
DUST TO DUST
NIGHTWALKER
DEADLY GIFT
DEADLY HARVEST
DEADLY NIGHT
THE DEATH DEALER
THE LAST NOEL
THE SÉANCE
BLOOD RED
THE DEAD ROOM
KISS OF DARKNESS
THE VISION
THE ISLAND
GHOST WALK
KILLING KELLY
THE PRESENCE
DEAD ON THE DANCE FLOOR
PICTURE ME DEAD
HAUNTED

* * * * *

Look for Heather Graham's next novel,
DEADLY TOUCH,
available soon from MIRA.

HEATHER GRAHAM

SEEING DARKNESS

mira

mira™

Recycling programs
for this product may
not exist in your area.

ISBN-13: 978-0-7783-6094-0

Seeing Darkness

Copyright © 2020 by Heather Graham Pozzessere

All rights reserved. No part of this book may be used or reproduced in any manner whatsoever
without written permission except in the case of brief quotations embodied in critical articles
and reviews.

This is a work of fiction. Names, characters, places and incidents are either the product of the
author's imagination or are used fictitiously. Any resemblance to actual persons, living or dead,
businesses, companies, events or locales is entirely coincidental.

This edition published by arrangement with Harlequin Books S.A.

For questions and comments about the quality of this book, please contact us at
CustomerService@Harlequin.com.

Mira
22 Adelaide St. West, 40th Floor
Toronto, Ontario M5H 4E3, Canada
BookClubbish.com

Printed in U.S.A.

R0457035547

To Dr. Cuevas and Southwest Animal,
and for
Caitlin, Danielle and Sean.

Their compassion for all creatures is amazing,
and I'm so grateful to them for Ozzie, Nimh, Rocket and Z,
and the care they gave all my creatures
throughout many years!

SEEING DARKNESS

PROLOGUE

In his life, Jon had never heard anything as horrible or heart wrenching as the mother's cry when she first realized that her child had been taken.

It happened just off Essex Street, by the Charter Street Cemetery, or Old Burying Point. Just a block or so from the heavy pedestrian traffic near the Peabody Essex Museum and the hordes of tourists who enjoyed the unusual shops and restaurants in the heart of the city of Salem, Massachusetts. Some were coming and going from the wax museum; some were buying the herbs and whatnot that made Witch City so famous.

The tragic history of the 1692 witch trials, of course, made the city *infamous*.

Even at twelve, Jon knew the city's history, and he also knew there was a decent-size population in the city who were truly Wiccan. He didn't quite get it; he liked the earth well enough, but he didn't ascribe it any magical properties. His parents weren't Wiccan—they were Episcopalians—but they never disparaged the Wiccans.

Jon's father had told him, "What a man believes comes from

his heart, mind, and soul. And our great country is founded on freedom of religion—something we must thank our founding fathers for having assured us. The Puritans hanged Quakers as well as those they accused of witchcraft, sad affairs indeed. So, unless it causes pain or injury to others, we respect every man's belief."

Having grown up in Salem, Jon and his family tended to avoid the heavily touristed area. There were *normal* things to do in Salem as well. Even if his Little League team was called the Broomsticks.

Their coach was a newcomer to the city, with a slightly twisted sense of humor, in Jon's mind. But he liked his teammates. Jon was the pitcher, and a good one. And that year, as he approached his thirteenth birthday, he was becoming more appreciative of the fact that Amy Larson, a knockout blonde, liked to sit in the stands to cheer him on. They'd gone to their first dance together.

Jon had mentioned to his father that his coach was an atheist.

"And that's his right, too," his father had said.

The woman screaming nearby with such fear must be a tourist, Jon thought. He was only in Salem's historic center because his mom's cousin had come in from New York with friends, and they were showing them the sights. He was a good tour guide. He knew his city well; it was impossible to grow up in Salem without having its stories drummed into one's head.

But they weren't on his mind now.

The sound of the woman's scream erased all else except for compassion for anyone who could cry out in such pain. The sound seemed to rip through his gut. There had been several kidnappings in New England lately—two bodies had been discovered. Jon's parents had even discussed it with him so he could be on his guard. It was scary.

This woman probably hadn't been thinking it could happen to her—she'd have her daughter's hand the entire time they were in the city. But somehow, in the blink of an eye, someone had spirited her child away.

Jon understood, innately, there could be no agony greater in life than losing a child.

At first, he stood there, horrified with the others, as the woman screamed. Someone rushed off and found two police officers who happened to be walking the beat past the cemetery.

Jon wound up shoved back by the growing crowd, but he was tall for his age, almost five-ten already. He could clearly see the devastated mother, hysterical as she talked to the father. Police tried to calm her and figure out what had happened.

The family had been in the cemetery, the woman managed to tell them. Tracy was ten, old enough to read the gravestones and take a few steps away. She had been right there—and then she was gone.

While Jon stood in the back of the crowd, he heard a man say, "Now, one of you must see... Now, if you don't stop him now, he'll have her! Get to that van, block the road, don't let him drive away!"

He turned to look. There stood a man in traditional Puritan garb, from his black hat to his white socks and navy vest and breeches.

Jon stared at him. "If you know something, you have to tell the cops."

The man looked at him, his eyes widening. "You heard me?"

"Of course, I heard you. Tell the cops what you know!" Jon said impatiently. "Someone took a little girl—go help!"

The man shook his head. He strode toward Jon and took his shoulders.

Jon never knew if it was the feel—or the lack of feeling—

when the man seemed to touch him, or the sound of his voice, as raspy as the wind in a nor'easter... Or maybe it was just the chill that swept through his body.

But he suddenly knew the man facing him was a ghost.

He was a dead man. A dead man who hadn't walked the streets of Salem for hundreds of years.

"You tell the police," the man urged him. "Tell them you saw a man sweep the girl away and out on the street by the old house—do it now! You saw him dragging her to a white van with an ad for a dog-grooming business, and he'll get away with her if they don't act immediately!"

For a moment, Jon stood frozen.

The dead man couldn't shake him; his touch was like a breeze. But then it seemed that he did.

Jon burst into action. He forced his way through the crowd and over to a police officer.

At first it appeared that the cop didn't want to hear him or believe him. But another policeman said, "Sweet Jesus, Matt, let's get to that van. We got nothing else!"

"Aw, come on, the kid didn't see anything. No one saw anything. The little girl just ran away, she's hiding some-where, she's—"

Jon didn't wait for more. He leaped the wall of the cemetery and ran across the graveyard to the house and street behind. And there was the van, just as the ghost said. Jon catapulted himself toward the van when he realized the driver was just about to take off.

He caught hold of the rear door handle, wrenching hard just as the driver tried to veer into the street. His feet flew off the ground. He wouldn't let go, even though he felt a surge of terror.

By then, the cops had caught up. One of them jumped in front of the van. The driver didn't slow down and seemed as though he was about to bulldoze over them, but then a shot rang in the air.

Jon wrenched the door open. A little girl was lying on the floor of the van, unconscious.

Next to another girl. One who…

He closed his eyes; he'd never seen anything so horrible. She was decomposing. She looked like something that might have been a prop at a Halloween haunted house.

Except that she was real.

Jon fell away from the van. He wasn't needed anymore. Cops were swarming the van. More sirens rang out nearby; someone was calling an ambulance.

His own family surrounded him. "Oh my God, Jon!" his mother exclaimed. She wrapped him in a hug as though he were still a toddler.

In the following days, they let him know repeatedly that they were proud of him. They couldn't understand his reticence to talk to reporters, or even to accept thanks. He had surely saved a life.

But he had also seen the other girl. The one who hadn't been saved.

He was also embarrassed. He didn't want to be hailed as a hero. He wasn't. A dead man had come to him and told him what to do. The dead man was a hero, but it was hard for a dead man to accept any acclaim. And it was hard for Jon to accept what he'd seen.

Jon lay awake, night after night, wondering if he had really seen the man in Puritan clothes, if he'd been mistaken, if it had been an actor.

Years later, he again met the man who had helped him. The dead man.

By then, Jon was looking at sports scholarships to just about any college he might want to attend. And it wasn't anywhere near Essex Street, the cemetery, a museum, or the memorial. He had just spent a good day at Dead Horse Beach with friends, and was zipping up his backpack when he heard a voice.

An unmistakable voice.

"You'll be heading out soon, eh, son? Leaving this place."

Jon turned around slowly. He was dressed in the same Puritan garb, a harsh-looking man of about forty-five. Not harsh; maybe *weathered* was a better way to describe him.

"No," Jon said simply. "You're not... You're no Puritan. I'm not hearing a thou, or a thee. You're an actor, and why you chose to make me crazy—"

"I was a Puritan. I've been walking these streets for...well, a very long time," the man said. "And why I haunt you? Haunting matters sometimes. We saved a life that day. Be thankful for your gift. It's rare."

"What gift?"

"You see the dead."

Jon shook his head. "I've seen *you*. I don't see the dead. And whoever or whatever you are—"

"Obadiah Jones," the man said. "Feel free to look me up. Everyone remembers those who were hanged, and old Giles Corey, who was pressed to death. They forget how many were arrested—how many died in jail, how many were ruined for life, who went on to die, their bodies ravaged with disease and malnutrition from imprisonment. I died in prison, but I was never convicted, so I lie in holy ground. And I watch, and I do my best to see that such horrible injustice never comes to this place again."

Jon stood still. His friends were still out on the sand. He waved to them and forced a smile.

"This can't be real," he murmured.

"Open your heart and soul, my dear young fellow—open to the possibilities of this world. Use your talent. Use your *gift.* You have the rare ability to listen and see, and maybe not change the world, but maybe change the world for some."

"I…"

"You'll know what to do," the man said. He walked away, disappearing into the sun and sky.

It couldn't be real.

But as Jon watched him go, he knew that the man—apparition, ghost, whatever—had certainly changed *one* life forever.

Jon's own.

CHAPTER ONE

Kylie Connelly could feel it.

First, the terror.

Then the knife, slicing into her flesh, slamming into her bone. It was agony. As the blade rose and fell, again and again, she began to feel a strange numbness, the unbearable pain lessening, fading, the light before her eyes...

But her mind fought the vision. She couldn't remember exactly where she was, what she was doing, how she was seeing this...

She had to see and feel something else: the past, the future, anything. This place, her friends, the laughter that had come before.

As if in a little bubble, she could see the immediate past; her friend, Corrine Rossello, third up with the hypnotist for their bizarre bachelorette party. Like a small screen before her eyes, she could again envision what she'd seen. Corrine, happy as a lark. Under hypnosis and enjoying her beautiful vision.

"I'm walking... I'm walking along, and the day is bright. I'm in a park... I can feel my dress, I believe it's satin, and it makes a delicate little swishing sound when I move. And in front of me... I see a carriage," Corrine said in the bubble of Kylie's memory. "It's a beautiful carriage, and there's a man who steps from it, but not before he's assisted by a footman in a truly regal costume. And then...he has his hand stretched out to me. He's so good-looking, gorgeous actually, and he's waiting for me. I start to hurry... A maid is following me, she's my maid, but we're very good friends, and she's happy!"

Corrine was a beautiful young woman with raven-dark hair, broad cheeks and deep brown eyes. She looked like she was in rapture, lying on the hypnotist's couch, her head and shoulders on a bed of pillows...

No. Kylie knew that *she* was now the one lying on the couch.

But the bubble of the memory fell back into place. Corrine's eyes were closed; she had consumed her tea—something that helped with regression, or so the hypnotist had told them—and she was smiling as she recalled her former life.

"Yes. You're making us see you," declared the hypnotist, Dr. Sayers. "You, as you were. I believe it's Hyde Park. And you are going to the man you love. Your husband, I believe, and he's...he's a duke!"

Kylie had to keep seeing this recent past, Corrine's turn on the couch, with the hypnotist. It was something she could cling to as she fought against...

The knife.

No! Something inside her screamed, fought the new images that were not the past, but now.

Fight it, fight it, fight it!

Kylie saw the little bubble-movie of the recent past again. Sighs and murmurs of amazement and pleasure went around the little group who had come to Dr. Sayers, a psychologist/hypnotist who specialized in past-life regression. Her friends were enchanted.

But Kylie couldn't help but think, *What a pile of...*

Yet, she had agreed to come. Her friends were dear to her, and Corrine was the bride-to-be, and this—regression to past lives—was what she had wanted to do that day.

So Kylie had smiled the whole way. They were in Salem, a haunt they had all visited multiple times in the past, for parties, for history, the Peabody Essex Museum, fun ghost tours, even shopping.

They were all from Massachusetts and had met at Harvard. None of them had come from money; they had worked hard for their scholarships and had kept jobs to pay their way through their school years as well. That had made their little jaunts extra special.

They had come here, close to all their homes, so many times. They all loved the city. They took a ghost tour every time but avoided the obvious tourist traps. They didn't usually come for tea-leaf or palm or tarot readings. The town, with its incredibly sad past, was a natural backdrop for every manner of Wiccan, New Ager, or occultist. They had fun with it. And Salem was, at a certain time of the year, Halloween heaven.

When they'd started out that morning—she and Corrine Rossello, Nancy Ryman, and Jenny Auger—Kylie had assured them that she didn't believe in past-life regression. However, Corrine had already made the appointments, and this little weekend together was Corrinne's concept of a bridal party or shower—she had no interest in dance clubs and strippers. She just wanted their group to do something special together; this was her version of a bachelorette weekend.

The knife.

He'd caught hold of her and spun her around. Despite her hatred for him, she wanted to live. She begged, she pleaded, she cried. She'd have done anything, said anything, to stop him. And yet she knew, even as he held her there, that there was no chance, that the knife would fall, that she would look into the hatred in his dark eyes as he brought that blade down, ripping into her flesh again and again, she knew that he would want her to suffer even past death...

Back to the bubble. Back to the immediate past.

Kylie fought to remember where she was. Her mind was in a strange place, switching between screens, the memory of the hypnotist's office, and the memory of the knife in the alley...

She struggled hard to stop it, not to see the image of the knife, the pain and the numbness, the look in the eyes of her murderer.

"It will be new for us! I hear it's fun, and you're going to love it!" Corrine had assured her, when she had first suggested it on the drive up.

Kylie had smiled through it all. She hadn't loved it, but she did love her friend, and this was what Corrine wanted. She had been last to go under with the hypnotist; Jenny discovered she had been a Norse princess, and Nancy had ruled a pirate ship until she'd married a legitimate sea captain and lived happily on a Caribbean island.

Apparently, none of the three had been poor, nor maids or servants of any kind—or lived lives of any hardship or remarkable trauma.

Or died beneath the fury of a razor-honed blade, cutting flesh and blood and bone.

"Oh, my God!" Corrine had said, her eyes closed. She almost sat up, in love with the vision in her mind. "It's Derrick—it's my Derrick! He was a duke in his previous life, and now I'm running to him, and he sweeps me up and..."

Corrine's voice faded. She lay back, exhausted—and smiling. Of course, she was smiling; she was about to marry Derrick.

A great guy, solid, but rather staid. He was working for an attorney as he made his way through law school. He was the kind of guy to give Corrine the life she wanted, with a picket fence, two-point-five children, and a cat and dog in the yard. They would settle in a suburb outside either New York City or Boston. Kylie knew that because they had all told one another their dreams often enough.

Dr. Sayers had smiled, saying, "Corrine, I'm bringing you back now. I will count slowly to ten, snap my fingers…and you will wake up."

He was somewhere between thirty and thirty-five, Kylie thought. Neatly dressed in a blue pin-striped suit, with sleek sandy hair combed back and a surprisingly…*mundane* look about him. The lights in his office were kept low, but he'd had no problem with all of them sitting in for each other's "regressions."

The tea, Kylie thought. *He had something in the tea. But that can't be legal, can it?* As the hypnotist counted, Kylie couldn't help but think, *Are they all really falling for this? Seriously?*

Her friends were all professional women; they had met as freshman at Harvard, for goodness sake! Corrine was the regional manager of an incredibly popular restaurant chain. Nancy was working on Wall Street, and Jenny was head of accounting for a small group of boutique hotels. Kylie had just been hired away from the Met to manage all the newly opened Trelawny House, a museum that featured New York's Colonial period through the present—including a historic-themed tavern.

"Ten," Dr. Sayers said, and snapped his fingers.

Corrine's eyes flew open and she stared around at the others. "That was amazing! I was there—that was me! Oh, I did live before, and Derrick and I… We were in love over and over again. It's so wonderfully right!" She jumped up and caught Kylie's hand. "Your turn, Kylie!"

And then Kylie was on the couch, and Dr. Sayers was talking to her, telling her she would never do anything that she wouldn't do naturally, that she would search back into the hidden recesses of her mind and memory.

As she slipped under, she thought, *I didn't even drink the tea.*

But then she was somewhere else.

She was *someone* else.

The bubble was gone; she'd lost the fight to escape whatever was happening to her. To the *her* she had become.

"I'm by the graveyard… It's dark…and he has me…"

Kylie couldn't believe the words coming out of her mouth, but she could see herself moving down the dirt road by the forgotten graveyard just outside the city. She shouldn't have come this way—the road was isolated.

A cat screeched.

She knew she had made a mistake, the worst mistake of her life, the mistake that would bring about her death.

Someone was coming after her.

And she knew it was him.

When she turned and saw him, she screamed, but no one heard…

He dragged her into the cemetery surrounding the small church. She saw the old gravestones around them as he jerked her along by her hair.

For a moment, one of those little bubbles of reality broke through. *Where the hell am I?* Kylie wondered.

But she knew where she was. Not in the center of Salem, not where the tourists went.

The knife! Oh, God, ripping through her flesh, making that terrible noise…

They'd warned her he would kill her. And he was doing it. She could feel the numbness setting back in, a terrible cold, a horrific sense of loss…

"Ten. Wake up, Kylie."

Her eyes flew open. They were all there—Corrine, Jenny, Nancy, and Dr. Sayers. They were staring at her with concern.

"Kylie, you scared us—you were screaming and scream-ing, as if you were being skinned alive!" Corrine said, her eyes wide, her face contorted with concern.

"I don't think she met a prince or a duke or anything," Jenny muttered, hazel eyes narrowed. Tall and slim, she had long sandy hair, a dry sense of humor, and often used sarcasm as a method of defense.

But despite her dry words, she appeared as concerned as the others.

"Miss Connelly, are you all right?" Dr. Sayers asked ner-vously.

Of course he was nervous. People came to him to find out they had been princesses or some kind of royalty or, at the least, had been very influential in some imaginary past life.

They didn't come to feel knives thrusting into their bodies.

Kylie made an effort to smile. She didn't know what the hell had happened, but she tried to touch her body surrep-titiously, to make sure she wasn't bleeding. It had all been too real: the feel of the knife; the terror, the sheer horror of knowing she was being brutally murdered.

"I'm fine, I'm fine," she said, laughing desperately to shake the feeling that had come over her. "Sir, you're very good," she told Dr. Sayers to ease his fear. After all, he had made the bride-to-be very happy. "It's just like I was there," she said.

"And?" Corrine asked nervously.

When Kylie hesitated, Nancy, a petite redhead, spoke up, "You were screaming, crying for help…begging."

"Well, sadly, I guess my last life wasn't so good," Kylie said lightly. "I apparently had something going with a gorgeous monster of a man—and he killed me."

"That's awful. I'm so sorry," Corrine said with distress. "This was all my fault."

"No one's fault—a truly unique experience!" Kylie said quickly. This was supposed to be a wonderful weekend. Corrine wanted to go to Salem and do some of the old things that had helped them escape the stress of final exams, like staying at their favorite inn and strolling through the funky shops—so many of them witchcraft themed, some owned by true believers and some by smart capitalists. And that night, they would have drinks and dinner at their favorite witch-themed restaurant on Essex, the Cauldron. A packed itinerary.

Which gave Kylie an out now.

She offered Dr. Sayers her most effervescent smile. "That was great—and reminded me we've still got a lot to get done tonight. Guys, I'm so sorry if I freaked you all out! But it was really amazing. Truly. So..." She paused, looking at her threesome of concerned friends. "Onward?"

She wasn't seeing any visions and she wasn't feeling the agony of the knife, but she was anxious to move and go—anywhere. Out of the doctor's office.

And forget.

"We have to take care of the bill," Nancy said quietly.

"Looked after it with the receptionist when we got here," Kylie said, never so happy she had chosen to take care of a bill—and that she had done it discreetly ahead of time.

Corrine protested, but the rest of them argued that this was her special weekend, and they wouldn't hear of her paying for anything. But Nancy and Jenny turned on Kylie—she shouldn't have paid the whole thing.

"You guys get dinner," she said breezily, standing and collecting her purse and jacket.

Assuring Dr. Sayers once again she was all right, Kylie managed to herd the others out to the street. Slowly, she got them all moving through shop after shop, looking at charming local art and handmade jewelry, along with the T-shirts, bumper stickers, incense, and souvenirs that could be found just about anywhere in the city.

At last, they headed to the Cauldron.

They ordered their first round at the bar. One of the bartenders was named Matt, and he was friendly, tall, dark, and charming. His partner, Cindy, was just as cute and perky. Eventually, as a dinner table cleared, they settled into one of the restaurant's upholstered booths.

"You know, it was Laurie Cabot who made it all what it is today," Nancy said, looking back at a painting of a typical evil witch—a crone in a black hat and cape, stirring a cauldron—at the entrance to the restaurant. "In the 1970s, Governor Dukakis gave her the title Official Witch of Salem. And, of course, the practice of Wicca has nothing to do with the devil-worshipping, dancing-naked-in-the-moonlight witchcraft those poor people were accused of. I mean, I remember as a kid…it was always so sobering. How horrible to imagine people were convicted on *spectral* evidence!"

The four of them knew all the theories regarding the 1692 trials. Nancy was from Marblehead, just a stone's throw from Salem and, at one time, an area caught up in the witchcraft hysteria as well. Her family was all but entrenched here. Her mother belonged to the Daughters of the American Revolution and wanted Nancy to belong as well.

Jenny's parents had come from Germany as children but settled north of Boston, in Lynn. Corrine had been born and raised right in Boston, and for Kylie, it had been Swampscott—a tiny place just outside of Salem.

"Well, I, for one, do not agree with the idea about the mold in the wheat in the least," Jenny said. "Everyone in the area would have eaten the same wheat."

"Just the art of suggestion," Kylie countered. "I mean, seriously, there were a zillion property disputes going on at the time. And kids were bored out of their skulls. It was dark as all hell at night, and the girls had Tituba telling them all kinds of tales. Mix that with the fact that you got into trouble for just about anything, you were afraid of native attacks, the woods were terrifying—and you could hear authority figures talk-ing about their problems with their neighbors. Not to men-tion the fact that in Europe—"

"Hey," Corrine said, "you weren't being attacked as a witch back in the seventeenth century, were you, Kylie?"

Kylie shook her head.

"It drives me crazy when people depict them as being burned!" Nancy said. "No witches were burned here in America—they all went to the gallows."

"Salem has a long history, and not all to do with the Witch Trials of 1692," Kylie reminded them.

Just then, a tall man with shaggy blond hair walked over. "Hey, ladies. Just stopping by to say hello and welcome to Salem. I'm Carl Fisher. I lead ghost tours. I start out just down the street in about an hour. I hope you'll join me. I mean, I really hope you'll join me."

"Maybe tomorrow night," Corrine said politely.

Carl looked them all over and smiled. "That'll be nice. Oh, if you want some lowdown on the town, I come back here after. I'd love to help you out."

"I'm from Marblehead," Nancy said, staring at him. "And we've all been here many, many times. But thank you."

"We're all from the great Commonwealth of Massachu-setts," Jenny added.

He was cute and friendly and obviously interested in them. Kylie knew her friends were trying not to be rude. But Cor-rine was getting married, Nancy was in a serious relationship, Jenny had just gotten out of a relationship and wasn't ready for even a rebound. And Kylie had been working hours and hours per day, getting up to speed at her new job. She was too busy to date. Then again, she hadn't been interested in the dating scene for a while now.

Carl looked at them all hopefully for a moment longer.

"Girls' weekend," Kylie told him, wincing slightly. She

hoped her tone and body language were right—they thought
he was fine, they just weren't ready to welcome a stranger
into their evening. "Corrine here is going to be married."

"Ah, well. Congratulations," he told Corrine, who smiled
and nodded her thanks. "But I do give an amazing ghost
tour—chock-full of history. Which you guys probably already
know. But I tell it well, if you should change your mind or
maybe tomorrow night or whenever."

"We love ghost tours. And we will look for you tomorrow
night," Jenny assured him.

"Great. See you then," he told them, and moved on. He
headed back to the bar, where, obviously, the bartender and
several regulars seemed to know him.

"Slow to take a hint," Corrine murmured.

"Hey, he's cute," Jenny protested. "You're getting married.
That's not on the horizon for the rest of us yet."

"Ouch. And, hey! Nancy and Scott have been together a
long time now," Kylie said.

"Doesn't mean I don't appreciate a handsome man," Nancy
said, grinning. "Besides, he was looking at you, Kylie."

She tried to smile; she still felt odd. She'd been trying to
shake what had happened during her "regression" all afternoon.

"She's right. He is cute, and he was definitely into you,
Kylie," Corrine said.

"He was into all of us," Kylie said. "We're women, and
we're young. Anyway, we're here to celebrate our last time
together as a foursome of single women. We're here for Corrine to go crazy as a bride-to-be. So what if her crazy is a little
tame. Past-life regression, shopping—museums! And dinner.
And we're all into it." She grinned at Corrine.

"You guys are the best," Corrine told them. "Thank you
for doing that regression thing. But…oh, Kylie. I'm still so
sorry that yours was awful. Mine…my life under hypnosis

was truly spectacular. I could feel the breeze and sunshine, and I knew I was hurrying to meet my love! But, Kylie, we were worried. Dr. Sayers tried to get you out—he counted and snapped his fingers, because you were literally screaming. It was really scary."

Kylie waved a dismissive hand. She just wanted to forget. "So what is everyone going to order?" she asked, turning to the menu.

As the others discussed what looked most delicious, Kylie fell silent, her attention elsewhere. She stared at one of the wide-screen televisions over the bar. The news was on, and something inside her seemed to freeze.

He was on the news.

The man she had seen under hypnosis.

The man viciously dragging her into the graveyard, the man who had shoved the knife into her, time and time again.

Kylie stood, heedless of the looks from her friends. She approached the bar.

On the television, the man was nicely dressed in a designer suit. His hair was conservatively cut and framed his face—a handsome face, lean, with broad cheekbones and a square chin.

Kylie couldn't hear the sound, but the words were close-captioned at the bottom of the screen.

"I will serve Massachusetts—and this country—with my full heart, soul, and energy, all the power within me, if elected. I know what lies in the heart of my people, I know my people. I make a point of knowing my people. I like nothing more than taking to the streets to talk about the economy, gun control, foreign relations—anything and everything that matters, and we need to know what matters most to all of us. I am a family man. My wife and I know the trials and tribulations of raising children, and believe me, we are dedicated to improving our schools. Our schools must be safe."

Kylie quit reading and simply stared at him.

"Kylie?" Matt, the charming bartender, said curiously.

She barely heard him speak.

She knew the face on the screen too damned well. She had seen how he looked when he was furious and determined; she had seen the pleasure he had taken in stabbing her over and over again.

Corrine was behind her, truly concerned again. "Kylie, what..."

Kylie shouldn't say anything—she knew it. She was just so confused and unnerved. She turned to Corrine. "That's him. That's the man with the knife. The man who was... murdering me... I saw his face. I knew him. Corrine, I saw him so clearly!"

"Him?" Corrine said. "Girl, where have you been? That's Michael Westerly. He was a state senator. He's campaigning to be a United States senator for Massachusetts."

Kylie wanted to laugh. She wanted to say something like, *Of course it can't be him, then*, and go back to their table and talk with her friends and make Corrine happy.

She couldn't speak.

"That's it," Corrine said. "You've seen his picture—you've seen him campaigning. And somehow, under hypnosis, you transferred that into...whatever it was you saw. Hey, come on. He's even your political party!" Corrine tried to joke.

Kylie felt weak; the sense of cold, of blood draining from her...of *death* seemed to be slipping over her again.

"No! I saw him," she said urgently. "He's a murderer! He killed me...with the knife..."

Corrine and the bartenders stared at her as if they needed to rush her to the nearest psych ward.

Why couldn't she keep her mouth shut? Why couldn't she have been hypnotized to believe she had been a Regency

heiress at the very least? Anything other than a victim, brutally stabbed to death.

And now, just seeing the man and his easy smile, his assurance…the sensation was horrible. She fought it desperately.

No good.

She was going to fall, slip down to the floor, into pure
black oblivion.

Someone took hold of her.

She turned; it was a man. When he touched her, her fear
increased at first. It was him… Michael Westerly, the man
who had murdered her!

But it wasn't. It was someone else entirely, someone she'd
never seen before. Tall, strong in his hold, and somehow
fierce. He had ice-blue eyes and dark hair.

Something about him both scared and somehow assured
her, even as he kept her from falling. He was good-looking,
not quite as classic in his looks as the would-be senator. His
jawline was rock hard and his look more rugged. His arms
were powerful, as if he were half made of metal beneath the
fabric of his dark suit.

She didn't like the way he was looking at her.

He eased her onto one of the bar stools.

"Oh my gosh, thank you," Corrine said for her.

Kylie still couldn't speak. Those icy eyes of his seemed to
be staring into her, into the place where she had been that
day, somewhere in her soul, in a strange reality.

"Murdered?" he said. "You appear to be alive and well to
me, but what's this about murder?"

Corrine laughed nervously. "We did 'regressions' today and
saw our past lives. It's all just silly. But seriously, thank you.
Kylie could have gotten hurt. She was a little freaked out. You
know, the rest of us were all cool princesses or whatever, and
Kylie was some poor woman who got murdered."

The man wasn't looking at Corrine. Those ice-blue eyes of his were still on Kylie.

"There was a murder today," he said quietly. "Out in the old St. Francis graveyard, between here and the Rebecca Nurse Homestead. A young woman was found stabbed to death. Knife went into her twenty times."

As if on cue, the news story on the TV switched. Just in— there had been a murder. Annie Hampton, twenty-four, of Peabody, had been found just an hour ago, brutally stabbed and left among the gravestones.

Fear settled in, and darkness clouded over the world.

Kylie passed out cold.

CHAPTER TWO

The four young women were an intriguing group.

They'd been deeply distraught when Jon Dickson had produced his identification and asked to speak with them. He had done so in a way that suggested—just *suggested*—that they had no choice.

The woman who had so drawn his attention was still in his arms as he juggled his ID, and then everyone was scurrying about, trying to determine if 911 needed to be called or if she had imbibed a little too much of the Cauldron's signature drink, aptly named the Witch's Brew.

She began to come to almost immediately. Her eyes opened—a mix of green and something like gold—and landed on him. Alarmed and startled, she nearly landed a good punch on his face, but he caught her arm in time.

He tried to reassure her as the crowd looked on. His badge indicated he was a *very* special agent with the government, and he heard people beginning to wonder aloud about what was going on.

So there he was, holding a stranger who'd made a small

scene about a recent murder, being stared at by her wary friends.

This case meant too much to ignore any possible leads.

He was already angry with himself. He'd come with the deepest hope he could prevent a murder. But a murder had taken place nonetheless.

As soon as he was able, Jon ushered the young women out of the bar and restaurant—drawing only a little more attention than they already had. The women were still flustered enough by their friend fainting and his Federal ID that they came along without resistance.

Jon had taken office space right on Essex Street—not that he wasn't welcome at the police precinct; he was set up there as well. And he could always call on Detective Ben Miller, his local contact—and friend from the time they'd been five or six and starting out in kindergarten. But Jon had known he'd need his own place, and a shop had been empty, the windows blackened, and it had seemed perfect—right in the middle of town, perfect to watch the comings and goings around him.

"This is harassment," insisted the woman who had identified herself as Corrine. "I'll have you know we all went to Harvard!"

"And her fiancé studied law," muttered one of her friends—Nancy, he thought.

"But still, I mean, you have to tell us what's going on," said the third woman—Jenny?

"I need your help," he said flatly.

He hadn't realized he'd taken the hand of the fourth young woman—Kylie Connelly, now perfectly fine on her own—to lead her down the street until she suddenly balked, trying to jerk away from him.

He stopped short, staring at her.

"I don't know what kind of government agency you're really with—or if that's a badge you bought in a souvenir shop," she told him. She stood very straight, and in her defiance, she reminded him of an Amazonian warrior—ready to go to battle for all that was right and just. She was about five-eight, with a headful of rich, chestnut hair that seemed to naturally curl around her shoulders and beautifully frame her face.

All four of the young women were attractive. Maybe they were just of an age to be attractive, somewhere between twenty-five and thirty, professional, certainly, and at ease with themselves and the world. Confidence could be an attractive asset.

They were obviously close friends as well, and were quick to rush to one another's defense, as siblings and best friends were prone to do.

He didn't want to scare them more than necessary, but he'd been hunting a serial killer for almost a year—hopping state lines as if those lines were a blueprint for getting away with murder.

Which was why, of course, the FBI had gotten involved.

And since the first victim, Deanna Clark of Fredericksburg, Virginia, had been seen by her sister hours after her death, begging for help, the Krewe of Hunters had been called in. Jon was here, following in the wake of that murder—and the murders of Willow Cannon of New Haven, Connecticut, and Cecily Bryant of Warwick, Rhode Island.

Jackson Crow, field director of Jon's unit, had called him in as a liaison after the first murder. He'd been hoping to get a step ahead of the killer by coming to Salem.

He'd failed.

He'd seen the latest victim, the young woman an odd splash of color in her cheerfully patterned dress against the gray tombstones and the haze of the day that had seemed to settle over the area—blending with the tombstones and the jagged rock that surrounded the place. Yes, her dress had provided color, as had her blood, spilled upon the stones and the ground.

He'd seen her dead; he'd been too late, a step behind.

No, in truth, dozens of steps behind, and if he didn't discover the truth...

They'd find more bodies among the gravestones.

Maybe that was why he was grasping at straws, seeking any shred of information that might help.

He decided that the truth was going to serve best with this group of women. The truth—more or less—and nothing but the truth—more or less.

"It's a real badge," he said. "I'm with a special unit of the FBI. You're welcome to check my credentials with my superior. I'm on the heels of a murderer. And you seem to know a great deal about a murder that was just committed. The news coverage you saw was the first out. The body was discovered just about two hours ago."

Kylie shook her head, her defiance and assurance slipping.

"We know nothing about it," she said, her voice husky and pained. "I saw the newscast. And it was horrible, and—"

"And I heard you clearly. You identified Michael Westerly as a murderer. You mentioned a knife. What I want to know is what would make you say that. What do you know about this murder?" Jon demanded.

The others gathered around Kylie Connelly as if they were a trio of nuns protecting an abandoned infant.

But she was having none of that. She maintained her pose of utmost dignity, glaring at him with distain. "I know nothing about a murder. Really," she said. "My friends and I have been right here, in the heart of Salem, all day long."

"We can prove it," Corrine said.

"Corrine is getting married," Nancy informed him. "This is her bachelorette weekend."

"She isn't into strippers," Jenny explained. She glanced

over at her friend. "Although, maybe in retrospect, Corrine, it might have turned out a heck of a lot easier if you'd been into the concept of a few naked bodies."

"Jenny!" Nancy snapped.

"Look, I'm sorry to cause any distress," Jon began, "but this is very serious, and horrible and tragic. Will you please just come with me to the office for a few minutes? We can sit down and clarify all this."

Kylie started walking again, in the direction he had been leading them. Even if she didn't know where they were going. For a moment, Jon was as still as her friends, who were looking at one another in confusion.

He turned and took the lead again, no longer attempting to take her hand. Everyone followed.

He produced a key to the ground-floor space he'd taken on Essex Street. Soon enough, it would be rented out to another gift shop, but for the moment, it was his space.

He opened the door. Kylie Connelly walked in, still ramrod straight and indignant.

Her friends balked.

"How do we know *you're* not an insane murderer?" Corrine demanded. "The windows here are all covered. And there's a sign that says Lola's Little Lollipop Shop, Coming Soon!"

"There are four of you," Jon said simply. "I've shown you my identification. If you'll just look inside, you'll see you're fine. The street is filled with Friday night tourists, and—"

Kylie popped her head back out of his office. "Hey, just come in. Let's get this over with."

The others filed in. He followed behind them.

The room was set up sparsely; he had a desk with his computer, several folding chairs, fridge and microwave, and a file cabinet filled with hard copies for the case. Against the wall was the air mattress he'd been using since he arrived two days ago. His duffel bag of clothing sat on the floor.

The last clue—found near the body of Cecily Bryant, in a historic cemetery on the border of Rhode Island and Massachusetts near Fall River—had led him here. It remained in an evidence bag at Krewe headquarters in northern Virginia.

Their *only* clue.

He was glad the photos from the earlier crime scenes remained in his desk in an envelope.

He indicated the chairs in front of the desk. The four young women perched nervously. He took his position behind the desk—an automatic position of authority, or so they had claimed in one of his academy classes.

"As you saw on the news, a young woman named Annie Hampton was found in the old St. Francis graveyard, just about two miles from here. I don't believe this is the killer's first murder. We've been tracking a man up the coast from Virginia. Four known murders to date now with Annie, all young women, all killed in historic graveyards. Three unsolved murders from previous years might have been the work of this same killer, but they weren't grouped together at the time because they took place almost a year apart from each other.

"If it's the same killer, they've escalated at a frightening pace. It's my deepest regret we haven't caught this man yet. We have questioned hundreds of people, investigated family disputes, work disputes, random drifters, all to no avail. If we just had something… That young woman shouldn't have died today. We are desperate to catch this monster before anyone else is killed, so I beg you, tell me anything at all you know." He stared hard at Kylie.

She met his gaze fiercely, and then sighed and shook her head.

"I don't know anything about the murder," she said. "Seriously. We have been here—within six blocks of where we are right now—all day. We came in this morning, checked into the hotel, had lunch, and then went to our appointments with Dr. Sayers." She seemed to wince. "He's a psychologist and hypnotist known for his past-life regressions. It's Salem, right? Then we shopped, mostly right there on Essex Street. In absolute truth, there is nothing we can tell you that would help to solve a murder. Any of us would help if we could. What you're saying is horrible. Don't you think we'd help if we thought we could give you any information that would bring in someone who was doing something so horrible?"

Jon leaned forward. "When the image of Michael Westerly came on the screen, you identified him as the murderer."

The other girls were silent. Uneasy. They glanced over at Kylie, letting her do the talking.

"Corrine suggested I had seen his face somewhere before. Listen, I'm not sure I even believe in past-life regression. Everyone gets to be a princess. Except me," she murmured, sounding a little bitter. "I was hypnotized. Trust me, I'll never be hypnotized again. I pictured something awful."

He kept eye contact with her. "Tell me, please, what did you see?"

She shook her head, as if what he was suggesting was impossible. The she sighed. "All right, I saw him—that man—Michael Westerly. And he was…killing me." She hesitated. "Stabbing me to death."

She paused for a moment; Jon could see she was remembering every brutal second of the attack. Whatever the experience had been, the terror of it had been real for her.

"But," she continued, "I'm telling you, we were here. All day long. Whatever I saw was just… I don't know…suggestion. Something evoked by his words or his tone, maybe. Not real. Obviously. I'm here. I'm alive and well. And you can check with Dr. Sayers. I doubt if he's still in his office, but it's just around the corner."

"What happened, though, in this imaginary scene? Step by step," Jon encouraged.

She looked at him as if he was asking something entirely ridiculous of her. "I was walking—"

"Walking where?"

She inhaled and seemed to grit her teeth before going on. "By a cemetery. Not the Old Burying Point here in the historic district, or even the Howard Street Cemetery. But it was very similar to those. The markers were from the 1600s and up. Pretty place. Old trees growing through some of the old stones, many weathered with no words left... Revolutionary soldiers, Civil War soldiers... Death's-heads on some markers, a few newer ones...some angels and cherubs. Overgrown. A little sad, really, and by a church. I wouldn't know which cemetery since there are at least thirty in the area that are so old... Salem is old."

"But it had a little square-shaped church?"

She nodded uncomfortably.

"The little box church—deconsecrated—now a tiny museum that sits between here and the Rebecca Nurse Homestead?" he asked. "If you've been here often and traveled more than the usual tourist treks, you might know the church and old graveyard."

She looked pained.

"Think about it," he pressed softly.

"Of course, she knows it," Jenny burst out. "We're all *from* Massachusetts, we went to *Harvard*. Kylie even spent a summer working at one of the museums, playing Bridget Bishop for their interactive program. Yes, we all know the area. Look, we're not a pack of silly girls out trying to cause a ruckus. We went to—"

"Harvard, yes, I got that," Jon told her. "I have absorbed that from the many times you've shared it with me. I'm not implying you're silly in any way. I don't know how this could be, but…" He broke off, frustrated.

The young women were all from Massachusetts. He could beat that; he'd been born and raised right here in Salem, and he still had friends and family here.

The first call to the Krewe's office had been when Deanna Clark had been found. The body had lain in a cemetery outside Richmond, an hour and a half drive for the Krewe. Her sister had told the police that Deanna's ghost had come to her, which had prompted one police officer who had heard rumors about a special FBI unit to reach out.

While they'd been asked for help and advice, the lead in the case had remained in the hands of the local police.

Then they'd been alerted about a similar murder on the outskirts of New Haven, Connecticut. Willow Cannon's body had been in the morgue by the time he arrived, and the local police had been handling the case as well, allowing for FBI assistance.

Then Angela Hawkins—Jackson's wife, and the agent in charge of deciding which cases should be handed to the Krewe and which ones would best be left to local authorities or the main offices of the Bureau—had discovered that a year earlier a woman had been found murdered in a similar fashion in Macon, Georgia. The year before that, one had been left in a small family graveyard near Raleigh, North Carolina. And a little more than a year before that, a slightly different scenario—a victim had been found *near* a graveyard in St. Augustine, Florida.

The geographical differences and the time gaps might have suggested different killers, but Angela had a theory that their killer had started out slowly. Perhaps honing his ability to kill and disappear, or perhaps discovering his need to kill had gripped him ever more tightly.

When the third victim in the latest rash of murders had

been found in Rhode Island, the case had fallen under Federal jurisdiction. Jon never forgot any of the victims—he had studied each of them.

Deanna Clark was the first. Tragically, her death might have gone unnoticed if it hadn't been for the dogged determination of a second cousin to find the truth; Deanna had been lost to most of her family for a long time. A musician, she had stumbled upon heroin along the way, and then prostitution, and her murder had been chalked up to a very bad trip—surely some other junkie had committed the deed.

He had seen pictures of her in life, and he had heard her recordings. Whatever need for alcohol and drugs had taken control, she had once possessed a beautiful smile. She'd been kind to children, and she'd been known to rescue abandoned pets. He'd quickly become determined to find justice for her, and had meant to search around Richmond until he found the truth.

Then, Willow Cannon had been found outside of New Haven. Her history had been similar. In Willow's case, she had fallen in love and followed the object of her desire to Connecticut. He, however, found love elsewhere. Willow then fell into the vices far too easy to embrace, especially for the down-and-out, in certain areas of New Haven. She'd had a record; petty theft. She'd started off young and sweet and trusting…and wound up with twenty-one stab wounds.

Thankfully, a local detective had resolved that her death would not go into the cold-case files. Even now, he was still working the case, keeping in touch with Jon, sharing info, letting him know any little step forward—and every frustration as well. That was all right.

Then there was Cecily Bryant, a student at a small college in Rhode Island, young and naive—and tripping into the excesses available in a college town.

She had been killed in an abandoned cemetery just at the

border of Rhode Island and Massachusetts—and that was where they had found their first real lead: a matchbox underneath the body.

A matchbox that advertised the Cauldron, in downtown Salem.

So, Jon had come here to set up his office just yesterday, with the help of Jackson Crow, who'd worked through all the red tape and arranged for governmental rental of the shop. Then Jackson had hopped on a flight back to the main offices.

But to Jon's dismay, he still hadn't acted quickly enough, or with enough knowledge, to stop the murder of Annie Hampton. He was willing to accept any help in apprehending the murderer—no matter how bizarre it might seem to others. He had long ago discovered many things in the world were not apparent to everyone.

If Kylie Connolly had somehow seen this murder, he had to know everything she knew.

He had seen Annie Hampton when she'd been found in the old churchyard. He had seen her bright colors against the gray of the stones and the graves and the sky. And he'd seen her blood.

She had been found by a tourist wanting to do a stone rubbing of the grave of a soldier killed at Yorktown. She'd hysterically called police. Jon's old friend, Detective Ben Miller, had been called, and Ben had called Jon right away. The two of them had held a quick meeting when Jon first arrived.

"You really think he's going to strike here next because of a matchbox advertising a restaurant?" Ben had asked.

"Yes," Jon said.

Sadly, he'd been proven right, and tragically, he'd been proven right with a terrible speed.

Jon kept his gaze steady on Kylie. "I am not seeing anything foolish or silly in any of this. I need to know what you know."

"You can't seriously think Kylie channeled a murder!" Jenny said.

"I don't know what I think," he said, leaning forward on the desk and looking at each of them one by one. "I know a woman is dead, and Miss Connelly saw the image of Michael Westerly on a TV and said he'd killed her. She'd seen it."

"Obviously not true! I am here," Kylie announced. "I'm right here."

"But you know something."

Kylie stood. "All right." She took a deep breath and started pacing. She crossed the narrow room and back before she went on. "Under hypnosis, I felt that I was walking by a graveyard and a church, and I knew the church wasn't open. Then, he was there—and he dragged me into the cemetery. I could feel the stone scratching my legs as we went over the wall. I was crying and begging and screaming and it didn't mean a thing. He was enraged, but almost methodical. Then he pulled out a knife. He stabbed me and stabbed me. I could feel it. The man I saw was Michael Westerly."

She paused. "It's all about the power of suggestion. I'm sure I've seen his picture before. Maybe I don't like something he's done as a politician, and while I didn't recognize him in my regression dream, I might have held his image in my subconscious. I have no idea. I majored in history and minored in hospitality, not psychology. So I don't really know what that experience was all about. But it was just a weird bit of fun. Now, if you'll excuse us, we're here on a special weekend to celebrate Corrine's upcoming wedding, and we'd very much like to make it a nice occasion for her. If there's nothing else we can do for you, please, you'll understand we have to go."

Corrine, Nancy, and Jenny stood as well. He rose.

He was about to thank them for their time—and to ask them to contact him if they thought of anything else—when

Nancy snapped, "Check out our alibis! Just call Dr. Sayers. We were here all day!"

"I never doubted that, though I will reach out to Dr. Sayers," he said. He looked at Kylie then, and reached to a pile of cards on the desk. He handed her one, hoping she would take it. "Please, be aware there is a very dangerous killer out there. Be careful. And, again, if you see anything, hear anything, anything even remotely suspicious, I will be grateful if you call me."

"Sure," she murmured.

He walked them to the door and watched as they headed out to the street—still somewhat busy. A few of the shops stayed open late, and the ghost tours were still going about the historic district.

He was worried for the group.

Yes, he thought dryly, they'd gone to Harvard. But they were four women, alone… They might be successful at their chosen fields, but he felt certain they had never known brutality or experienced any of the factors that might have led them to suspect the worst in others.

At least none of them would be wandering around alone. The killer—thus far—was taking only one vulnerable woman at a time, and until today, he had chosen women on the fringes of society, those who had become lost to loved ones, who might be gone days before their absence was even noted.

Today's murder was different. Jon had left the cemetery—and the medical examiner and the forensics crew and his friend, Deputy Ben Miller—just before heading to the Cauldron. There'd been no mystery as to the victim's identity. Even Ben had known all about her.

Annie Hampton had been a school teacher, loved by her coworkers and students. A starry-eyed idealist, fighting the good fight. She'd had a good education, been cherished by a good family, and she had also enjoyed the camaraderie of many close friends.

The killer was upping his game.

And the women Jon had just met seemed to be very much like the most recent victim. *Lambs*, he thought. He could only pray they would not be easily led to slaughter.

He hesitated a minute before letting himself out and locking the door behind him. There was one friend he hadn't met up with yet in Salem.

He'd told the girls he'd accept any help.

And his old friend—his dead friend—Obadiah Jones was out there somewhere. Maybe, just maybe, he could help.

"The nerve of the man!" Corrine exclaimed as they headed back down the street.

"Well…" Nancy started, apparently ready to come to Jon Dickson's defense. Special Agent Jon Dickson's defense. "To be fair, I mean, it's so horrible—that poor woman. And Kylie did walk up to the bar and say the politician had killed her. You can't blame him. It's like having a fit over something on an airplane today. You just can't do it. The whole world is jumpy."

"Let's try looking him up, see if we can find him. We'll make sure he's totally legitimate," Corrine said.

"That's a plan," Jenny said. "What if he's just…whoa. What if he's a killer himself? He's tall, dark, wickedly sexy… Isn't that what some serial killers have supposedly been like, gorgeous on the outside? They're just all twisted up inside. Oh! And if that politician did kill you—or someone else and you saw him killing you—then he's kind of like that, the same thing. Michael Westerly is a very charismatic politician. You just don't know that, Kylie, because you've been living in New York. If you'd hung around Boston, you'd have recognized him instantly. Not that there's anything wrong with living and working in NYC, you just haven't been here."

Kylie stared at her friend, acutely uncomfortable, and yet trying very, very hard to smile. Jenny had just put into words a deep-seated dread that had been growing in her.

What if she had somehow experienced not a past life, but the present life of someone else? The life and death of someone else?

If she had, Michael Westerly wasn't a man dedicated to bettering the world for everyone. He was worse than a man just out to better his own world. He was a stone-cold killer.

"We'll head to the room and whip out our computers," Corrine said.

"We never ate," Nancy said. "And this may be wrong—I mean, a woman was killed—but I'm hungry as hell."

"Room service," Jenny suggested.

"We can get all comfy and order food and it will be great," Corrine said.

"We're supposed to be celebrating," Kylie reminded her. "We're supposed to be going out and imbibing at least one silly cocktail. I'm ruining this party. We're supposed to be having a great time."

Corrine looped an arm through hers. "This is going to be fun. We were all but dragged out of a bar by a mysterious dark-haired hunk of a man. Now we're going to go and find out just who the hell he really is."

"Do they list FBI agents online?" Jenny wondered, frowning. "I mean, wouldn't that kind of put a whammy on the whole thing, if people know who you are? Oh, maybe that's just if you're undercover. This dude isn't undercover."

"Let's just head up," Corrine said. She gave Kylie a heartfelt smile. "This is fine, it's cool. My one big wish was to visit Dr. Sayers. I had no desire to have a wild party. Us spending time together is my idea of a great way to head into marriage.

Really. So, let's go up and put on comfortable T-shirts and sweatpants, order up food, eat whatever, and see what we can find out about this guy."

"Jon Dickson," Nancy said gravely.

"Okay," Kylie said. She hated to admit that if she could actually do what would make *her* happy, she'd lock herself in a room alone and try to sort through her feelings.

Fear.

Empathy for the stranger who had been murdered.

Guilt for ruining Corrine's party.

Horror at what had been done.

Confusion that an FBI agent seemed to give credence to her words, even though she'd been miles away when the murder had occurred.

Once they got up to the semi-luxurious suite they'd taken, Jenny read through the room service menu. "Steak!" she declared.

It was an old hotel; it could only be so luxurious. But their suite did have two rooms, a dining area, and a newly installed whirlpool tub.

"You know I'm a vegetarian," Nancy reminded her.

"Only because you're dating a vegetarian," Corrine said. "And you're a pescatarian. You wolfed down a lobster grinder at lunch."

"Pescatarian. Because fish are cannibalistic little monsters," Nancy said. "Have you ever seen a cow eat a cow? Nope. But fish… Trust me. I've been diving. Those little suckers are ready to turn on each other at a moment's notice."

Kylie was only halfway paying attention to her friends. She already had her computer out.

"Kylie, what do you want to eat?" Corrine asked.

"Anything. Just order two of whatever you're getting," Kylie told her. She logged in to the hotel's internet as she spoke, starting a search for FBI Special Agent Jon Dickson.

Nothing came up on the FBI website. Then again, she hadn't really expected it would. She wasn't sure how to do a further search; she tried a few social media sites and came up with a dozen men with the name Jon Dickson—none of whom seemed to be the Jon Dickson they had met. Putting his name into a general search engine yielded tens of thousands of hits; too many to start scrolling through.

Nancy, leaning over her shoulder, murmured, "That might not even be his real name."

"He might not be for real at all," Jenny suggested. "I mean, he met us in a bar and then dragged us out to a weird, obviously temporary office in a place that's supposed to be a candy shop soon."

"He's real," Corrine said decisively. "You can tell."

"How?" Kylie demanded, looking up at her friend.

"Confidence, authority. He's polite, but he behaves in a way that defies...defiance. I believe he's for real. He was definitely mysterious, though..." She broke off, staring at Kylie. "Come on, Kylie. You must admit the whole thing is very weird. I mean, the way you behaved under hypnosis and the things you were saying... The way you were screaming. It was terrifying just to watch. I thought something terrible had happened to you in a previous life. But now, seeing what happened... Except you're talking about Michael Westerly. That's impossible. But then, what is an FBI agent doing here? So, what is going on?"

Kylie stood, feeling guilty again. "Something terrible happened. But as horrible as it may be, happens every day. That's life—good and bad. And bad will happen...okay, this isn't coming out the way I intended it to. I'll try again. Yes, something terrible happened but we're here to celebrate your marriage to a great guy. A guy you love. So, let's get going with champagne and dinner and forget all this for now."

"Hear, hear! To Corrine and Derrick," Nancy said, and the others echoed her.

As if on cue, there was a knock at the door.

Dinner had arrived, and with it, a bottle of champagne. Jenny did the uncorking. Nancy was ready with the glasses. They all toasted Corrine and Derrick, and then, as they had planned, they grouped in one of the bedrooms and ate and talked and ordered more champagne and talked some more, about the men they had dated, their trials and tribulations through college, and how Corrine was lucky, the wedding would be amazing, and she and Derrick would certainly live happily-ever-after.

Much, much, later, Corrine fell asleep, Nancy and Jenny retired to the second bedroom, and Kylie lay wide-awake for an hour before she got up and tiptoed back out to the little parlor/dining room of the suite to open her computer again.

She found a news story on the recent murder; that was no surprise. The police had barely managed to cordon off the area where the body had been found before the media descended. Kylie swirled around in the desk chair, the remote control in her hand, and turned on the television.

Annie Hampton had been beloved in her community. She had lived just ten minutes south of the Rebecca Nurse Homestead. She had taught grade school in Swampscott. Local residents were devastated and anxious that whoever had perpetrated such a deed be brought to justice immediately.

They interviewed friends of the victim—a cruel thing to do, Kylie thought. Reporters played sympathetic, but they still filmed people fresh in their grief, with tears in their eyes and streaming down their faces.

Some suggested a horrible monster had come to Essex County. Others speculated about a mystery man in Annie's life. Someone she had talked to friends about, a man who was wonderful. Rumor had it they were just waiting for the right time to announce their love to the world. No one thus far seemed to know who the mystery man might be. Not even her closest friend, a woman who was crying her eyes out as she spoke to a reporter.

Kylie flicked channels; almost every local station was covering the murder.

She finally found a national channel, where an astute young anchorwoman was giving statistics on murder rates in the country—unsolved murder rates. They were staggering, and frightening. She noted that similar murders had taken place along the Eastern Seaboard, from Virginia through DC, and on up.

"Officials now suspect there is a serial killer at work," the anchor said. "Several members of law enforcement believe Annie Hampton might well have been attacked by a murderer moving north and leaving a river of blood in his wake. Please call the tip line shown on the screen if you have any information regarding this murder or suspicious behavior in your area. Any and all help will be greatly appreciated by authorities."

Kylie turned from the television back to her computer and began to research recent unsolved murders. As the anchor had suggested, they were numerous. She narrowed her focus to young women who had been stabbed to death. She found a handful of stories about stabbing murders, the bodies left in abandoned graveyards up and down the Eastern Seaboard.

She hesitated.

And then she looked up Michael Westerly, trying to find his events calendar.

She blew out a breath, frustrated. Michael Westerly had not, according to his calendar, been in Virginia. Or New Jersey.

She sighed. What was she thinking? That this senator was a serial killer? Based on what? A weird vision? As Corrine had theorized, Kylie had probably just seen the man's picture somewhere. And while her friends had envisioned beautiful past lives for themselves, she had somehow imagined an act of violence.

But she could still see his face, see the fury in his eyes, feel his determination and his cold rage and she could feel...

The knife. Ripping into her.

She stood, slamming her computer shut.

Before heading into the bedroom, she picked up what remained of their second bottle of champagne and drank it down in gulps.

Stupid. Champagne shouldn't be guzzled. Now she didn't feel like sleeping; she felt like she had swallowed a giant air bubble.

She made herself try anyway. Eventually, she sank into darkness.

She could feel the cool air on her face. Saw herself standing in a field of forgotten graves.

She was a short distance from the deconsecrated church, plain and stark among the stones. Many of the gravestones bore death's-head carvings; they were wearing away, just like the memories of those who had lived and long been buried in the earth and by the passage of time.

She walked down the overgrown path that led to the old church, covered in faded graffiti.

It was a strange place to meet, and yet, so safe. No one ever came here; if anyone did, they could each explain being there.

She felt the breeze again, felt the dying sunshine, bearing down on her. Winters could be so harsh and brutal here, but when the sky was clear, it was a beautiful blue, and when the soft touch of the wind moved in from the water, it was as wonderful as a sweet caress, especially when the afternoon waned, and night was coming.

She arrived so happy, in love with love, anxious to see him.

Then, he was there, and the expression on his face stunned her. The way he wrenched hold of her was startling at first.

And then terrifying.

There was that first astonishing kiss of the blade…shock and agony.

Kylie woke with a start. She realized she was trembling; she was thankful she hadn't cried out. In the bed opposite from hers, Corrine was still sound asleep.

It was barely six thirty. Kylie hurriedly rose and peeked in the other bedroom. Jenny and Nancy were still asleep. Of course. For a weekend vacation morning, it was ridiculously early.

Kylie knew she wasn't going back to sleep. She showered quickly and snuck out of the room.

She was going to go back to see Special Agent Jon Dickson—whoever he might be—and try to make some sense of it all.

CHAPTER THREE

"This will change things," Ben Miller said glumly to Jon over the phone. "The killer has changed it for us—and for the country. They're going to have to start watching for this man all the way up in Canada, if we don't get somewhere. I mean, there are differences, but it has to be the same killer, right? Victimology—troubled women then, now a happy one. Annie Hampton was stabbed at least twenty times—medical examiner says he can be exact after autopsy—but man, that's some kind of wicked mean anger, right? You came here afraid this killer would strike again. I pray we don't have more than one person stabbing women like this at work on the East Coast. When you were telling me about the murders you've been following...solving...trying to solve..."

It was the crack of dawn, but Ben hadn't had the least hesitation in calling him. He'd known Jon would be awake.

"It's all right, Ben, you're not going to offend me. I've been to the crime scenes. I've seen the bodies. But the first murder was considered a local affair, as were the second and by the third. We may have stepped in eventually, but a bright detective called us because he didn't believe in throwaway lives, which, sad to say, isn't an uncommon sentiment. When clues are nonexistent and there isn't a family member pressing the police, a case can go into a cold file with painful speed. I wasn't officially on this case until the third victim was found, though I did backtrack to the beginning," Jon said.

He was quiet for a moment, then added, "Geographically, it was close enough for us to step in, but at that time, there was nothing to suggest it was a Bureau case. Knowledge that he might have started several years ago and killed four or more previous victims didn't make it through all the channels until we were just about headed this way."

"You knew, though," Ben said. "You knew it was going to happen here. And we didn't even have time to get the media to post warnings—it happened. And to Annie Hampton. That's what I mean by it all changing things up. Don't get me wrong, every human life is precious. Except for, sorry, the life of a monster who kills like that. It may sound bad in some circles, but if someone has to shoot that bastard, I won't be sorry."

He sighed. "But the general population isn't as outraged when a sex worker or an addict is killed. It's not that they think they deserved it, but with the lifestyle they were living, those victims played a dangerous game. I worked a case once where a call girl had been killed— autopsy showed she was half eaten up with cirrhosis of the liver and she would have been dead in another six months. But those six months belonged to her. People don't see the violence and desperation that we see on a daily basis. Brings me back to this," he said. "Annie Hampton was no invisible victim. Do you think that, up to now, the killer believed he was killing women who needed to be killed? Who were suffering?"

"I'm not giving this guy any humanitarian attributes," Jon said.

"I've been going over it and over again, all night, working

with the information you gave me on the other murders and comparing what happened to Annie Hampton," Ben said.

Jon had spent the night going over the details as well.

With Obadiah Jones. A dead man, but one who'd stayed around and watched—and saw many things.

He had found Obadiah last night, sitting on a bench at the memorial at the Old Burying Point. He'd heard about the murder, but to his great regret, he knew nothing that could help Jon.

Now Obadiah would be watching and listening. Haunting the place with a passion.

Jon gave his attention back to his living friend, the county detective on the phone.

"There's a lot of talk at the precinct," Ben was saying. "You know, there were still those who doubted that one killer was committing all the crimes. Because if this is the same killer, he has an amazing capacity for movement, and an excellent knowledge of his surroundings, wherever he chooses to kill."

"That's true. He might be a trucker, or...it could be a woman trucker. Or a salesperson. Whoever it is, they're smart and careful. Not a cigarette butt, gum wrapper, hair, fiber, or scrap of anything was found anywhere near the first two bodies. Not a thing, until the matchbox at the last crime scene in Rhode Island," Jon reminded his friend.

"Yeah, I heard that. Except for that matchbox, the sites were so clean that plenty of officers believe the killer has to be a member of a police force or something like that. Or perhaps someone who worked in forensics and knew what would give them away. And there's no real proof the crimes were committed by a man, right?" Ben asked.

Jon shrugged, then smiled at himself, aware Ben couldn't see him. Good thing—he was at his desk in a robe and boxer shorts. "In profiling, the nature of the crimes suggests a man, but until a killer is caught, a profile is a guide, an assumption made through education on the human psyche—but never proof."

"Well, if you want to see our medical examiner, I'm heading over at 11:00. You can go earlier, if you want, but I'd rather be there for the end report—even though I don't believe we'll learn much we don't already know. She was stabbed repeatedly and bled to death."

"I'll join you," Jon said.

"Walk straight up off the pedestrian sideway. I'll meet you between the museum and the Old Burying Point," Ben told him.

Jon rang off, pensive. He couldn't help thinking about Kylie and the strange reaction she'd had to seeing Michael Westerly on the news. And then hearing about the murder. He'd watched her face; there had been very real horror written on her features.

He told himself he'd overreacted, putting so much faith in her vision. There was probably no way Senator Michael Westerly could be involved. The man had a wife, grown children, and a sterling reputation.

Jon shook his head thoughtfully; he'd started creating his case board last night. He had times and details, pictures of the victims in life and in death, statements from those close to them…

Jon had confirmed Westerly's schedule last night, reaching out quietly to an assistant in the senator's office. The man hadn't been anywhere near the other sites where the crimes had been committed. If the dates and times of the senator's meetings and other engagements were correct, Westerly couldn't be the killer.

Kylie had been hypnotized. Maybe she had mixed things up in her mind under the influence of a clever mentalist who could make people see "the past."

Except the murder hadn't been in the past, which made it

very curious. Still…it could be just a mind game played on a susceptible subject.

But Kylie had been convinced. In her mind's eye, she had seen Westerly murder Annie. She had, in her vision, *been* Annie Hampton. And Jon knew very well that there was more to the universe, and to the human mind, than most people realized. Which was why he believed that Kylie had seen *something*.

The killer just couldn't have been the man Kylie had seen.

Could the senator's schedule be off? Or had he disappeared by night to commit murder and then reappear in the morning? Were the logistics even possible?

Jon picked up his phone again. He made an appointment to meet with the senator, clearly identifying himself as being with the Bureau.

Apparently, that didn't cause the least alarm. The senator would be glad to see him that afternoon, or so the man's assistant assured Jon.

He hung up, drumming his fingers on the desk. He'd slept badly and was grateful that there was a shower stall in the small bathroom. And the water ran hot.

He was ready for a long shower.

It didn't matter that he stayed under the steaming water for a long time; he was spinning his wheels that morning. Having arrived just yesterday, he'd already met with Ben Miller, set up shop, and started to stake out the Cauldron.

He'd hoped to stop a killer here but the man struck before he'd found the least clue how to find him. Jon had barely come out of the shower, dried himself, and dressed when there was a knock at his door.

He answered it carefully—that was his instinct. There weren't many people who knew he was in Salem. And it was still ridiculously early for anyone to be out in a tourist town, somewhere between seven thirty and eight. He knew he would not be opening the door to a stray tourist who wanted to know when lollipops would be available.

To his surprise, it was Kylie Connelly. She offered him a weak smile. "Hey."

"Hey."

"Um, may I come in?"

"Sure." He opened the door wide, indicating she was welcome. Still, he felt awkward with her in his space, until they were seated on opposite sides of the desk as if in an interview.

Or an interrogation.

He looked at her hopefully. "You have something more for me?"

She sighed and shook her head, looking down at her hands for a moment and then back up at him. "I don't have more, I'm sorry. But I'm afraid I'm going a little crazy. I barely slept. There seemed to be so much to my vision, or whatever it was... I could feel the sun, see the sky, and I... Oh!" She leaned forward, as if remembering. "I knew I was supposed to meet him there. I met him there often, probably because it's in an area where no one really goes. Tourists occasionally, but it's not the beaten path, you know? Most people come downtown, and then they might drive out to the Rebecca Nurse Homestead or other sites associated with the witch trials, but... Sorry, I guess I'm digressing. Anyway, in my dreams, I was remembering more about the experience. More than what I saw with Dr. Sayers." She winced. "This sounds impossible, I know. I felt I was Annie Hampton, and I walked with her, waiting...until the killer came."

Jon frowned. "What do you do for a living, Miss Connelly?"

"I'm a docent—or a curator," she told him. "I was with the Met until recently. I'm going to be the head historian for a museum in an old mansion in New York City that's just been restored. Why?"

He had to admit to himself—he'd been afraid she was going to say she was a psychic or the like. Not that he disparaged any form of a living, as long as it didn't hurt others. He just needed to know she wasn't showboating for attention for her profession. And naturally, in his work with the Krewe, he'd come to be skeptical of those who claimed to have "powers." Those who really did have unusual abilities tended to keep their talents quiet.

Whatever this was, she wasn't making it up. She hadn't approached him with her vision. On the contrary, he had dragged her out of the restaurant where she and her friends had gone to enjoy an evening together.

"You're from Massachusetts," he said, "and you went to Harvard. But you're working in New York?"

She shrugged. "I was offered a good position after college. And I love New York. Of course, I love Boston, too. It's a great city."

"I see."

"Why?" she demanded.

"Just curious."

"I'm… I'm not prone to this kind of thing. I don't normally have visions or anything. But you pulled me out of the bar. You seemed to believe me. And then I had nightmares all night. I don't know… I thought you could help."

"Yeah. Sorry," he said. "Listen, I have to meet with a local cop in a while. But later, I'm going back by the graveyard. Would you come with me? Show me everything you saw and felt in this dream that you had?"

Kylie turned a strange shade of pale red and swallowed, then nodded slowly.

"If it's going to bother you, just say so," Jon offered. "It's probably a long shot on my part anyway."

"It's going to bother me, yes," she told him. She stood.

"But I'd like to go with you. Maybe I can knock it all out of my head that way."

He walked with her to the door. "Great. We'll just see what happens."

"What time? Or can we be a bit flexible?" She grimaced. "We're Corrine's wedding party, you know. I'm her maid of honor. I realize that next to horrendous murders and the work you do, a wedding must seem very minor. But it's important to my friends. Still… I want to go with you."

"I'm sorry this has happened, for what that's worth," Jon said.

"I just keep thinking about Annie. I'm truly sorry for her," she said. "And I want to help. I wish I was kick-ass. Like Wonder Woman—we all want to be Wonder Woman these days. But I'm a historian. I probably should have at least taken kickboxing, but Pilates is pretty much it for me. I guess I'm trying to say I wish I could do more."

"Meet me back here. We'll go from here," he told her. He held open the door.

She paused and turned to him. As close as she was, he noted again her exceptional eyes, green and yellow, made more luminous by the chestnut frame of her hair.

"Miss Connelly?" he said.

"Yes?"

He offered her a rueful smile. "For what it's worth, the Pilates seems to have paid off very nicely."

He could have kicked himself. It wasn't a comment a professional agent should have made, not in any way.

But none of this seemed to be going by the book.

To his relief, she smiled. "Thanks," she told him. She looked at him curiously, and then walked back out to the street.

Somehow, Kylie made it back to the hotel suite just as the others were beginning to wake; they assumed she had been there all along. She didn't correct them.

"Did you sleep okay?" Corrine asked her anxiously.

Kylie smiled. "Like a baby," she lied. "So, what are we up to this morning?"

"Oh, you know me. I love the Salem Witch Museum—I think they tell the story well without sensationalizing it or being, I don't know... It's a tourist attraction, but a really good one, in my mind."

"We all love it, and it's your party," Kylie said determinedly. "Breakfast first, though."

"And a ghost tour tonight. Touristy, but fun," Nancy said. "Then it'll be kind of late on a Saturday night. Latish, anyway, and we're going to go a little wild."

"I really, really don't want strippers," Corrine protested.

"And we really, really haven't hired any," Jenny said. "Our wild time is trying out the beer flights down at the brewery."

"The brewery tonight— Aww, too bad, in a way. There will be no Matt, the cute bartender, or Cindy, his speedy cohort," Nancy said regretfully. She grinned. "But we can take the ghost tour with that cute tour guide!"

"I'll bet he is a good guide. Outgoing. And dramatic, probably," Corrine said.

"Not as good as..." Jenny's voice trailed.

"Not as good as what?" Nancy asked. "Oh, oh, oh! I know who you're talking about. Tall, dark, authoritative, and mysterious. If Kylie hadn't been in shock last night, I'd have been tempted to...well, not defend him, but add him to the group!"

"Too bad he doesn't give ghost tours," Jenny said. "Because that's what we're doing tonight."

No, he certainly doesn't give ghost tours, Kylie thought.

"I truly do love a good ghost tour," Corrine said, "and just doing all these things we've done dozens of times is—maybe sadly and boringly—just what I want. Thank you all for understanding that I may be weird. Derrick will just be enjoying his Magic: The Gathering tournament, and we're both going to be happy as little larks, doing our own particular geeky brand of celebrating."

She had been smiling, but now she frowned, looking at Kylie. "Are you really...all right this morning?"

"I'm fine."

"Did you see any news? Do they have any idea yet of what happened to that poor woman who was murdered in the graveyard?" Corrine asked.

"I don't think there's anything new," Kylie replied. She hesitated just a minute. "Um, speaking of that agent, I'm going to duck out for a bit this afternoon. I'm going to go with him to the graveyard."

"You're going to what?" Nancy demanded.

"The graveyard? Where that poor woman was killed?" Jenny asked, horrified.

"Oh!" Corrine exclaimed. "Is that a good idea? Won't that make you even more...confused and miserable?"

"I think I need to go," Kylie said.

"And I think you should invite him to dinner with us," Nancy suggested thoughtfully.

"Sure, invite him to dinner," Jenny agreed. "But...the graveyard? Kylie, after you were so upset yesterday? Corrine, tell her she can't do that, she'll ruin your day. Not that we want to hurt you in any way, Kylie, but...you didn't see how scary you were when you were still under. Whatever you saw—"

"It's unbelievable, I know, but if I somehow saw something in my mind, I need to tell Special Agent Dickson what it was. What if it can help stop a serial killer? Please. I need to do this."

Kylie thought she was incredibly lucky then; her friends surrounded her, and each one of them gave her an encouraging hug.

"We're all on your speed dial, right?" Corrine asked.

"Of course."

"And 911, of course."

"I'm going to be with an FBI agent. I should be fine no matter what," Kylie said. "But I'm a big girl, I know how to dial 911, my phone is charged…and as for this killer, I don't think I'm in any danger. I don't think he's ready to go up against anyone strong. I mean, he took a young woman completely by surprise when she was alone. I know that. And if he's the same guy who has killed others, it's always been the same. He gets them alone. He has a knife—they're defenseless."

"Ah!" Nancy said. "Hang on!" She disappeared into the bedroom and then reappeared holding something that looked like a super-large lighter. "Pepper spray. Take it."

"I'll be with an agent. You guys—"

"Let's order breakfast. I've another plan—just a cautionary plan," Nancy said. She hesitated. "I'm calling my cousin, Andrea. She's dating a Peabody cop. She'll find out if this too-good-to-be true agent is really an agent. I mean, if he's not undercover or anything. Someone must know something."

Nancy disappeared into the bedroom again. Corrine called room service for breakfast and they all decided they needed to start with a giant pot of coffee. They'd have eggs and bacon and pancakes and fruit—a nice mix for a good start to the day.

When Nancy reappeared, she looked a little surprised.

"No. Don't tell me there's something wrong with him," Kylie said.

Nancy shook her head. "Quite the contrary. Jonathan Wolf Dickson was born right here in Salem. He went to Yale after a stint in the military. He's been with the Bureau almost ten years, and he was selected for an elite unit. He's also good friends with an Essex County cop, a guy named Ben Miller, who is friends with Andrea's boyfriend, Ernie. So, yeah, he's the real deal."

Kylie was grateful for the information. "So, he's a local?" she asked.

Nancy nodded. "He's been elsewhere since he was eighteen, but yeah, he's from right here. And… Corrine, she should invite him to our dinner at the brewery tonight, don't you think?"

"Yes, she should invite him!" Corrine said. "It will be wonderful."

"To our girls' night out?" Kylie asked.

Corrine laughed softly. "In my mind, he's way better than any stripper. But back to me being basically boring and strange, let's get going to the Salem Witch Museum. While you're on your graveyard trek, we'll head to the wax museum and the New England Pirate Museum—gotta love me some pirates, too—and we'll probably be into dinnertime by then. Keep in touch, okay?"

"Of course," Kylie said. They were all still staring at her. "Yes, yes, I will," she promised again, and she turned quickly to answer the door to the suite; their breakfast had arrived.

Lizzie Borden took an ax
and gave her mother forty whacks
When she saw what she had done
She gave her father forty-one.

Jon couldn't keep the old rhyme from rushing through his head as the medical examiner spoke to him and Ben about his findings regarding the death of Annie Hampton.

Lizzie Borden hadn't really given her mother forty whacks—she had given her nineteen. And she had hacked up her father with ten or eleven—assuming she had done the deed, despite the fact she'd been acquitted. Just about any kid who had grown up in Massachusetts had heard the facts regarding the murders.

As for Annie Hampton…

The killer never touched her face, a fact Jon had noted at the crime scene the day before.

She had been twenty-eight years old, with a round face and soft blond hair. The damage done to her appeared to have been done in fury as well. Both methodical and determined.

She'd received exactly twenty-two blows from the knife that had killed her. It had pierced her heart—causing the pools of blood—and also ripped into her abdomen, tearing apart her liver, stomach, and pancreas.

This was the first time the killer had completely missed the victim's face. It had never appeared before that he had purposely destroyed the face, but a person being murdered usually tried to stop the knife from piercing their chest area or vital organs; there would be slashes on the arms as the victim tried to avoid the blows. In every case, including this one, there were slashes on the arms.

But there had also been at least one wound on the faces of the previous victims. Was his aim getting better? Was he improving his method of killing?

There would be tests on her blood and stomach contents; the results from the lab wouldn't be back immediately.

The medical examiner, Dr. Custis Margolin, shook his head when he left his assistant to sew up the body. He looked at Jon and Ben and said, "This is truly sad. I know the family. This was a lovely young woman." He studied them both and added, "Please, get this bastard." He stared at Jon, and he clearly attempted to keep his tone bland, but there was something of an accusation in it as he asked, "You were here on the trail of this man, or so I understand. There should have been warnings out. This is a serial killer, and he's been heading up the coast."

"Dr. Margolin, we're still trying to ascertain if we're looking for one man or not," Jon told him.

"Seems to me you might as well move on," Dr. Margolin said. He had a hangdog face, heavy in the jowls, thinning white hair. "Doesn't he make one kill each place, and then move north?"

Whether he should or shouldn't feel it, Jon felt a rush of guilt. Could he have stopped this? "I've got no excuse to offer," he told Margolin flatly. "I arrived yesterday, just hours before...hours before Annie met her death."

"My office had been informed," Ben pointed out. "We were trying to arrange our facts and sort them from rumor before having a press conference."

Dr. Margolin studied them both and turned away. "I'll be in touch," he said.

Jon and Ben were both silent as they walked back to the car; it was a good twenty-five miles back to Salem from the morgue and they'd have plenty of time to talk.

"That's not on you, you know," Ben said at last. "You came to me. I'm the county detective here. I should have had a press conference. Thing is— "

"All we had was a matchbox," Jon finished for him. "I know you had to notify the family and you interviewed some of her friends. Was there any suggestion at all she'd been to the Cauldron?"

Ben shook his head.

They drove in comfortable silence for a while. After several minutes, Ben glanced over at him, barely taking his eyes off the road. "How do you like DC? Are you ever coming back?"

"I'm here now, aren't I?" Jon said lightly.

"To stay?"

Jon grimaced. "I love my unit. We're based in northern Virginia. I have a great director and I find incredible satisfaction in thinking that, at least sometimes, I can make a difference."

"And it's eating you alive that you feel you failed Annie Hampton. You didn't. I did."

"I don't think either of us failed her," Jon said. "We did, and we didn't. I can't touch it, but…there's something different here."

"How? Women knifed to death in old graveyards or cemeteries. No sexual assault. Left where they lay, in remote areas."

"She wasn't his usual target," Jon said. "And her face…he didn't touch her face."

Ben glanced at him. "The faces on the other victims were injured?"

"I don't think the killer was trying for the faces. But in the stabbing, they wound up with at least one slash."

"What about the number of wounds?"

"The most on a previous victim? Eight. And that included two defensive wounds on the arms. I'm not sure there is a difference between being killed with eight or twelve slashes, but… I don't know. It just bothers me. Something has changed. As you mentioned, the victimology. I'm waiting on your crime scene folks to let me know if they have anything, anything at all, to suggest where he might strike next." Jon was quiet a minute. "If this was *him*. The same killer."

Kylie had seen state Senator Westerly in her…well, it couldn't have been a regression, not if it had been happening when she'd been under. He really needed the exact timing on what had happened at the graveyard, and when Kylie had been "under." It seemed to jive, but could mean exactly nothing. Was he grasping at straws?

But that's what his unit often did.

"I'm going back out to the graveyard this afternoon," Jon told Ben.

"Our forensics people are good. If there's something to find, Jon, I swear they'll find it," Ben told him. He sighed. "I'm arranging interviews. According to friends and family, Annie was seeing a mystery man. But if this is a serial killer at work, one who has moved up the coast, I'm not sure how her mystery man might be involved."

"Hopefully the boyfriend will come forward," Jon said. "If you find anyone you think has useful information—"

"I'll bring you in on it right away, my friend, I promise. But what do you think you're going to gain by going out to the cemetery?"

"I don't know. I'm going with a new acquaintance."

"Are you holding out on me?" Ben asked, frowning.

"You know I wouldn't do that. No, this is a bizarre circumstance. She was in Salem all day—plenty of witnesses. But..." He hesitated, and Ben groaned.

"You're going out there with some kind of psychic? Jon, you believe a kook—"

"She isn't a kook, Ben, and I don't know if she can or can't help. That's why I'll explore this avenue alone, and you let me know about friends and family."

"Fine. Have fun. I hope you're not dragging along a crystal ball."

"We're not dragging along a crystal ball," Jon said, but he looked at Ben. "But if I thought we might get anywhere with a crystal ball, I'd damned sure give it a shot."

Ben let Jon out on the street near the office space he had rented. He saw Kylie approaching the office; she moved with a slightly hurried grace, as if she was afraid she'd be late.

He couldn't help but notice that movement; she had a slim build, and yet was curvy enough. She was, no doubt, an exceptionally attractive woman, and hard as he tried, it was almost impossible not to notice her in that way. She simply called out to just about everything primal in him.

He'd felt the softness of her chestnut hair on his arms when he caught her falling the night before. It had been a brush of velvety silk.

Jon watched as a child of about ten, bored and running

in circles as his mother looked in a shop window, ran into Kylie. She laughed and straightened him, and he smiled, and his mother smiled, and Kylie moved on.

She had a way about her.

He quickened his walk, as if he could reinforce his resolve to stay completely professional. He thought of Annie Hampton. And the others...so many lives, so sadly lost before they could ever really live.

"Kylie!" he called out to her.

She turned, saw him coming, and changed direction.

"My car is in the garage," he said. "We'll go straight to it and head out." He paused, looking at her. "You're sure you're still willing to do this?"

"Willing," she said, "and wanting. Let's hope..."

"For something," he finished.

She kept step with him, and despite his resolve, he couldn't help noting the scent of her perfume was just as compelling as her eyes, her movement...

Every single little thing about her.

CHAPTER FOUR

The graveyard was exactly as Kylie remembered it, having been there a few times over the years...and from her experience when she had been hypnotized. The abandoned church and burial ground surrounding it belonged to the county, but there were no signs warning against trespassing. There were signs that warned the area wasn't safe after dark. Kylie figured it was left for curiosity seekers. No one had been buried there for well over a hundred years, so family members wouldn't be bringing flowers to a recently lost loved one.

The cemetery wasn't in the center of town, and there were no known participants in the witch trials buried there. It was notable in the amount of Revolutionary and Civil War soldiers it housed. But Salem was a town where one history ruled over all others, and many visitors never ventured out of the old section of town.

As if reading her mind, Jon said, "No recent burials. No real reason to be here. Except there are records for this church that date back centuries, and there are online sites where you can find a grave. With the trend of finding about their ancestry through DNA, you have more people than ever searching out their family's past. Plenty of people around here can date their ancestry way back, so they might well have family here, and you have those from other places who just discovered that great-great-great-granddad is buried here. And then there are people who study the American Revolution and there are also a few Union soldiers buried here. Still..."

"It's not a heavily traveled tourist destination," Kylie said.

The road, almost empty, stretched out in both directions with only a few distant homes dotting the landscape. She could see a farm up a hill; cows were out in the surrounding paddocks.

They paused at the entry. It was much like any of the very old cemeteries in the area. Stones were crooked and broken, weeds hugging many of them. In places, trees had simply joined with the stones so that roots broke out jaggedly from them, eerie as new life crept over the death's-heads, reapers, and skeletons that had been the iconography prevalent in the graveyard's heyday. There were a few aboveground tombs, worn and grayed, but no mausoleums or vaults—just the occasional one-person tomb, big enough for one coffin and stark in the center of broken stones.

A path that had nearly disappeared led to a shell of a building that had once been a church. It had been built for a small Puritan flock, and it was simple in the extreme. Just a building with slanted roof, once white-washed.

There was nothing inside but fading graffiti. On weekends, the civic organization that tried to keep up the church and graveyard sold T-shirts and water from the little church. People likely came to take advantage of the solitude, high schoolers and drifters, but though the nearly abandoned building might have been filled with debris or garbage, it wasn't; court-ordered community service brought petty offenders through semiregularly and kept the place clean enough to be safe.

Safe.

It hadn't been safe for Annie Hampton.

As they stood there, Kylie thought the day—sunny so far—was becoming gray. She closed her eyes for a minute, clenching her teeth hard. "Now that we're here…" she murmured.

"Tell me what you remember from the beginning. You were walking…"

"Coming to meet someone," she said softly. "I didn't climb over the little wall. I walked alongside it and I came down the path. I headed straight for the church."

"Okay, shall we do that?" he suggested.

She nodded somberly.

They walked alongside the wall. As they moved, a feeling of immense dread began to fall over her.

"Stop," Jon said.

She halted, frowning as she looked at him.

"You're ashen. This isn't good."

"I'm fine. I'm a pale person."

He smiled at that. "Give me your hand," he told her.

She complied. His hand was large, his fingers long. They walked along again and while she still felt the sense of something terrible, she felt as if she had the strength to face it.

They came through the opening and walked along the overgrown path.

She paused and closed her eyes for a minute. She could feel the breeze, and a sense of anticipation. She shook her head, confusion plaguing her. "Annie… If I was somehow in her shoes… She was glad to be here. She came here often. She was excited at first. She came to meet someone."

"So she was happy," Jon said.

"Anticipating what was going to happen. I think she was waiting for someone. Someone she'd met here before… It was probably a natural place to meet for her. She didn't live far. She was a teacher and interested in old graves, in history, and from the little I know from the news, she was very happy here. She loved her home."

"And the person she was meeting?" Jon asked her.

She shook her head. "She was waiting for him, but what he was feeling, I don't know. Until he arrived, that is, until they were together."

She stopped walking just outside the church. "I think he found her just about here." She paused. An area of the graveyard was still roped off with crime scene tape. It looked as if large portions of earth had been dug up.

She recoiled inwardly.

Blood had seeped into the ground there, and the forensic crew had dug up the earth to test it, hoping Annie Hampton might have taken some of the killer's blood with a good scratch, and there might be his blood cells mixed in with hers, bits of skin…

"He dragged her," she said softly.

She felt his hand, holding hers tightly. "I'm here. You're safe," he told her.

She nodded and closed her eyes. For just a few seconds, she could see it again: the man, his furious face, and the way he dragged her.

She'd been stunned. It was supposed to have been a romantic interlude, something that broke up her humdrum life. Annie was a good girl, she went to work, she came home, she loved children and charities, and this… This was different for her. Wild and a bit crazy and new. She had been in love, perhaps, partially with the secrecy he demanded, with the mystery.

She'd been stunned by the fury in his face, and she knew right away something was wrong.

The knife. She had begged and pleaded.

She saw the knife, saw it coming for her, felt it…

She cried out, and the world began to go dark and she started to fall.

She felt his arms as he caught her, and she struggled around the darkness, finally finding light again.

Jon was holding her, and she was looking into his eyes, dark with deep concern.

"I think I found out all that I can," she whispered. "She was in love. She was meeting him here. She came because she wanted to."

He was still holding her; she hadn't tried to pull away. She wasn't sure she could. She couldn't read his expression. "You must think I'm… I don't know."

But he shook his head. "I'm not thinking anything. I've seen too much, and I… Well, let's get out of here, and then we'll talk."

She was silent as they headed back to his car. Finally, once they were on the road, she had to say something. "I don't understand this. At Dr. Sayers's office, we had tea, and at first I thought he'd drugged the tea. But I never drank mine. And then, when he hypnotized me…" She broke off and shrugged helplessly. "The most awful part is that it's as if I still *feel* it. As if I know what it's like to feel a knife in my flesh, and my blood…spilling."

"Now, you need to… Well, I guess you can't forget it, but—"

She looked over at him. "You believe me. I'm not even sure I believe me."

He watched the road as he drove, but she saw his jaw tighten slightly, as if he was contemplating his next words. "There was a case in Denver I worked a few months ago. A kidnapping. The husband swore he could see his wife, who'd been taken. He had a vision of a warehouse filled with computer monitors. He didn't know how he saw it… He dreamed it, dreamed her voice, calling to him. He was able to describe the warehouse in detail. We had to check out a few places, but we found her, because of what he saw."

"And you're sure the husband wasn't involved?" Kylie asked skeptically.

He glanced over at her. "The husband was in the military, deployed to an air base in Saudi Arabia, when she was first taken. He called us in a panic. No, he had nothing to do with his wife's kidnapping. So, while ideas that may be a bit *strange* aren't the first line of inquiry, we never discount anything. And on this case, we're desperate. We have so little to go on."

"But you knew he was going to strike here. He just did it ridiculously fast."

"If it is him."

She looked at him. "You think it's a different murderer?"

"Either that, or the greatest lover in history. You said Annie was expecting this man, that they'd met at the graveyard before. She was excited to see him, so he must have been the mystery man her friends knew about. That would lead us to speculate he picked up the other women, wooed them until they were comfortable with him… But he started this months ago in Virginia. And even before then."

"Maybe he'd been having an affair with Annie, and the others were just pickups."

He grimaced. "The other victims had substance abuse issues or were sex workers. They were, I imagine, easy enough for him to charm or coerce. Who takes a date to a graveyard?"

Kylie shook her head. "I think in Annie Hampton's case, she knew the place well. The graveyard was perfectly natural to her—she'd known it forever and ever. And whoever he was, if it turned out they didn't have the place to themselves, he'd have an excuse for being there. Playing tourist or doing some research." She hesitated.

She'd seen his face again, the enraged face of the politician.

She was afraid to speak her thoughts out loud.

But again, Jon seemed to be reading her mind. "I checked out Michael Westerly's calendar, including confirmed dates when he was seen by crowds of people. It doesn't allow for him to have committed the other murders."

"I guess my friends were right—I just saw his picture some-where," Kylie said. "That's what put him into my daydream or nightmare or whatever it was."

He glanced her way again. "I have an appointment with him in an hour."

She twisted to look at him. "And what are you going to say? 'A random woman trying to be regressed to a past life saw you murder Annie Hampton'?"

"I'm going to say an anonymous tip came in, and there are people who believe he was Annie's mysterious boyfriend."

"I see," she murmured. "The fact that he's married would account for the secrecy with Annie."

They reached town quickly. He parked in a municipal ga-rage and when they walked out, she asked, "Where are you meeting him?"

"Walking distance," he said. "The restaurant at your hotel."

"He's staying there?" she asked with horror.

"I don't know. His secretary set it up." He frowned. "I'll find out, if you want me to."

"I guess… Yeah, I'd like to know."

He grimaced. "You all are welcome at my place, but there's only the one bed."

She shook her head but couldn't help grinning. "There are four of us. I'm sure we'll be fine. And it's pretty ridiculous. I saw him during a regression. I'm not up on the law, but I don't think that would stand up in court. Unless we went to the witchcraft days and I could say his spectral presence mur-dered her."

"And he might have hanged for it," Jon said.

She hesitated. They paused at the intersection that would

take them by the Peabody Essex Museum and into the pedestrian walk on Essex Street—right by the Old Burying Point. It was ancient, for the US, at least; the second oldest cemetery in the country, right behind the Miles Standish Burial Ground in Duxbury. It was similar to the one they had just left; stones were awry and tree roots grew haphazardly through and around many, though some stones had been carefully preserved.

A memorial to those hanged as witches during the craze—and to Giles Corey, pressed to death—was next to the cemetery. Twenty benches had been created for the tercentenary of the trials in 1992; names of the accused and the dates of their deaths were etched into the stone benches. It was a simple and moving memorial, surrounded by trees and in the center of the tourist district.

Kylie had been to the Old Burying Point many times. It was moving, of course. The cemetery held the graves of a *Mayflower* Pilgrim and a witch trial judge—John Hathorne, great-great-great-grandfather of Nathaniel Hawthorne, a man so distressed by his ancestor's part in the witch trials he put a *w* in his name, as if that could dispel his association with such a man.

The Old Burying Point had never bothered her; rather it had fascinated her. So much history could be found there.

She had felt so differently that afternoon, at the graveyard surrounding the abandoned church.

"Are you all right?" Jon asked her.

"Fine. Really. Absolutely fine. I'm going to call Corrine and the girls and find out where they are and I'll just meet up with them." She hesitated before awkwardly adding, "Oh, I'm supposed to invite you to dinner."

"To a bachelorette dinner?" he asked, his mouth curving.

"It's not like we're the most exciting group out there,"

Kylie said. "I know you're really busy, but…you have to eat sometime."

He laughed softly. "They want me to come? I thought they were about to accuse me of abduction and forced confinement last night."

Kylie shook her head. "They understand. They're a bit scared by what happened. But okay, I'll be honest. Nancy has a lot of friends and family in this area. She checked you out. They like you now."

She wondered if she should have spoken—if her words were offensive.

But he laughed again and gave her a grin. "Well, I'm glad I passed muster. Sure, I'd love to stop by and eat with you and your lovely group. Just text me and tell me a time and a place. You kept my card from last night, right?"

"I have your number," she assured him.

A soft breeze was blowing; the temperature was pleasant, as if winter was only a memory. Tourists still flocked the streets, but she was surprised when he said, "Why don't you find out where they are? Can't be far. I'll walk you there, meet them, and then still have plenty of time to walk back to the hotel."

"Oh, you needn't bother—"

"Humor me," he said, "please."

She nodded and put a call through to Corrine. She and Nancy and Jenny were close, just down at the wax museum.

"You don't have to walk me," Kylie said again with a smile. "You can just watch me from here. They're right there." She pointed. "I think we're heading down to Derby Street after, to the Pirate Museum. History suggests that pirates of old weren't quite as romantic as we like to think of them these days. But Corrine loves pirates, so—"

"Museum on Derby Street, and you'll be right by the brewery," he said. "Get going. I'll be watching. And I'll meet you later."

Kylie nodded and turned to go, lowering her head with a smile, but she looked up as she walked away. She was surprised that she'd had…not a good time, that was impossible when the memory of a murder was still so strong within her. But she liked him. Many, many things about him. Not to mention the way he touched her, held her, and made her feel…safe.

She paused and looked back. He was still watching her. And that should have made her feel safe.

But there was something else in the air that seemed to disturb her. She couldn't explain it. It was as if someone else was watching her, too. And those eyes were not filled with care or concern, but rather something evil.

She straightened, gritting her teeth. What the hell was the matter with her? She'd been here so many times! Salem and witchcraft—past and present—had never done anything but intrigue her before. She was feeling so unusual.

No, she was right to be a little off-kilter. A woman had been brutally murdered. It was natural to feel uneasy when such a thing had happened so near. Uneasiness was good. It made people careful, smart, and aware.

She hurried on to the museum, wondering what Jon's meeting with the senator was going to be like. She was ridiculously pleased that Jon had agreed to have dinner with them; she was going to see him again.

Senator Michael Westerly was the perfect picture of a politician. He was maybe half an inch shorter than Jon's six-three; he was impeccably dressed in a dark blue suit and a lighter blue shirt. He didn't appear at all stuffy; for a casual meeting, he wasn't wearing a tie and the top button of the shirt had been left open. His hair was a soft brown, just beginning to gray at the temples, and his eyes were a clear gray, steady on Jon as they met.

His handshake, Jon thought, was firm, not crushing. He

wondered if even the handshake had been practiced, intended to instill faith in his strength and his steadfast abilities.

Maybe he was all that he seemed. A good man trying to do good things.

Then again, all political affiliations aside, Jon had to wonder if it was possible to go into politics with a completely pure heart, if the game itself didn't change a person.

"Sit down, please sit down," Westerly said. "Nice to meet you, Special Agent Dickson."

The senator had chosen the lounge area of the restaurant. He'd found a position right before the hearth—there was no frost outside and they didn't need a fire for warmth, but there was an electrical blaze that had been turned on for atmosphere.

"What can I get you?" he went on. "That's soda water for me—it's work and no play on the campaign trail—but please feel free to indulge in whatever suits your fancy."

"Coffee, thank you," Jon told him, smiling. "There's never enough coffee."

Westerly looked at his watch. "There's never enough time, either. But I'm always ready to help in any situation. So, what can I do you for?" he asked. "My secretary assumed you were a member of an outreach group for the federal government and that, perhaps, you intended to endorse my candidacy. To be honest, I'm not sure if I hired a sadly naive woman or if Miss Foster is simply forever optimistic. I looked you up, naturally. You're with a special unit involved in high crimes. You're here on a serial killer case, and it seems you're a hair too late, since we had a tragic murder yesterday."

He's certainly a smooth talker, Jon thought. "To my great regret, sir, we are admittedly stumbling in the dark here."

"Okay, we've established the facts. You're not here to endorse my candidacy."

"No."

"Why, then?"

"Senator, I am—along with excellent Massachusetts law enforcement—investigating the deaths of several young women,
and now specifically the murder of Annie Hampton."

"You believe there's a way I can help you?" Westerly asked.

"I'll be honest with you, sir. Your name came up in the
investigation."

Westerly was undeniably startled. He frowned, and Jon
noted his fingers tightened over the handsome claw arms of
the upholstered chair in which he sat.

"My name?"

"Yes, and I asked for a private meeting because of the deli-
cacy of the situation. Annie Hampton was seeing someone.
To friends, she referred to him as her 'mystery man.' It's been
suggested you were her mystery man. This may seem entirely
frivolous, but in keeping with standard procedure, it was necessary I speak with you."

Westerly was silent for a minute, and it seemed that he
was slowing growing red. His blood pressure was spiking,
Jon thought.

"How dare you?" he managed at last.

"Senator, please, I had to ask. Your name came up. Following protocol and procedure, it was necessary I ask you
about it."

Jon's words didn't seem to register for a moment. Westerly
still looked as if he was a rocket about to go off.

"How dare you?" Westerly asked again.

"Sir, I need to ask where you were yesterday."

Westerly's fingers gripped tighter on the arm of the chair.
"Home. Preparing for my speech in Boston."

"Can anyone corroborate that, sir?"

"What? Do you have the audacity to accuse me of lying?
Do I need to call my lawyer?"

"No, sir, I'm simply asking if anyone can corroborate your
story."

Westerly was staring straight at him—then, he wasn't. He was looking across the room, and for such an arrogant man, he suddenly had an expression of thankfulness and relief. "I'm afraid I'm going to have to cut this short, Special Agent Dickson. My wife has arrived." He stood and motioned across the room. "Sandra!" he called.

Jon stood as well. He watched a slim, well-groomed woman walk across the lobby and toward the lounge. She was about the senator's age, but she kept her hair a soft brown, worn in a contemporary short cut that framed her face. She was handsomely and conservatively dressed in a red shirt and tailored black skirt. She wore little black pumps that matched her little black bag. When she reached them, smiling a campaign smile, he thought that she might have had some work done. She was pretty, but also had a tight look about her, as if her skin had been stretched a little too far.

"Sandra, Special Agent Jon Dickson. Special Agent Dickson, I'd like you to meet the love of my life, my steadfast rock in thick and thin, my wife, Sandra."

"How do you do?" Sandra Westerly asked, her plastic-politician's-wife smile perfectly in place.

"My new friend here is working hard on the case of the poor girl murdered yesterday," Westerly said. "I was telling him about the campaign trail, how I was home working yesterday on my speech."

"He writes his own speeches, you know," Sandra said proudly. Then, frowning just slightly as she turned to her husband, she said, "And yes, he was working hard on his speech yesterday." She laughed softly, as if she'd shaken something off, taking her husband's arm and addressing Jon again. "He tries all those speeches out on me and frets over every word! He's an incredibly gifted man with words," she continued. "But of course, he was privy to an excellent education. He went to—"

"Ah, don't tell me," Jon said. "Harvard, right?"

"Harvard law," Sandra said proudly.

"Of course," Jon said, smiling.

"Well, Special Agent Dickson, I believe you'll find my lovely wife to be my corroboration. Will you be kind enough to excuse us? We have dinner and drinks with local business-people, and I sincerely long to hear their concerns for the future of industry in this great commonwealth of ours."

"Thank you for your time," Jon said. "Mrs. Westerly, a true pleasure to meet you."

Westerly took his wife's arm and they moved together through the lobby and out the front door. Jon watched them go and he wondered if he saw—or imagined he saw—Sandra Westerly look up at her husband with a slight hardening of the jaw.

She had never said definitively that her husband had been with her when the murder had occurred. She had talked about his speech-writing ability.

Would Michael Westerly have managed to change Sandra into something of a Stepford wife? A woman ready to agree with his words, whatever they might be?

Then again, even a Stepford wife might have a point when she cracked.

CHAPTER FIVE

Kylie found her friends at the Salem Wax Museum. By the time she arrived, they'd worked on their nautical rope tying and done gravestone rubbings. They'd taken a brief tour with a practicing Wiccan who talked about the hysteria of the witch trials, the Puritan view of witchcraft, and what the Wiccan religion was in the contemporary world, including the true insights of paganism, like a good harvest meant everything, and the earth itself was to be loved and worshipped.

Kylie joined them down in Frankenstein's Castle, a fun exhibit based on the literary talents of Mary Shelley. They wound through dark alleys and enjoyed the chills and thrills, and then, Corrine announced, "To the pirates! Derby Street, my friends, forward, ho!"

They left the Salem Wax Museum, chatting as they walked the several-block distance to the New England Pirate Museum. "It's something to think, while witches were being accused of terrible deeds and being hanged, pirates were busy just off Boston's North Shore, robbing, pillaging—and innocent farm folk being executed!" Corrine said, glancing at the brochure that advertised the museum. "Apparently, pirates were snowbirds, too—hanging out down South while the snow raged, and then coming back up to raid New York and Boston when the sun came out up here. Blackbeard, Kidd, Bellamy, and more."

"Well, if I remember right, Blackbeard was born in 1680, so, in 1692, he was twelve years old," Kylie reminded her.

"And Sam Bellamy was born in 1689. I'm not sure I ever heard of a three-year-old ruling the seas," Nancy said.

"Hey, quit raining on my parade," Corrine protested.

"Sorry, but yes. Right after the witch hunt, the pirates were busy in the same area," Kylie said.

"Well, of course Kylie knows. She's about to open Trelawny House. She has American history down from A to Z," Jenny said. "But Massachusetts is older."

Kylie shrugged. "The oldest building in New York is the Wyckoff Farmhouse Museum in Brooklyn. 1652," she said. "Trelawny House is one of the oldest buildings in Manhattan. It's really a miracle it survived, considering the way we like to tear down and rebuild. But it wasn't built until 1768. It has a great history."

"Yes, and you get to tell it over and over again in the near future," Jenny said. "What we'd like to hear about now is *recent* history—what happened at the graveyard?"

Kylie hesitated. She didn't want them to know it had been extremely disturbing, and she still felt haunted by whatever had happened. "It was fine," she said. "I just... I told him what I had seen. We walked around a bit, and that was it. We came back."

"And you remembered to ask him to dinner, right?" Nancy asked.

"I did."

"And?" Jenny demanded.

"He's coming."

"Cool!" Corrine said, her eyes dancing. "Wow. A girl's weekend, and you land an FBI agent."

Kylie looked at her with surprise. "Corrine, I haven't landed anyone."

"He likes you, it's obvious," Jenny said.

"It's obvious he's very serious about catching a killer," Kylie told them. "Come on, pirates! Yo, ho, ho! Let's go."

They were still on the street, several feet away from the entrance to the museum, when they saw their first pirate. It was a man dressed in stereotypical pirate clothing—breeches, frock coat, plumed hat, and high black boots.

He was entertaining children on the street when they saw him, making coins appear and disappear, growling "Arrr!" at every opportunity.

They paused to watch. Something about him was familiar.

"It's Matt," Kylie said, recognizing the bartender from the Cauldron.

"Yeah, it is!" Nancy said with surprise.

"He seems to be having the time of his life," Kylie murmured. "I wonder if he's just working on his own, if you need a permit to do this, or—"

"Quit complicating everything," Nancy told her.

The children moved on, and Nancy walked up to him, calling, "Yo, ho, ho!"

"Ah! A sassy wench, I say," Matt said. "Why, alas, missy, were my ship but near, I'd be takin' ye sailing—aye, the lot of ye," he said, grinning as he saw the others, "in the captain's cabin, were I a lucky man! I'm fond of sassy, that I am."

Nancy laughed delightedly. "This is great. Are you working for the museum?"

"Sassy wench, you'd question me, eh?" he demanded. Then he grinned and lowered his voice as Kylie, Corrine, and Jenny approached. "No, I'm not working for the museum, but they don't seem to mind me here. I'm opening in a show in a few weeks. We're doing a new musical based on the pirates off the coast. This is my way of helping out, getting into character—and getting local merchants to carry the advertisements for us."

"Well, you're doing a great job out here," Kylie said. "The kids love you."

"I love kids! And the ladies, of course. I pose for pictures with people out here, zillions of them. Hey, it's a tough job, but you know how that goes, someone may not *have* to do it, but what the heck, it's fun, and it may pay off."

"Busy man," Kylie said. "Bartending, acting, and pirating."

"Good thing I like people," he told them.

"Well, if we can get back up here, we'll see your show," Nancy promised, clearly enthralled.

"We need a picture!" Jenny declared. "No strippers, but maybe a pirate?" she asked Corrine.

Corrine laughed. "Sure!"

"Crowd round—I'm a selfie expert," Matt told them.

Corrine produced her phone and Matt, drawing them all in close and stretching out his arm with the camera, said, "Say *arrr*!" He took several pictures, telling them to "work it!"

He returned Corrine's camera, and Kylie noticed a woman with two children about six or seven waiting patiently for their turn with the pirate.

"Thanks," Kylie said, slipping an arm around Nancy's shoulders and easing her away. "Your public is waiting."

Matt nodded, but then he crooked a finger at Kylie. She paused. "Are you all right?" he asked quietly. "I was about to call the cops last night—you seemed really distressed. I figured that guy was someone in authority, but I worried afterward that I probably should have called the cops."

"The news was just really...horrible," she said. "I'm fine. You'd better go. Your fans are waiting patiently!"

She turned to join the others.

The way they lingered for her to join them reminded her of a strange classroom picture: tiny Nancy next to Corrine and Corrine next to Jenny. Small, medium, and large.

"What was that about?" Jenny asked protectively.

"He just wanted to make sure I was all right after last night."

"Ah, Kylie, an FBI guy and a pirate! You're raking them in," Jenny teased.

Kylie groaned. "May we just see the pirates?"

As they headed into the museum, Corrine reminded them, "No bailing on me. After dinner, we're going to find Carl Fisher's ghost tour—I'll bet he's good. And then Kylie can rake in a tour guide, too! They'll wind up arguing history all night."

Kylie laughed, shaking her head. "Yeah, do we know how to get wild, or what?"

Jon didn't make an appointment with Dr. Sayers; he simply walked the short distance to the man's office.

While signs on most businesses advertised tarot card, palmistry, tea leaves, and all manner of readings, there was nothing other than the doctor's name on his door.

An older woman sat at a desk in a small reception area, and there was one door behind her. The place seemed small, but pleasantly appealing. Copies of paintings by the old masters adorned the wall; they seemed to invoke the romantic, including literary characters such as the Lady of the Lake from *Le Morte d'Arthur*, and a mystical angel rising above questing knights from the Round Table.

"Hello," the woman said pleasantly. "Welcome. I don't have an appointment for Dr. Sayers on the books right now— would you like to make arrangements to see him? I'm afraid he's having lunch."

"I don't have an appointment. I just thought I'd try to see the doctor."

"He's a wonderful man, if something is troubling you. You're more than welcome to wait. You're aware that people see him as a therapist? As well as for past-life regressions."

Jon produced his badge. "I really just need a few minutes of his time."

"Oh. Oh!" she said and jumped up. "He is having lunch, but he's just in his office. Give me a minute." She started for the door and then stopped, turning back and frowning. "What...what is this in reference to? I can promise you, Dr. Sayers is a truly fine man, and his practice is perfectly legal."

"I'm just hoping he won't mind speaking with me. I don't suspect him of any wrongdoing in the least," Jon said. "I just need some help with something."

She looked at him a bit suspiciously another few seconds, then opened the door to the inner office and disappeared. She reappeared moments later and invited him in, "The doctor will see you now."

Jon thanked her and went in.

Like the reception area, the inner office was handsomely appointed. There was a desk, paintings on the wall, a chaise longue upholstered in a dark crimson velvet, and numerous matching chairs. Maybe he held group sessions for therapy or—as with Kylie and her group—allowed friends in while working with one or the other.

Dr. Sayers had cleared up whatever lunch he'd been having; the desk he sat behind showed no sign of any kind of leftover food. He stood, offering his hand. He was in his early to midthirties, dressed in a casual suit, tanned as if he worked on it, and quick to offer a grim nod.

"Sir," he began, "I'm happy to help law enforcement at any time, but I'm not sure what this is about."

Jon shook his hand. "Special Agent Jon Dickson, Dr. Sayers."

"Please, sit, what can I do for you?"

"I'm not particularly sure, but thank you for indulging me. You saw a young woman the other day—let me correct myself—you saw four young women the other day. Three apparently had lovely past lives. One believed she was being murdered."

Sayers arched a brow. "You know I can't discuss patients."

"People seeing you for a regression aren't exactly patients," Jon said.

"I'm not a palm reader—not to cast aspersions on palm readers. Many see things, help others see things, and guide them gently toward what would be right for their lives. But as you see, I am a licensed psychologist."

"I understand that. I've come for what help you can give me. I met Miss Connelly the other night. She was extremely upset when she heard about the murder of Annie Hampton."

Sayers's manner seemed to change from black to white. "Oh, my god! Yes, right… I'd love to help you, but I don't know what I can tell you. Poor Miss Hampton. I heard she might have been a victim of a serial killer. Kylie Connelly was in this office precisely when that murder was happening."

He paused. "Do you think I might have tapped on something real? Not that my therapy sessions aren't entirely real, or that past-life regressions don't happen with people as well. You see, I believe in past lives, Special Agent Dickson. I'm not playing at the paranormal in any way because I've set up shop in Salem. I'm a guide. I only take people where they are going into their own minds. But… I was here, and she was here exactly when they're saying Annie Hampton must have been attacked."

"Have you ever had anything like that happen with another client, such as with Miss Connelly?" Jon asked.

Sayers shook his head. "I still have reservations about speaking with you. Doctor-patient privilege."

"But you didn't see her as a doctor."

"I didn't see her as a charlatan, if that's what you're suggesting."

"Not at all. As I said, I'm just here for help. Do you think Miss Connelly really saw something? That it's possible she saw through someone else's eyes, and was somehow with Annie Hampton when she was murdered?"

Sayers sat back, looking at him with eyes full of wonder. "I do. I was with her. To be honest, we were frightened, her friends and I. She was fighting the air, crying out. I was this close to dialing for emergency help. It was so odd... She was smiling at first. She seemed so happy, and then scared, and then she was screaming. I had to work to break her out of her hypnotic state."

"Thank you very much, Dr. Sayers. I appreciate you seeing me."

"This is no quack situation, I assure you. Yes, I believe Kylie Connelly saw whoever murdered Annie Hampton. I believe she saw a serial killer at work."

The pirate museum offered all manner of artifacts, a fun cave to explore, and all kinds of interesting tidbits of information. They had a great time exploring, and since they'd decided on dinner at about seven, they hopped over to another favorite museum and store, Count Orlok's Nightmare Gallery, where movie monsters and explanations regarding them were on display.

Movie monsters were fun.

They weren't real.

Jenny bought a few T-shirts, as did Corrine—her beloved Derrick would love them.

When they were about to go to the brewery, Kylie texted Jon Dickson. He was already at there, he texted back; he'd go ahead and get a table.

When they arrived, and the hostess came out to greet them, Jon stood and waved as he saw them. He greeted them all pleasantly, asking about their day. A waitress brought them flights of beer to taste and promised to be back soon for their orders.

Naturally, Kylie wanted to know how his day had gone, but she was polite and sat—perhaps too quietly—as the others went on about the things they'd been doing.

Then out of nowhere, Jenny, sitting very tall, as if she were standing and using the authority of her six feet—asked Jon point-blank if dragging Kylie to the graveyard had helped in any way.

"Yes," he answered simply.

"You caught him? You know who did it?" Jenny demanded with surprise.

"No, but I feel Kylie is helping me put puzzle pieces together."

"Are you any closer?" Corrine asked. "It's so sad, really. I didn't know Annie Hampton, but I feel guilty having my bachelorette weekend when something so terrible happened. I wonder if that makes me strange."

"It makes you human in the best way possible," Jon assured her. "But regrettably, there are forty to forty-six murders a day in the U.S. alone—statistically."

"Oh, that's horrible," Nancy said. "Almost one a day per state!"

"Well," Jon said, "it's not per state. So, how much longer do you have in Salem?"

"We leave Monday morning," Corrine told him. "We all go back to work on Tuesday. Except for Kylie. She has the week, if she chooses to take it. She was handpicked to oversee tours and research at the Trelawny House. It's a historic property that's undergone tremendous renovation and preparation. The last of the inspectors come through this week, and her boss—some billionaire who bought the property—insisted she take time after all the work she did getting everything up to par. Oh, and there's a tavern—Colonial food, of course. Kylie did all the food research, too."

Jon looked over at Kylie and smiled. Was he wondering what she intended to do with her week? She felt her color deepening, but before she could be put on the spot, he asked the others what they did.

"I work on Wall Street. I'm a stockbroker," Nancy told him.

"Nice," he told her. "That must be intense."

"I love it," she informed him.

"She's tiny, but fierce," Jenny assured him. "I'm not so exciting—I'm an accountant."

"Don't let her fool you," Kylie said. "Jenny is head accountant for one of the largest hotel chains in the country. No, the world, right?"

Jenny shrugged.

"And Corrine is head manager for one of New York City's largest restaurant chains," Kylie said.

"And I'm looking forward to taking time off for my honeymoon," Corrine said.

"When is the wedding?" Jon asked politely.

"November," Corrine said. "We're really excited. "We've rented Kylie's place—well, Trelawny House—for the reception. And we're being married at Grace Church. You've met my bridesmaids… Derrick will have my brother, his brother, and his best friend stand with him. And we have little relatives as ring bearer and flower girls. Kind of traditional, and kind of not."

"Sounds great," Jon said.

"Yes, doesn't it?" Corrine said. "Now, Special Agent Jonathan Wolf Dickson, I think we need to know more about you and exactly what you're doing here. You're a local, but you've rented weird space in a building on Essex Street. Where's your home? Where are your family?"

"Corrine!" Kylie protested.

"Well, he cornered us yesterday," Corrine said. "It's our turn to corner him."

"I'm from here," Jon said easily. "I grew up about two blocks from the Salem Witch Museum. My parents still own the house, but they're at the Cape half the time, and when they're gone now, they rent it out. I'm on Essex Street in that weird little space because it's where I wanted to be."

"You have something against hotels?" Nancy asked.

He grinned. "I like my own space."

"Hmm." Nancy looked at him, drumming her fingers on the table. "Okay, we know you went to Yale."

"Yes, I did."

Nancy looked at Corrine. "Not Harvard, but..."

"I went to community college first. I finished at Yale after a stint in the military."

Nancy laughed. "Hey, in my opinion, the college doesn't matter as much as the teachers and what you choose to put into your classes. Still, if people are trying to make you feel insecure, it's nice to have the fallback of a great school."

"Did I try to make any of you insecure?" he asked.

"Not your fault," Corrine told him. "You walk into a room, and...well, you have an air about you. You scared us last night."

"I'm sorry."

She smiled, then let it fade. "But you came here because you've been following what you believe to be a serial killer. So it makes sense if you're a little intense about it."

"If that's what you want to call it," he agreed.

"So now what's going on?" Jenny asked.

He hesitated, and then drew in a long breath. "I'm not

sure about Annie Hampton. Her murder may not be tied to the others."

"A copycat?" Kylie demanded, leaning forward.

He shrugged. "I can't say definitively. And because of that, I'm going to ask you all to be very careful. Don't split up. Whatever is going on, he preys on lone women. So don't go anywhere alone, don't wander off from one another." He hesitated for just a second, as if deciding how much to tell them. "Detective Ben Miller, Essex County, was on the local news tonight. He's putting out a warning, extending it to all surrounding areas. We're waiting on forensics from the burial ground, but this killer—or *these* killers—are good. They know how to clean up, how important it is that they leave nothing behind. ME's haven't found skin beneath nails, no hairs or fibers. The killings have been quick and vicious. But completely clean."

"Oh, not to worry! We'll stay with one another like glue," Jenny promised. She looked around the table. "Safety in numbers. Now, should we order?"

"Yes, let's eat," Corrine said. "We need to make the ghost tour."

Their waitress must have heard them. She was at the table at once, smiling, giving them suggestions, and writing down their choices.

When she was gone, Jon grinned at them all. "Ghost tour?" he asked. "You haven't taken one of the tours here before?"

"Of course, several times," Corrine said. "Nancy even gave tours one summer to help pay for college. We still love them. We consider ourselves connoisseurs of ghost tour guides."

"Ah, well," Jon murmured.

"And we met a fun guy last night who said he was the best, so, we'll check it out," Nancy said.

"At the Cauldron?" he asked.

"Yes, he was a little in-your-face, but he seemed fun," Jenny said.

"So, Jon, where do you live in Washington?" Nancy asked.

He spent the next few minutes answering a barrage of questions. He lived in Northern Virginia. His unit had their own offices, separate from the main FBI building. They worked with the amazing technical staff that served the main office, but his was a smaller team, comprised of field agents doing a lot of traveling. They stepped in when it appeared that danger threatened at certain levels, and a new approach was needed.

"I have a pretty amazing field director," he said. "He's willing to look in many directions, listen to any possibilities, and he's great at making arrangements with local officials."

Their food arrived. As they ate, Kylie stole a glance at Jon and found he was looking her way, smiling. He wasn't making fun of her friends, she knew. He was enjoying the fact they were checking on him and his credentials since he had been spending time with her—even if that time had been tensely spent in a graveyard.

She felt a pang, something clenching tightly inside her, and she was surprised it hurt so badly to realize that this dinner could be it—they might never see him again. He would go back to Virginia, or wherever the next lead in his case was, and she would head back to New York. Her life and work were there.

Her job was wonderful, but it had just about consumed all her time and attention for the past few months. That had kept her from thinking about any other aspect of her life, and shielded her from feeling.

She liked Jon even more as he spoke easily with all of them.

He insisted on picking up the check. "A small repayment for crashing a bachelorette weekend," he said.

When they were out on the street, they chatted casually.

They were all headed back to Essex Street: Jon to his office, and the women to meet up with the ghost tour.

Jon caught hold of Kylie's elbow, keeping her back slightly as they all walked.

"I'll be at the Cauldron in a bit. You should come back there after your tour, if you're up to it. If not, will you call me when you're all safely back in your room?"

"Yes, sure. But I imagine we'll be happy to stay out a bit tonight. It's the wild wicked Saturday night of our wild wicked bachelorette weekend," she said dryly.

"Great," he said, then he waved to the others and left for his office.

Kylie and her friends moved on, heading toward the pedestrian walkway where people were gathering in groups, ready to meet up with their different guides. Kylie asked if they needed to pay someone or get tickets, but Corrine had made the reservations and gotten their tickets earlier.

"Remember, we stick close," Jenny said. "Oh, there's our guy. Carl is with the History Most Haunted group. Looks like we can stick close with about fifty people!"

Too many for one tour, Kylie thought.

Carl hopped up on a box he carried with him so he could speak over the crowd. He had a deep, booming voice, and was easily heard. First, he welcomed everyone, and then announced they would split up.

He was dressed in Revolutionary clothing, similar to what Matt had been wearing as a pirate, but somehow a bit less swashbuckling. It suited him, and Carl looked dignified in the period costume.

"The tales we have to tell tonight are enough to chill your bones. But lest we leave anyone too far back to hear—and in order for us all to make it across streets when we need to— we will split up. My very excellent assistant, Charles, will be taking half of you. If you all will be so kind… Kind of move more to the left on this side, and more to the right if you're over here... You'll be Charles's group."

"Great," Jenny said. "We took this tour specifically for this guide—little did we know just how popular he is."

But as she spoke, Carl looked at them.

"He saw us!" Nancy said happily. "Thanks to your height, Jenny."

"Yeah, I'm a beacon," Jenny muttered.

"He's motioning for us to follow him," Corrine said.

They were on the wrong side, but Carl excused their move. "My cousin and her pals!" he lied to the crowd.

No one seemed to mind, but Carl hopped down from his box to greet them with hugs as if one of them was his cousin and the others long-lost friends.

"Thanks! You came," he told them.

"We're excited to see what you do with the tour," Nancy told him.

He winked, then launched into his speech for the crowd. "Okay, we're going to start with the Clue house!" he told them. "Why is it the Clue house, you ask? Well, let's move down the street a bit, to 128 Essex Street, to one of the loveliest and grandest manors on the avenue. The game Clue was called Murder by the inventor at first, and then, it was released in the United Kingdom as Cluedo—a play on the word clue and the word *ludo*, Latin for *I play*.

"Clue was invented in England by Anthony Pratt, who applied for his patent in 1944, but the world was a mess—World War II, you know—so it was 1947 when he received his patent, and then 1949 when the game was produced. Parker Brothers, a company that began its illustrious existence right here in Salem, had the rights and put the game out in the States.

"Why is this man babbling about a game, you ask? Aha! Because this beautiful house, deeply haunted by a cruel story of murder, might have made its way into the American version of the game. On April 6, 1830, Captain John White was bludgeoned and stabbed to death in his room on the second floor. The murder turned out to be a conspiracy with the most heinous of objectives—the old man's money! Before it was all over, Daniel Webster himself gave fiery oratory to see the conspirators brought to justice, one man committed suicide, knowing himself damned, and two hanged from the neck until dead.

"And many, many years later, George Parker, arranging for the American version of the game, certainly knew all about the murder and the weapons and the many rooms of this house."

As he had promised, Carl was an excellent guide, ready with historical facts and figures, as well as being a talented showman. But no matter how excellent a guide he proved to be, Kylie found herself watching everyone on the tour with them. One man nearby said to his wife that he felt odd, heading out on a ghost tour when a woman had recently been the victim of a cruel and brutal murder.

Many of the stories, however, were distant—and part of Salem's more ancient history. The group walked to the Howard Street Cemetery, and heard about Giles Corey, victim of the witch trials, who had been pressed to death—refusing to plea, since any plea would allow the confiscation of his property.

The old man who had died so pathetically—but given testimony against his own wife at her trial—was said to haunt the place.

They saw the old Salem Jail, which had been converted into luxury apartments—but naturally they were haunted, too.

The tour was good, and still Kylie had watched the other tourists.

At one point, she had the strange feeling she'd had the night before: a feeling that she was being watched.

When the tour ended, and Carl had collected his fair share of tips, the guide joined Kylie and her friends and asked, "Well?"

"Excellent," Corrine told him.

"I knew all the stories, but you gave them a great spin," Kylie said.

He smiled at her broadly. He certainly was appealing in his costume and with his friendly manner. If not for her current circumstances, Kylie would have enjoyed his obvious attempts to flirt with her. She wasn't entirely sure what was holding her back…except that she was attracted to Jon Dickson. And while there was nothing between them except for a strange partnership, she felt almost as if she would be cheating if she indulged another man's flirtation at the same time.

Thankfully, her friends didn't notice.

"I'm heading to the Cauldron," Carl mentioned. "Can I possibly get you to come along?"

"Sure!" Jenny said, and the others agreed.

"We were already planning to grab a drink there. We might have another friend joining us as well," Corrine said.

"Another beautiful woman?" Carl asked hopefully.

"He really can flatter," Kylie said to her friends, amused. He had such an open and charming way about him.

"A man. Tall, dark, mysterious, and handsome," Nancy said.

Carl shrugged. "Okay. I'll meet him. I probably have lots of friends hanging out in there now, too, so I can introduce you," he said. "You'll have lots of friends in Salem."

"Nancy is from Marblehead," Kylie said.

"*Almost* local," Carl said, and then he laughed. "I'm actually from Springfield, Missouri."

He linked arms with Nancy and Jenny, who were closest to him. He laughed, saying he had to twist a little to accommodate the foot of difference in their heights.

Corrine led the way.

Kylie paused for just a minute. The great throng from the many ghost tours was beginning to thin out. Old buildings stood tall; shops had only their dim lights on, and their displays seemed ghostly: rams' heads, pentagrams, and witch mannequins here and there with conical hats, black capes, and broomsticks. The faint sound of chatter echoed down the street, and the night air was deliciously cool. She looked around, noting one shop with Styrofoam headstones and a display of sticker-ghosts attached to the glass.

It was strange. She didn't feel the least touch of anything frightening or evil. No one was actually watching her. But she couldn't shake the feeling someone was out there. Perhaps she'd grown paranoid.

She hurried to join her friends. Kylie knew that Jon would be at the Cauldron, and she felt something inside her quicken a bit, and her skin grew warm.

She was foolish to be falling for such a man, especially under the circumstances. He lived in Virginia; her life was in New York.

She couldn't help it. She was glad to be seeing him. No one could change what they were feeling. She could only decide she wouldn't show it in any way.

CHAPTER SIX

Jon quickly befriended Matt Hudson and Cindy Smith; it was always good to get to know your local bartenders. People confided in them, and customers who didn't had a tendency to ignore them as if they were part of the bar, and often talked in front of them without really realizing they were being heard. Through the years, Jon had received invaluable help from bartenders and waitstaff.

He'd arrived at the Cauldron and grabbed a stool at the bar shortly after he said goodbye to Kylie and her friends after dinner. All he'd done in his office was change his clothing.

Thinking about the ghost tour the girls were on had given him an idea; tour guides might be the type of people to travel easily and still keep a job—and might have a secret affair with Annie Hampton.

Matt already knew the names of all the local tour companies, but Cindy supplied him with the most popular guides—Carl Fisher on the top of the list. Jon sent the names and info back to his technical staff at the Virginia offices, grateful his unit had an amazing on-call staff who could be asked to research anything at almost any time of the day or night.

Matt and Cindy kept checking in on Jon between other customers. Both asked him about the night before, about the young woman who had all but passed out in his arms. Matt wondered if they were long-time friends.

"Saw their little foursome today," he mentioned. "They were heading to the pirate museum. All of them are so sweet! Nice group, but almost intimidating. Like a foursome of supermodels. Well, one would be a short supermodel, but really...wow." Matt shook his head. "Anyway, last night was scary."

"Yeah," Cindy said, pausing with two drinks in her hand. Then she laughed softly. "That poor woman. First, she's just staring at the TV and whatever politician was talking, and then the news about the murder. She was fresh-fallen-snow-white. Good thing you came up when you did. You saved her from falling. You didn't know her already?" Cindy asked.

"No, I was just trying to help, and it worked out. I know her now," Jon said lightly.

"Nice," Matt said, and his look seemed to silently note that Jon was lucky to know Kylie now.

Jon just nodded. "Really, all the girls are my friends now. I'm expecting them in here soon, and you're getting so busy. Not to give you more to do, but I noticed some counter seating across the room over there—"

"Say no more, friend, I've got you covered," Matt assured him. He found a reserved sign beneath the bar and hurried out with it, securing the space just before a flood of people entered the bar.

Jon lowered his head, smiling slightly. He'd liked to think it was his winning personality that brought such compliance; however, it probably had more to do with the number of drinks he'd bought for some of the locals he met the night before. For himself, he'd been sipping the same near-beer all night.

Near-beer was best tonight; it still felt as if his mind was on a constant reel. If he went by the case history, a woman had already been murdered here, so the killer would move on. But something wasn't right this time. And instinct led him back here, to watch and to listen. And that was best done with a clear head. Which meant no bartender would really warm to him...unless he kept his tab going by other means.

Cindy came by again to check on him. "You doing okay?"

"Great, thanks. Hey, will you and Matt do me a favor? Those friends who are due soon...make sure I get their tab."

"Of course."

"You two work really amazingly together," Jon told her. "Are you long-time friends?"

"Matt's a great guy, but no, not a long time. I'm from Concord. He's from the Plymouth area. I love working with him." She lowered her voice. "Matt is definitely my favorite coworker. The other jerks, they think I should handle it all. One of them even said female bartenders can make more money, just showing a little...well, you know. I wanted to trounce him or tell my boss or...whatever. I need the job. I'm going back to school. I just wish Matt didn't travel so much."

"He travels a lot?"

"Oh, yeah, he's an actor and takes jobs wherever he can. He never misses his shifts, but every time he has a few days he can put together with one of the other guys picking up his shifts, he takes off. Ah, still, I do love him! Not a sexist or mean bone in his body."

"Good to hear," Jon said pleasantly.

"Do you want a fresh bottle of near-beer to not actually drink?" she asked him, grinning.

"Sure," he told her.

She smiled, replaced his bottle, and moved on.

An older man Jon had talked to before came in, along with a little crowd he introduced as his nephews and nieces. Jon ordered drinks for them and they chatted easily, until some-one brought up the murder, and one of the girls looked upset.

"You knew Annie Hampton?" Jon asked her.

"Best teacher ever. Oh, and please, don't worry. I am twenty-one now," the girl told him, indicating her beer. She offered her hand to him. "I had her a few years back. I'm Brittany."

"Jon," he told her, taking her hand. "Do you know if she was seeing anyone? I heard she was dedicated to her students, and she didn't have much time to go out, but she told friends she was seeing someone. She wouldn't tell anyone who it was. Said she was seeing a mystery man."

Brittany shrugged. She didn't seem curious that he was ask-ing such specific questions. "She was dedicated. Best teacher possible. But everyone is human. I heard rumors about her seeing someone, too. I wondered if she was just making it up so people would leave her alone. But you know, maybe she was seeing someone who came and went and didn't demand much of her time."

She hesitated, looking around as if assuring herself her uncle wasn't listening. "I think she was seeing him just as a…um. A quickie. A booty call, you know? Or maybe she was into him, and he was just using her. Or he might have been mar-ried. And so she wouldn't have introduced him to her family or friends. Not a BFF with benefits—an occasional acquain-tance with benefits."

"Too bad. If this man stepped forward, he might be able to help." As he spoke, Jon noted Dr. Sayers come in, accompa-nied by a group of friends. Or perhaps clients. They moved quickly to a booth in the back.

"I hadn't seen Miss Hampton in a while," Brittany was saying. "My classmates under her are all out of school and haven't seen much of her because we're moving on with life. But maybe now we're breathing a sigh of relief because the distance means we don't have to feel the pain as much. Anyway…"

She paused and looked over at her uncle, who was gesturing at her to get the check. "Uncle Jared! Hey, no, we don't have a check—Jon picked up the bill."

Good old Uncle Jared slapped Jon on the back. Jon grinned and lifted his drink in a toast.

Then the door opened again, and Kylie was there with her group—including the tour guide.

Jon's heart gave a little slam. He had been worried, even though the women had all been together on a busy Saturday night, surrounded by people. It was ridiculous, but he had been worried nonetheless. Corrine, Jenny, and Nancy were all attractive, filled with energy and blessed with young and lovely appearance.

But there was something about Kylie.

He wasn't the only one who noticed it. Heads turned when she walked into a room.

And that, he realized, was what made him uneasy. He wondered just what lay in the hearts and minds of those who watched her.

And if anyone watching her suspected there might be something very special about her indeed.

It was a Saturday night, and the Cauldron was a busy place. It stayed open until 1:00 a.m., so their arrival at 10:30 meant they had plenty of time to enjoy the crowd and their newly acquired friends.

Kylie spotted Jon the moment they arrived. He had changed into casual jeans and a gray flannel shirt, and appeared like any tourist. Although there was probably nothing he could do about his commanding presence, no matter what he wore. He was seated at the bar, surrounded by a group that included men and women, young and not so young.

Watching him hold court, Kylie noted he had a great smile. He had the ability to charm. But she knew why he was there: he was probably still working. Maybe he was finding more pieces of the puzzle. Maybe she had even helped.

Matt—minus his pirate apparel—was behind the bar, shirt-sleeves rolled up, collar open, curly dark hair casually falling against his forehead. He was serving quickly alongside Cindy. While it was busy, the two of them worked smoothly and ably, engaging with their crowd.

"Wow, our little gang is all here," Jenny said quietly to Kylie. The two of them were a few steps behind the others.

"I knew Jon would be here," Kylie said.

"Jon, eh?" Jenny teased. "Not Special Agent Dickson?"

"We did just have dinner with him," Kylie said.

"We did. Yes, I'll call him Jon now, too," Jenny said. "But I wasn't referring to Jon. Look. Over in the far corner."

Kylie swiveled.

Dr. Sayers—also in casual dress, dark sweater and jeans, was at a table with friends. Two women and two men, all in their thirties. The tail end of a plate of appetizers was on the table before them along with a few empty pitchers of beer.

"Do we say hello, or do we pretend we don't see him? I guess it would be rude to interrupt. Let's just head to the bar," Jenny said.

"Pretty crowded there," Kylie noted.

"Want to see if Special Agent Dickson will make room for you?" Jenny asked.

Kylie didn't have a chance to answer. Jon had risen, laughing and responding to something being said by Matt, but he was turning toward her and pointing down the bar. There was a section with a Reserved notice set on it.

Jon reached them, shaking hands with Carl as Corrine introduced the two—not using Jon's title, just his name.

"You were in here last night, right, over at a table?" Carl asked politely.

"Guilty as charged," Jon said. "Nice to meet you. You do a great tour, I hear."

"I do!" Carl told him. "And there was some pressure on me, too, with these ladies. They know their stuff, but they're here for a bachelorette party. No chance of getting really friendly with this crew—they'll be moving on," he warned Jon. "But they're bright and sweet and I enjoy just looking at them and talking shop. They know as much about the place as I do."

"Well, I'm glad I bribed my way into holding some extra seats. The tour went well tonight?" he asked, ushering them over to the empty stools.

Kylie's friends made sure she was seated by Jon Dickson. "Told you he was into you," Jenny whispered to her.

Kylie could only hope they hadn't made it too obvious.

Nancy started right in asking Carl about himself. "So, you just fell in love with Salem and decided to stay?" She turned to look at Jon. "He's originally from Missouri."

"I just talked for two hours. What about you ladies? Oh, yes, sorry, and you, too, Jon," Carl said.

"Sounds like your story is more interesting," Jon told him. "You came from far away and moved here and became a ghost guide?"

"I think it's one of the most interesting places in the country. Maybe the world," Carl said. "I remember the first time I learned about the fact we had witches in the US—I was just a kid. I read about Laurie Cabot and how she became the Official Witch of Salem, and when I finally came here, it was so different from my hometown—cool shops, not the same chains you find everywhere."

"Are you Wiccan?" Kylie asked him.

"No, but I have friends who are, and it's just all about nature and good things, certainly not anything evil. The Puritans... Those suckers were pretty misguided, but if you're ever out at night around here on some of the roads where the forests are dense... Well, you can kind of understand how they might have seen the devil in everything. There is a theory that the whole mess was over property disputes and petty arguments, but I think they let themselves believe it was all true. Some of them, anyway. Over in Europe, the belief in the devil and the fires of hell and pacts and imps and all that was way worse than here."

"I think you're right," Jon said. "The entire community was swept up in the frenzy, and those who suggested it would end if the girls were stopped or punished wound up accused themselves. But I don't think so many people were truly so messed up they'd execute that many people over greed. Maybe because I don't want to believe it. But we're still like that, aren't we? If we don't like someone, it's easier to believe bad behavior out of them."

"Jon is from Salem," Kylie said.

"Really," Carl said, as if that was a cool bit of information. "Then you know all the stories. The witch trials are tragic history. So much more went on here."

Nancy laughed. "And you don't ever get tired of it all?"

"Oh, I do, but I love the real stories we get here. And I go other places. Great cities with great stories." Carl shrugged. "I was into acting. Los Angeles just wasn't giving me an income. I can be in all kinds of theatrical things here and make a living. And travel around when I want to."

Kylie glanced over at Jon; his face revealed nothing.

The conversation turned to different places: Boston, New York, DC, and then Richmond.

After a moment, Jon excused himself to use his phone. Kylie watched him walk toward the door, but then made a point of joining the conversation, which turned to Corrine's wedding.

She didn't stare after Jon—she really didn't. But she did look up a few minutes later.

He had come back inside and was over at another table talking to someone. Kylie twisted around to see who was at the table.

She was surprised to see it was Dr. Sayers.

"Kylie?" Corrine said, giving her a nudge.

"Um, yes, what? Sorry," she said.

"You love books, but hate Ouija boards, right?" Corrine said.

"There are some really great boards in Salem," Carl said.

"Yes, I've seen some," Kylie said. "And I don't hate them. I just don't want one."

The conversation went on. She wasn't really paying any attention; she was too curious regarding the fact that Jon seemed to know Dr. Sayers.

But in a minute, Jon was back. Smiling, chatting, casual. Just another visitor to a bar.

The night wore on with him excusing himself now and then and making rounds. At one point, Kylie saw him talking to the bartenders. Everyone seemed to accept his mingling easily. After all, Jon was from Salem.

She noted he'd picked up a matchbox, and he was tapping it absently on the table, conversing with the others, pleasant, and yet she couldn't help but feel his mind wasn't really there. Something was going on behind all his light banter.

Corrine seemed to be having a good time, and Kylie was happy that her friend was having the weekend trip she'd wanted. But it came to a point where Kylie wanted to scream. It was growing late. She'd slept badly. She was tired.

And yet, she was afraid to sleep again.

She suddenly felt as if the bar was obnoxiously loud. She desperately needed to escape. The bar would close soon, but not soon enough for her.

Jon took his seat beside her again, but even that didn't ease whatever had started to plague her.

She stood and yawned elaborately, then apologized. "I'm so sorry. I'm going to have to leave. Please, everyone else should stay. We're only about three blocks from the hotel—"

"I'll walk you," Jon said quickly, rising. "I'm ready to call it quits, too."

"I wouldn't mind walking you back, either," Carl said.

"I didn't want anyone else to have to leave," Kylie protested. "This is Corrine's big weekend and you should all have fun."

"Noise was getting to be a bit much for me," Jon said. "Seriously, you four stay, I'm happy to get going. Oh, the tab's taken care of. Whatever you order."

"Thank you! That's not necessary," Corrine told him.

"My pleasure. Please, stay. Kylie will be fine with me," Jon said. He took gentle hold of her elbow and led her toward the door.

Dr. Sayers was still at the booth with his friends. He watched them go, nodding and lifting a hand as Kylie turned to look his way. He offered a weak smile.

Outside, Kylie demanded, "How do you know Sayers?"

"I went to see him."

She stared at him, stunned. "You were...regressed?"

"No," he admitted. "I went to ask about you."

"Is that even legal?" she demanded.

"Kylie—"

"You think I faked it?" she asked angrily.

"No. I needed to see if he could explain what happened, if he'd led you where you went in your state," Jon said. He stopped in the near-empty street and looked at her. "I believe you. I'm the one who asked for your help today, remember? I never thought you were making anything up. That's obvious, I would think."

She was still for a minute. Then she asked, her voice barely a whisper, "Why? Why would you believe what I don't even believe myself?"

He stepped close to her, smiling. He touched her face gently, and then withdrew as if he had gone too far. "I'm with a supposed 'elite' unit of the criminal division. In truth, we're the last-resort, desperate unit. I told you… I've seen things that shouldn't be. Not by the laws of science as we know them now. I believe you because I pride myself on knowing people, and I think you're honest and caring and have integrity. I saw Sayers because I needed to know what he felt, what he saw, and what he did."

He was quiet a minute. "I've thought about asking you about the possibility of going under again, to see if you can recall more, bring the vision any further. On the one hand, that's not fair to you. I don't want to make you go through all that again. On the other hand, if you're strong enough to do it, you might save a life in the future."

He was so earnest. He spoke of caring and integrity, and she realized those were the qualities in him that seemed to draw her, along with the physical draw she felt. Especially standing this close. He smelled good, his scent both clean and musky, something that hinted of the earth and the woods and something compellingly male.

And she liked him. Really liked him. More and more each time she saw him.

Part of it seemed so wrong. A woman had been murdered. No, several women had been brutally murdered, and somehow she had witnessed a murder. No, she had *felt and experienced* a murder.

"I'll continue to do anything I can to help," she said quietly. "But I'm not sure I can go through that again."

He surveyed her for a moment. He nodded. "Okay. Come on, let me get you back to the hotel."

They reached the hotel and right before going in, she found that she balked. "Is he staying here?"

He didn't ask her who.

He knew who she meant. But still, she made sure. "The senator," she said. "Michael Westerly. The man I saw during my regression."

Jon grimaced. "I just found out. I stepped outside because I had a call from my office about his movements. Yes, he's staying here. But the thing is, we still have nothing concrete on him, and he's using his wife as his alibi. But I don't believe you need to check out of your hotel—he doesn't know you and would have absolutely no idea you suspect him of anything."

"Or that I believe I saw him kill Annie Hampton in a *dream*."

"Right," he said. "There's no way he could know. I don't think. I mean, no one knows about what you saw when you were hypnotized, right, except for me, Dr. Sayers, Nancy, Jenny, and Corrine?"

"Correct."

"Well, let me walk you all the way up. I can hang out in the hall and watch your door until your friends come back."

She smiled. "It's a suite. We have a little living room/kitchen combo thing. No need for you hang out in a hallway, but…yeah, if you want to stay until they get back, it would be super."

"Sitting on a sofa, standing in a hall… Sitting on a sofa does sound better. Let's go."

She thought he was going to reach for her hand; maybe he had been about to. Apparently, he remembered they were on the trail of a murderer, following a most unusual path. He turned and walked with long, quick strides, and she kept pace.

The hotel was quiet. Most people were probably sleeping or out enjoying their Saturday night.

It was a little strange when he entered the room behind her. She was surprised to feel flustered. He was a man who would never press anything, and he might not even find her appealing. She had something he needed. And he intended to protect that by protecting her.

Still, the air seemed charged when he was near. Now that they were alone together, she was a little alarmed to acknowledge just how attractive she found him.

She offered him something to drink; he opted for coffee.

They hadn't been there more than a few minutes when there was a knock on the door. Kylie started toward it, but Jon put up a hand and walked over to the door. She realized he had taken a casual stance, but one that would allow him to reach back to his weapon—in his holster, she thought—in a split second.

He looked out the peephole, and then frowned and threw the door open, stepping out into the hall. "Lock the door."

As he headed down the hallway, toward the bank of elevators, Kylie shut and locked the door, then bolted it. She was too surprised to feel any kind of fear. She hoped he would return quickly, that it would be nothing, that Jon was just playing everything safe.

A second later, there was a huge thud.

CHAPTER SEVEN

The hotel was nowhere near as old as the area in general, having been built in the 1920s, but it was iconic for Salem. It wasn't as luxurious as modern standards, but it did offer a penthouse level that had suites, all considered worthy of the best patrons. They were named after four of the magistrates and justices who presided over the witch trials: Stoughton, Hathorne, Gedney, and Corwin.

Corwin was the best known and studied, perhaps because his home remained on the tourist and "haunted" trails. That suite was the largest and considered the best in the hotel. Naturally, Michael Westerly would be in one of those suites—most likely the Corwin suite.

Following the oldest trick in the book, Jon watched the needle atop the elevator doors; only one was moving, heading for the penthouse.

He raced for the stairs.

He had just reached the stairwell door when he heard the reverberating sound that might have been something like a sonic boom. Whatever it was shook the hotel itself.

Striding swiftly to the window at the end of the hall, Jon

looked out on the street below. He heard the commotion before he saw the cause: a car had jumped the curb and driven into the front of the hotel.

He knew the area well enough to be thankful the car had crashed into the front corner of the old hotel. The little boutique and souvenir store nearby closed by seven, meaning it was unlikely anyone within the hotel had been hurt.

Of course, he didn't know the fate of the driver. He had his phone out, though he was sure others were already dialing emergency services as well. Still, he put through his call.

He knew he should head down to the street; his military days had given him a basic knowledge of emergency treatment. He was still torn. He needed to know if Westerly had been tapping at Kylie's door.

The right thing to do was hurry down without checking on Westerly's whereabouts. But as he made his way down the stairs to street level, he kept thinking, what if Westerly had instantly opened his door? What would it prove?

And if he didn't—what would *that* prove? That he was hiding in the suite somewhere and had no intention of appearing at the sound of a knock? Jon had reason to force his way into the man's suite.

He dialed Kylie's phone. She answered on the first ring.

"Accident in the street below. Stay locked in. I'll be right back."

"The hotel was hit...by a car?" Her voice sounded incredulous. "I just looked out—"

"Yes, that was the bang. I don't know much, but I'm checking on the driver or any pedestrians who might have been in the way. Keep your door locked."

She was silent—probably just for a second—but he was hurrying.

He repeated, "Keep your door locked," and rushed down to the street.

★ ★ ★

Seconds dragged like hours.

The minute the car hit, people on the streets had gathered, coming around but keeping a distance. Apparently, someone in the crowd had medical training, a young man who rushed to the car.

Kylie prayed no one had been in the path of the runaway car. She thought not, because the young man raced straight for the driver's seat.

She watched as Jon rushed out from the front of the hotel. He went to the young man, who spoke to him quickly. They opened the driver's door but didn't attempt to remove the driver. He must have been bleeding from an injury; she saw Jon rip up the tails of his shirt and hand them over to the young man who proceeded to use the fabric to staunch blood.

A siren screamed; police cars and an ambulance were quickly on sight. She watched as the EMTs approached, briefly conferring with both Jon and the other man. A collar was set around the driver's neck and he was stretched out with as little trauma as possible and laid on a gurney.

Then, the ambulance took off, one policeman in the back with him. Several more stayed behind, evidently to speak to witnesses. One officer seemed to be questioning Jon and the young man who had helped. Other were seeking help from the gathered crowd.

Kylie saw her friends were part of the crowd now, on the sidewalk staring and talking to one another. Of course. The Cauldron was almost directly across the street from the hotel, not much of a walk. Those in the restaurant would have heard the noise.

Minutes had passed; it seemed like forever. Then, even while the officer was still speaking with Jon, Kylie saw that Corrine, Jenny, and Nancy had seen Jon, and they started toward him, looking anxious, certainly worried about the accident and probably about her as well.

Kylie thought she heard footsteps hurrying along the hallway and she turned from the window, afraid she'd hear those footsteps pause by the door.

She realized she was afraid to stay inside, even though the door was locked. She wanted to be downstairs, trying to understand what was going on along with what now appeared to be several people staying in the hotel and dozens of workers and tourists from the late-night venues.

The footsteps continued…right on past her room. She breathed a sigh of relief. She was letting her imagination run away—but it was hard not to.

Growing increasingly anxious, Kylie looked out the window again. Jon was still speaking with a policeman. She didn't see her friends anymore.

There was a knock at the door and the sound of a key sliding against a lock; her heart seemed to stop.

Nancy called out, "It's us!"

Kylie dashed over and took off the deadbolt. Nancy entered, followed by Corrine and Jenny, who were both talking at once.

"Incredible! I've heard of cars driving into yards and houses, but this is Salem. There's no big highway here—not in the historic district," Corrine said. "We heard the crash in the restaurant!"

Jenny picked up where she left off. "The driver really slammed into the place. They have structural engineers coming out now, but it seems he got an area with no support walls, or whatever—he hit that area by the door. Some guy in the street was explaining that wasn't where the support structure or whatever was. So the hotel is safe, or so the night manager has assured everyone. Can you imagine the paperwork on this, or what a mess it's going to be?"

"Was anyone hurt on the sidewalk or street?" Kylie asked anxiously.

"No, it's a miracle. It happened so late."

"The driver?" Kylie asked.

"He's alive. From what we gathered, there was a paramedic on vacation from Colorado on the scene—along with Jon!" Corrine said, before pausing to sigh a little dreamily. "Your boy popped right in, helping the paramedic stabilize his position—you have to be really careful about the neck and the back—but so far, the man is alive. Not conscious, and no one knows now just how badly he was hurt. Some people were speculating he might have had a heart attack while driving and lost control of the car. Jon said there was no smell of alcohol, but that doesn't mean he wasn't on drugs or... Well, it's all speculation right now."

Kylie would have protested that Jon wasn't *her boy*, but Corrine had moved on so quickly there was no point.

"We do need sleep," Nancy said. "But now we're all so wired!"

"We can watch the news," Jenny said, "until we wind down a little. I doubt they'll know anything other than a man crashed into an iconic hotel, but I'm willing to bet there will be some coverage."

"Great idea," Kylie muttered. "Let's watch more about what's keeping us all up."

"You didn't come down," Nancy said thoughtfully. "That was good. Jon told us he suggested you stay here. He also told us that Senator Westerly is staying here." She frowned. "He is very protective of you. Well, all of us, I think. But mainly you. He's a good guy." Corrine walked over to Kylie, setting her hands on her shoulders. "What are you going to do? Are you going to stay on for the days you have left?"

Kylie didn't have to answer—there was a knock on the door. For a moment, she felt her stomach tighten, but Jon called out, saying it was him.

Corrine ran to the door to let him in. "You finished with the police? What happened? Or how on earth did it happen?"

He shook his head. "I didn't see the accident," he said. "Same as you, just the aftermath." He looked across the room at Kylie and said, "No one knows. The driver is unconscious, and the police will speak with him, I'm certain, as soon as possible. The doctors have the say on that. Anyway, you're all here and set for the night."

"Yes," they all said in unison.

Jon nodded with satisfaction. "Then I'll leave you for the night." He still hesitated.

Nancy said, "You can watch TV with us for a while."

He smiled. "That's okay. I was just checking... Kylie, everything is all right?"

She managed a smile. "Despite a hole in the hotel and a poor man gravely injured in the hospital, yes."

"Anything...else?"

"No. I stayed locked in. Watched you all from the window."

"Well, then, good night," Jon said.

"Wait," Corrine said firmly.

Jon paused, arching a dark brow.

"We leave tomorrow. And Kylie—"

"Maybe Kylie should get back to New York," he said softly.

"Yes, yes, we can all leave together then," Jenny said.

"No, no. Kylie isn't going," Kylie said firmly.

"Kylie," Corrine said, "on top of everything else, a car just drove into our hotel! I love Salem, but at this time, it seems Salem is dangerous for you."

"Oh, come on," Kylie protested. "I'm a little nervous, yes, but as I said, this has to be solved for me ever to be sane again. Oh, Corrine, forgive me. I wanted this weekend to be so perfect for you, and I'm afraid that—"

"The weekend has been perfect for me. You all were wonderful. You did exactly what I wanted. As far as I'm concerned, it was all great. And so what if things are weird? Maybe the car crashing into the hotel did have something to do with all of this. You just never know."

Nancy cleared her throat. "Seriously? I want Kylie safe, too, but I don't think that a car driving into the hotel can have anything to do with anything. And while it seems bizarre to even contemplate that Michael Westerly is in the hotel, he is a politician. And what's that thing about politicians? Want to know when they're lying? When they open their mouths."

They were all silent. "Yes, Michael Westerly is in this hotel," Kylie said at last. "But I don't have to stay here. There are dozens of places nearby. But I'm not going to leave. Not until we know something."

"Kylie, that's silly," Corrine protested.

"No, it's not."

"You should stay away from Westerly. He speaks in Boston on Tuesday. If you're in New York, you'll be safe. Not that he knows you think he's a murderer anyway, but still, there's safety in distance."

"Is there?" Kylie asked, stepping forward determinedly. "People heard me in the bar, people who might have talked. He may know it was me who suggested he was a murderer. And, if I'm not crazy and it was him, then he doesn't hesitate to kill. And he'd find me in New York—or anywhere. This must be solved if I'm ever going to feel safe again. I tried to explain that to you. And the best way for me to help see that it's solved is to stay here."

"Alone?" Jenny gasped with horror. "Maybe I can find a way to call in and get out of work. I can at least try—"

"She won't be alone," Jon said.

They all turned to stare at him. Assuming, maybe, that he intended to move right in with Kylie. And while they all liked him, they were also protective, and might be a little worried about a man making such an easy assumption.

He smiled ruefully, his head lowering for a minute, amused. "Two more Krewe agents are due to arrive, Devin Lyle and Craig Rockwell. We'll keep this suite. Devin and Craig can take the second room. They're a married couple," he added quickly.

Silence greeted his words.

Then Jenny gasped. "Devin Lyle? I know that name. She writes children's books. And she's an FBI special agent or whatever?"

"She's still a writer. She's on the books as a consultant. We do that often, making use of people's...talents, while still allowing them their dreams." He shrugged. "Adam Harrison, who is the director in charge of our unit, also owns a theater and is involved in other endeavors. We're a varied group."

"Uh—great. I wish I was going to meet her! My nieces are in love with her books," Jenny said.

"I'm sure it can be arranged sometime."

"Wow," Jenny said.

Another awkward silence followed.

Kylie said, "Well, I'll be with people, well protected. Great. That's wonderful."

"I'll see that Devin and Lyle arrive as quickly as possible. They've been assigned to this already," Jon said. "And Devin owns a home just outside the historic district, toward Danvers. We might wind up out there. We'll see. Also, my field supervisor, Jackson Crow, was here before—he could be heading back. And there is another set of agents from this area as well who might come in when they finish with their current assignment. There will be no need for Kylie to be alone."

Corrine, Nancy, and Jenny turned as a threesome to look at Kylie, as if they were parents about to allow their teenage child a sleepaway trip for the first time.

"I guess..." Nancy began.

"That will be all right," Corrine finished.

Kylie laughed. "Yes, it will be fine. I'm a coward. But I'll be surrounded, with FBI! And I'll never feel safe again if I'm not able to see this through to the end."

Everyone was silent again. They all knew there were murders that were never solved.

"This will be solved," she insisted.

"Yes," Jon agreed. Then, because no one spoke, he added, "Good night, then. I'll see you before you leave."

"We won't leave her alone," Corrine said loyally.

"Of course not. I'll be here between nine and ten in the morning. Will that do?"

"We aren't in a hurry. We don't really have to leave until early afternoon," Corrine said.

"Between nine and ten," Jon told them. He stepped out.

Corrine went over to the door and locked it.

"It's almost 3:00 a.m.," Nancy murmured. "I guess we should try to get some sleep."

"I'd have slept better if Kylie had just asked him to stay here tonight," Corrine said, turning away from the door. "Kylie, you could come home with me." She put up a hand to stop any protest before she could finish. "Yes, I know, you live alone. But you could come and stay with Derrick and me—"

"No, no, no, Nancy, please! I've explained the way I feel. And I really have faith in Jon and his group of agents. They won't leave me alone."

"Great. You're going to be protected by a woman who writes children's books," Corrine said.

"Really, really good children's books," Jenny said.

"I think that if she's a consultant, she has to be good at something important. And I'm going to be fine. I swear it," Kylie said.

"Hey, it won't be bad getting to know tall, dark, and FBI a little better, too," Jenny said.

"You two do look good together," Nancy commented.

Corrine laughed. "Either one of them looks good, together

or not. That's beside the point. Anyway, it's a doomed romance. Kylie just got her dream job. Jon Dickson is with a special unit that's in Northern Virginia or Washington, DC, and long-distance relationships don't really seem to go…the distance. But seriously—"

"Seriously, I'm staying," Kylie said. "And, I'm going to get some sleep!"

She headed into the room she shared with Corrine and quickly got ready for bed. She could hear the others talking, but the night had taken its toll.

Although she thought she might lie awake for hours, she felt herself drifting almost as soon as her head hit the pillow.

It was strange, but she still thought she was awake—or at least, half awake—when she started dreaming. She wasn't hypnotized, so that was no excuse.

But she could swear that she opened her eyes and looked up—and saw Annie Hampton standing by her bed.

In any conscious realm, she surely would have screamed. But she didn't.

The woman just looked down at her, smiling sadly. It almost seemed that she brushed a lock of hair from Kylie's face. And she said very softly, "Thank you. Thank you for seeing, for believing, and for trying to help."

Then she was gone, and once again, Kylie wasn't sure if she was awake or asleep, but it quickly proved to be sleep.

She hadn't drawn the drapes and the sun was just starting to shine into the room when she awoke. Apparently, Corrine hadn't thought to close them, either. It was barely the crack of dawn.

Kylie crawled out of bed, closed the drapes, and crashed back into the bed. It was far too early to be awake and her body must have agreed. She wondered for a moment about her strange vision.

Wonder didn't last long; she quickly found that sleep was her only answer.

CHAPTER EIGHT

Jon returned to his office; Essex Street was very quiet by the time he arrived. The bars and shops were closed, and the last of the gawkers of the bizarre accident had headed to their homes or hotels.

Inside his little room, he found he had no desire to sleep. So he pulled out his computer and went over every note he had on the murders and studied the crime scenes again. He shook his head, muttering to himself.

It was impossible for Michael Westerly to have murdered Deanna Clark, Willow Cannon, or Cecily Bryant—unless he could be "beamed up" in a manner that defied science. He'd been several states away each time, in full view of the public.

And yet the murders were alike. To a T.

Copycat?

Or was it simply a step too far to believe that a woman had been hypnotized and *seen* herself as Annie Hampton being murdered?

The sun was beginning to rise when he heard a tap at his door. He jumped, aware that he was letting his fear and feelings for Kylie effect his usual levelheadedness.

But who the hell else might be looking for him when the sun was just rising?

He hadn't shed his clothing or his holster; he instinctively felt for his Glock as he walked toward the door, checking through a hole in the cardboard that covered the window.

Then smiling, he eased back and opened the door. "You knocked," he said.

His old friend was back. The man who had first haunted his youth and basically propelled his direction in life, Obadiah Jones.

"Polite, my friend—in my day, and yours," Obadiah told him.

"Well then, sir, please, do come in."

Jon figured that he'd never really know if ghosts got tired of standing and preferred to sit, although he was aware that they could grow weary sometimes, trying to manifest themselves to those who saw them for long periods of time.

Obadiah had been around a long time. He was good at being a ghost.

"Have a seat, please," Jon said.

"Thank you."

Obadiah found a chair in front of the desk as if expecting Jon to take his place behind it, so he did.

"I saw that accident tonight," Obadiah said.

"You did? What did you see?"

"You didn't see anything? I saw you talking with the police."

Jon shook his head. "I was in the hotel. I felt the impact. I ran out to see if I could help."

Obadiah nodded with pleasure. "I trained you well."

The ghost hadn't actually trained him. Apparently Obadiah knew that because he was smiling. "Sorry, you were always decent. I do pride myself on reminding you of that fact. But you had it in you. That's why I could...well, manipulate you a bit. And it worked. Well, in my mind."

"Thanks. So, what did you see?"

"When he was driving down the street, the old fellow grabbed his chest—then, I imagine he thought he was hitting the brakes but hit the gas instead."

"A heart attack," Jon murmured.

Obadiah inclined his head with a bit of a shrug. "Yes, but possibly, a heart attack brought on."

"I don't even know the man's name yet, but he had to be in his sixties. A heart attack at that age—really, at any age—isn't that much of an anomaly."

Obadiah shook his head. "I know the old fellow. Jimmy Marino. Well, he doesn't know me, but I know him. A nice fellow of Italian descent. His family has been in the area about a hundred years or so. Not as far back as some of the folks around here, but long enough."

"And?"

"Heart attack seems odd to me. He has an apartment down near the wharf. He and his wife had one of the big old Victorian houses in town, but she passed away young or youngish—she was just fifty. The cancer, you know. His kids are in Boston now, though they're good kids and come and see him. Thing is, he was talking to Mrs. Martinelli—a sweet Italian widow—at the memorial the other day. The two of them like to go sit at that memorial, you know, by the Old Burying Point."

"Yes, of course."

"And I hang out there, you know that."

"Yes."

"Well, the old fellow was happy, telling her that he'd just been to his doctor. He'd aced something called a 'stress test' and the doctor had told him he had the heart of a young man—not just a young man, but a football jock."

Jon leaned back in his chair, frowning. "Who would want to cause anyone to have a heart attack and drive into a hotel? Doesn't make any sense."

"I don't know. And I don't know much about modern medicine or science and I'm wondering how you could cause such a thing. And if you could, how you'd manage to get someone to have that heart attack and drive into a building. But it struck me as so odd that a man glowing because he'd passed a 'stress test' and had the heart of a football 'jock' could suddenly have a heart attack."

Obadiah paused for a minute, adjusted the scarf he wore around his neck as if he could really feel it. "I'm deeply distressed that the poor young woman was murdered. I haven't found anyone —" he paused again, grinning "—any dead friend, that is, who witnessed anything. Such a giving young woman, so young, to have something so terrible happen to her. Since I rather pushed you into your direction in life, I thought I should come to you with anything. And so I'm here."

Jon nodded thoughtfully. Odd, he thought. One of the girls had also mentioned the fact that it was bizarre, though none of them thought that it could have had anything to do with a murder.

And he still couldn't fathom it. An attempt at murder perhaps, but by a different culprit? Stabbing a woman in a cemetery and drugging someone into a heart attack were two very different things.

"Well?" Obadiah said.

"Food for thought. I have friends from my unit coming in tomorrow. And I'll certainly talk to Detective Ben Miller about it. You know that he's lead here on Annie Hampton's murder."

Obadiah nodded grimly. "You should go to bed. I never told you to give up sleep."

Jon smiled. "I'll do that. And thank you, my friend. Food for thought. Thank you."

"I'm keeping my eyes open," Obadiah promised, and rose.

Jon didn't have to let him out; he vanished on his own.

Jon went ahead and stripped down to his boxers. He lay down, even though he didn't think he'd sleep. What could the murder and the car accident have to do with each other?

He must have catnapped; he awoke to a pounding on the door. He leaped up, stepping into his pants and reaching for his small belt holster and Glock again before going to the door.

He needn't have worried; it was just Devin and Rocky. He welcomed them warmly. It was good—really, really good—to have more Krewe in town.

He had promised to keep Kylie safe. And it was certainly reassuring to have a greater sense of surety where that promise was concerned.

"I can't believe we're really leaving you," Jenny said, surveying her overnight suitcase and carryall bag in the center of the suite. "Well, I suppose the good in this is that if I've forgotten something—which I am prone to do—you'll be able to get it for me."

"Of course," Kylie said.

Corrine came out with her little suitcase and bag as well, shaking her head. "This is scary. We're not leaving you behind because you're working on a historic find, we're leaving you behind because of a horrible murder. I'm still—"

"I'll keep in contact every day, I promise," Kylie said.

"Do that, because if we don't hear from you—" Corrine began.

"We'll be calling in the militia," Nancy finished, dragging her bag out as well.

Kylie smiled. "You'll hear from me, I promise."

"We're beating a dead horse here," Corrine said pragmatically.

"Right. So where are we going to lunch?" Nancy asked.

"Nowhere yet," Corrine said firmly. "It's still early, and I'm waiting right here until that FBI man shows back up."

"I'm hungry," Jenny murmured. "We could call down—"

"They have a great brunch downstairs," Nancy suggested.

Kylie's phone rang then, and she hurried back into the bedroom to get it. She answered and returned to the others in the middle of the suite. It was Jon Dickson, telling her he was almost there. Even as he spoke, there was a knock on the door.

Corrine opened it, and Kylie was surprised to see a woman there, tall, in a pantsuit, and stunning with a wealth of long dark hair. She was accompanied by a tall man, athletically built, also in a suit, and breaking the intimidation of his size with a warm smile.

She started to frown, her fear receptors working overtime, but she quickly saw Jon right behind them.

"Hey," he said, coming around the other two as if ready to introduce them.

But the dark-haired woman smiled at her. "Hi, I'm Devin, and this is Rocky. Special Agent Craig Rockwell, to be more professional, I suppose."

"Wow!" Jenny said happily.

"I'm not that cool," Rocky said with a grin.

Jenny quickly flushed. "I, um, I didn't mean you. I mean Miss Lyle. It's so amazing to actually meet you!"

The dark-haired beauty made a face. "I'm really Mrs. Rockwell now, but thank you. You mean—you know my books?"

"I do. I adore them—my nieces adore them. So charming!"

"Well, thank you so much," Devin said.

"Okay, all right, I'll introduce in the other direction," Jon said, smiling. "Kylie Connolly, Corrine Rossello, Jenny Augur, and Nancy Ryman."

"A pleasure," Devin said, and her husband echoed her words.

Kylie looked over at Jon, curious about the pair. Before she could say anything, Rocky told them, "We're both from the area, too. Devin still has a cottage, inherited from an aunt, just outside the city. My folks still own a place here, though they spend their time in the South now and keep it rented out." He glanced over at Jon, then added, "Rest assured, we're well prepared to watch over Kylie."

"That's good to hear," Corrine said. "But, Devin, you write children's books?"

"I do."

"Then…" It was clear she had some doubts about a children's book author being an effective guard.

Devin smiled and said, "I'm also a consultant for the FBI. I've spent hours at the gun range, and since Rocky and I have been together, several self-defense classes, martial arts, and so on. Talk about your couples who fight," she added lightly.

"That's great," Kylie said, ruing the fact that the greatest training she had was in several dance classes—and a nice, peaceful form of yoga.

"We are so glad we got to meet you," Corrine said, although it was evident she was still weighing the two newcomers with the critical eye of a mother hen.

"Food!" Kylie said. "Jenny was talking about being hungry."

"Right, you all can join us if there's time? We don't have to be on the road for a while," Nancy said. "I mean, I know you're here because of what happened, and there are things you need to be doing… Although, I'm not sure what you can do at this point, except go over what you know and try to make sense of it. But maybe it's good to take a bit of a break and refresh your mind…?"

"We eat. We just got here, so a meal would be great," Devin assured them. "And the brunch here is really excellent."

"Let's head down," Jon said.

Over the meal, Jenny and Nancy wound up quizzing Devin about her books. When it appeared they were behaving a little too much like stalker-fans, Corrine broke in and asked Devin to talk about her cottage.

Kylie had ended up at the end of the table with Jon at one side and Rocky the other. While Devin and the others talked among themselves about the cottage and the surrounding area and its history, Rocky told Kylie quietly, "Please, do have faith in us."

She gave him a reassuring nod. "I appreciate you coming here. Did you and Devin know each other growing up?"

Rocky glanced at Jon, who must have given him a subtle hint just to tell the truth.

"We met over a dead body, just a few years ago." Rocky smiled grimly. "A murder occurred on her property…just like one that happened when I was in high school." He hesitated. "I'm afraid old friends did wind up being involved. It was rather heartbreaking. But… Well, it's over, we're together, and so familiar with this area that we should really be helpful on this. And you will be safe with us."

She smiled at him. "I'm glad. I insisted on staying. I am a total coward with no skills whatsoever."

Rocky glanced at Jon again and Kylie wondered just what Jon had told him. *This crazy woman thinks she was channeling a murder victim as it was happening.*

"I know we discussed staying on at the hotel," Jon said, "but now we're thinking that the safest thing to do is for you to pack up and head out to Devin's cottage."

"We'll both be there," Rocky said.

Kylie looked from one of them to the other. It would get her out of the hotel where Michael Westerly was staying. "I—I guess that would be a good thing."

"Great," Jon said. "We'll see Corrine, Nancy, and Jenny off, and then get you moved for the day."

"Isn't that kind of a wasted day for you?" Kylie asked.

Jon shook his head. "Devin and Rocky will drive you out

there. I have a detective friend in town I want to see about a few things. And it won't take all day to move you. We'll meet back up at the Cauldron for an early dinner."

"Westerly will be in Boston tomorrow," Kylie said.

"He won't drive there until morning. We looked at his schedule," Rocky said.

"Which will give us some time to make sure he's out of Salem," Jon said.

Kylie wasn't sure what that meant, other than they wouldn't have to worry about the man for a day.

Brunch went long; they all joined in conversation about the area, growing excited about visits to Gloucester, arguing over the best chowder, and arguing trivia about the Founding Fathers and Massachusetts in the Revolutionary War.

Then Corrine sighed at last and said, "Okay, we have to get on the road." She stood and addressed Rocky and Devin first, saying, "Such a pleasure to get to meet you. We do feel better about leaving Kylie. And, Jon...you may be a hotshot FBI guy, but if anything happens to Kylie—"

"You do strike terror in my heart," he assured her, his tone grave, "but with or without the threat, I swear, I would give my life for her."

"It's in the job description," Rocky said more lightly.

After a few more goodbyes, they all left the dining room, heading to the elevators—Kylie to pack, and Corrine, Nancy, and Jenny to get their bags so they could leave.

Jon paused in the lobby, explaining that he had to go talk with his friend, Detective Ben Miller. He told Corrine, Jenny, and Nancy goodbye one more time, receiving ardent hugs from all her friends, Kylie noticed. She was amused, and then not. This was a case. It would be solved. It had to be solved.

Then the man would most probably be out of their lives for good.

Before he left, Jon paused by Kylie, his head low, and spoke softly. "You're okay, right? I swear by these guys."

She felt him close, breathed his scent…and lowered her head slightly, unnerved by the strength of the attraction she felt for him. "I'm fine. Rocky looks like he could knock over the entire Patriots' football team. I'm good."

He nodded and smiled. "Rocky is the best. So is Devin. Don't let the knowledge she's a children's author allow you to doubt she's badass."

"I won't. Maybe I can take some lessons from her."

The others were waiting for her at the elevator. When the doors opened, to her dismay, Michael Westerly walked out, accompanied by his wife and a couple men she assumed to be aides—or bodyguards. The politician beamed a smile and a good morning to everyone in front of him.

Kylie froze. The others muttered good morning. Maybe it was obvious that, at least, he wasn't getting their votes.

But when he looked at her, she felt as if his eyes became all-seeing. As if he *knew*. As if he was fully aware she knew beyond a doubt he was a murderer.

The moment ended; he walked into the lobby, greeting others. Smiling, dignified, a handsome mature man.

"Kylie."

She felt Devin's hand protectively on her shoulder.

"Elevator," Devin whispered.

Luckily, Kylie's group was alone in the elevator car.

"That man!" Nancy exclaimed. "Smiling like that!"

"We really have no proof," Corrine murmured unhappily.

"*We* have proof—Kylie saw him!" Jenny said.

"We need proof that will stand up in a court of law," Rocky said quietly. "This may be Salem, but the days when a court allowed any kind of spectral evidence in are, thankfully, long gone. Please don't worry. There will be a way. Westerly will

make a mistake—there will be someone out there, somewhere, who knows something. We won't stop."

Kylie still felt numb.

When they reached their floor, her friends' obvious distress broke her out of her terror. "Quit acting as if we're never
going to see one another again," she chided. "I'm going to
be fine. I swear!"

"Yes, yes, yes, of course," Corrine agreed, wiping away
tears. "And she's reporting to us every night. Let's go—I have
to be at work tomorrow!"

And just like that, her friends were gone.

Kylie looked at Rocky and Devin and smiled weakly.
"Thank you. It does make me really uncomfortable to bump
into the man."

"A pleasure," Devin assured her. "He doesn't know anything about us, or the cottage, so it will be a much better
place to be. And you'll have me and Rocky and Jon, and we
do know what we're doing. And what we're up against."

"And you don't think I'm crazy?" Kylie asked.

They glanced at each other—a bit oddly, Kylie thought—
but they both shook their heads.

"Trust me. Not in the least," Rocky said.

"I'll just need a few minutes to pack," Kylie told them.

She headed to her bedroom door, opened it, and paused,
looking back into the suite to see if her friends had left anything obvious. They'd only come for the weekend; they hadn't
brought that much.

As she stood there, she heard Devin speaking anxiously to
her husband.

"I'm still so worried about this. The poor woman must be
freaked out by her experience already. What do we say when
she meets my dead aunt? Do we tell her now? Jon should have
talked to her and told her about this and—"

"All our dead friends?" Rocky interrupted.

Dead friends?

Kylie froze, her nerves electrified with fear. What the hell was she getting into? These people were… Well, they'd seemed like the real deal. But they must be crazy.

Panic seized her. She needed to get away from them. She needed people around her. Hundreds of them. Living people. Tourists.

Rocky and Devin were by the window in the suite, their attention on one another.

Kylie's bag, with her wallet and everything essential, was already over her shoulder. She left her little overnight suitcase where it was and slipped over to the door of the suite and out. She eschewed the elevator and tore down the stairs as quickly as possible. She fled out the back door of the inn and raced down the first few blocks of Essex Street, veering off when she realized she was getting close to Jon's office.

Within minutes, she realized she had come to the Old Burying Point. A tour guide was giving a speech by the memorial; others were exploring the cemetery.

She hurried into the cemetery and found one of the huge old trees that had grown through the tombstones. She leaned against it, gasping for breath. Wondering how in hell all of this had become so insane and terrifying.

She saw a man coming toward her and her breath caught in her throat. Then she smiled. She had wanted people; normal people.

And it was just Matt, their friendly evening bartender from the Cauldron.

Detective Ben Miller met Jon at the little makeshift office on Essex Street. Jon filled him in on the fact that Special Agent Craig Rockwell had joined them along with a consultant, his wife, Devin Lyle.

Ben grinned and leaned across the desk. "I know all about Miss Lyle."

"You know her? I'd never met her—we weren't in the same schools. Then, I didn't know Rocky, either. I know they were involved in a case here together that went back to when they were both kids."

Ben nodded. "Sad state of affairs, that. But solved. And Devin did keep her Aunt Mina's cottage. I'm glad. I just worked on the edges of that one. An old friend of your fellow agent had lead detective on the case." He was quiet for a minute. "So, you think there's something odd about this case."

"Odd..." Jon mused. "Yes. Four women we know of have been murdered in the same way, and if you look closer, there have been other such murders, years before, that weren't solved. You have anything more? Forensics of any kind?"

"Strange thing there," Ben said.

"What's that?"

"The gentleman in the accident last night—good work on your part, by the way."

"Thanks. What about him?" Jon asked carefully. "Jimmy Marino. I should have asked right away. Did he make it?"

"Hanging on by a thread. Doctors won't allow us near him right now."

Jon held his silence, letting Ben talk—and remembering every word that Obadiah Jones had said to him.

"He was supposed to be coming down to the station today," Ben said.

"Oh?"

"He'd called. The officer on the phones called me, said someone wanted to talk to me and only me. I did talk to him briefly. He said he wasn't sure that what he had to say meant anything, but he wasn't saying it over a phone line. He wanted to see me alone, and face-to-face."

"You think he might have known something about the murder of Annie Hampton?" Jon stared at his friend.

"Well, he wanted to speak to me because he knew I was the local heading up the investigation. So, yeah, it's an assumption, but a fair one, I think."

"Any possibility his heart attack might have been brought on?"

"So far, tests at the hospital haven't proven anything." Ben made a face, leaning back. "They say it's easier to run some tests at autopsy than it is to run them on a living man. Sad, eh? But I have asked that they try to determine if there was anything in his system that might have caused it."

"But that's what it was?"

"Acute myocardial infarction, yes."

"Interesting. I wonder if he talked to any of his friends about whatever he was going to say to you."

"And," Ben said, "I wonder if those friends might be in danger. If the old man did know something and he spoke to anyone, that person might be in trouble," Ben mused.

"Mrs. Martinelli," Jon said.

"Who is Mrs. Martinelli?"

"Just talk I heard on the street last night," Jon said. It wasn't really the truth, but it wasn't that big a lie. "From what I heard, Jimmy was a widower—and he spent time with a widow. I don't know her first name. Mrs. Martinelli. I'm willing to bet she's tried to get into the hospital to see Jimmy, so we might find her that way. The family has been called? Jimmy has children living in Boston, I believe."

Ben nodded solemnly. "Boys got here last night. I don't know about Mrs. Martinelli. We can find out."

Jon's phone rang and he glanced quickly at the caller ID. Rocky.

"Problem?" Jon asked by way of greeting.

"Yeah, and our fault, I believe. Your girl bolted. We're on the street now, trying to figure out which way she went."

"Bolted?" Jon repeated, standing at once.

Ben rose as well, eyes narrowing as he watched Jon.

"We failed you and I'm sorry as hell, but I can't just try to fix it—three of us are better now than two. It went bad right after you left," Rocky explained. "We headed to the elevator and Michael Westerly was coming out of it with his wife and party. Smiling away. The politician in action. But it must have been exceptionally disturbing for Kylie. Then, we thought she was packing in the bedroom, and Devin and I were talking about her dead Aunt Mina, worrying about how she joins us whenever she feels like it. We have no idea if Kylie heard, but it might have been too much for her. Devin and I have split up—I'm on Essex, she's headed toward the wharf—but I figured you might want to get out there, too."

"I'm out the door. Keep in close touch." As he disconnected, Jon turned to Ben. "I've got to go. I've got to find a friend who may be in danger." He started toward the door, then winced and turned back. "Find Mrs. Martinelli. I think she might be in danger, too. She and Mr. Marino were seen together often enough."

He didn't wait for Ben's response; he was out the door and onto the street, starting toward the hotel. He willed himself to understand what Kylie might be thinking, feeling…and just where she might be running.

She was all right; she might not know kickboxing, but she was smart, and she knew Salem and she would stay where there were people, where no one could get to her alone.

Westerly…

He was a politician. He'd left the hotel with his wife, in full view of dozens of people.

She would be all right; Kylie would be all right. They just had to find her, and then he had to find a way to explain what he hadn't yet been able to talk to her about. It might have made her run a hell of a lot faster and a hell of a lot sooner.

But if anything happened to her...

On Essex, he paused. She had to be close, but they needed all the help they could get. He hurried toward one of Obadiah's haunts.

The Old Burying Point.

CHAPTER NINE

"Kylie, you're all alone! Where's the posse?" Matt asked with a curious smile.

"My friends had to head back. They have work tomorrow," she told him.

"And you?"

"Not until next Monday."

"Ah, so you're wandering by yourself?"

"I like coming here to the Old Burying Point. Makes us think—and appreciate the fact the country moved on from these Puritan roots," Kylie said. "I can never envision heading across a dangerous ocean to find freedom to worship, and then hanging Quakers if they dared to walk the same earth."

"They did hang Quakers," Matt agreed. "Puritans were intolerant." He shook his head. "Thank God for our Founding Fathers who guaranteed us freedom of religion in the Constitution. I'm grateful we can be what we want to be."

She nodded her agreement.

He grinned. "I come here often enough. You know what? No matter how many times I take a tour, walk around on my own, visit the museums, there's always something new I discover. Like that one grave—back over there, behind that tree and tomb, by the wall."

"Oh, what is it? I thought I'd seen everything here."

He smiled like a conspirator. "I don't know if you read about it or not, but recently there was a letter found in someone's attic. It was written in 1730 by a woman who survived the frenzy of the witch trials—she was just a kid when it all went down. Her mother was arrested. Anyway, I think I've found something fascinating. Come on, over here."

She pushed away from her tree. He set a hand on her shoulder, leading her toward the back wall. She felt a moment's hesitation, but then figured she was with a friendly bartender she'd met before, and they were in a public place.

"So, this woman," he went on, "Elizabeth Simon, wrote about the terror she felt when her mother was arrested, how horrible it was to watch people hang. Townsfolk went to the hangings—you would in essence be watching the devil get his due. They were terrible—people were pushed off ladders to hang from branches, and if they didn't die quickly from a broken neck, they strangled. Anyway, I digress. I found a broken stone I believe to have been her mother's next to one that I'm certain must be hers."

"I'm sure that someone in the historical society would be able to tell you—"

He brought his fingers to his lips. "Yes, as soon as I can get to them. But come on...kind of hide. There are people out and about and I want to keep this as my discovery."

She followed him behind another tree and one aboveground tomb.

"There... Kneel down, you'll see it better."

Kylie knelt on the ground by the wall, behind the tree and the tomb, scanning the earth for the broken tombstones. Matt was behind her, leaning low.

And she saw he was reaching for a knife.

★ ★ ★

Jon didn't have to look for Obadiah. The ghost was hurrying toward him as he left his office.

"She's in the cemetery," Obadiah announced. He set a ghostly hand on Jon's shoulder, trying to get him to move along as quickly as possible.

"Who?"

"Your lady friend. And she's with that young barman, Matt something. I've been hanging out there, watching for Mrs. Martinelli after what I told you about Mr. Marino. And I'm a wicked suspicious old coot."

Jon was running, weaving his way through tourists crowding the street by the Peabody Essex Museum and hurrying past Charter Street. He sprinted to the cemetery with Obadiah on his tail and leaped over a piece of the wall at the memorial.

At first, he didn't see Kylie. He ran through the tombstones, pausing occasionally to scan the area. There were trees, but not big groves of them, and he searched quickly.

And then he saw them.

Matt was bending down beside Kylie—and he had a knife in his hand.

Jon cursed and raced for him. He tackled him from the back, shoving him to the side and away from Kylie.

Stunned, she crawled away from them backward on the ground, staring at them both.

"What the hell?" Matt shouted.

Jon wrenched the knife from Matt's hand and pinned him to the ground. "Not another!" he snapped.

"What?" Matt protested.

"You've got a knife!"

"I was going to cut away some weeds!" Matt exclaimed.

Obadiah, who had caught up, yelled, "Who the hell brings a knife to a historic cemetery?"

Matt, of course, didn't hear a word.

"Matt Hudson," Jon said. "Traveler. Did you travel to a few cities where a few other women might have happened to die, stabbed to death?" Jon knew he had to get control of himself; he had no proof, no evidence whatsoever against this man—just that he was here, he'd had a knife, he'd been behind Kylie…

And with his traveling, he might have been in Virginia, Connecticut, and Rhode Island.

"Hey, come on, up! Both of you!" a voice boomed. Ben Miller was beside them.

Ben Miller was a damned good friend, and a really good cop. Jon figured Ben had been heading to Jon's office and seen him running, realized something was wrong, and followed.

Ben stood over them, demanding as an officer of the law to know what was going on.

Jon stood, dragging Matt up with him.

"I swear, this was innocent," Matt said.

Kylie was still on the ground, propped up on her elbows, staring at them with confusion and alarm.

"He had a knife out over your back," Jon said.

"I did, but—" Matt began.

"You're under arrest," Ben told him.

"For what?" Matt cried.

"Assault," Ben said.

"I wasn't assaulting her, I swear. I was going to cut the weeds away from the grave. If anything, this guy assaulted me," Matt protested.

"All right, then. Let's get down to the station and straighten it all out," Ben said. "It might all be up to Miss Connelly here."

"I have to be at work in a few hours," Matt protested. "Ask her. Just ask her. Kylie, I was telling you about the grave, right?"

Jon reached a hand down to her. She stared at him for a moment, and then accepted it. Once she was on her feet, he felt her resist his hold and he let go instantly.

She said to Ben, "He was telling me about this grave. I came here with him to see it. I—I don't know what went on behind my back."

Ben looked at Jon.

"We'll go to the station," Jon said. "Long enough to compare some travel dates."

"Not going to cuff you, sir," Ben said. "As long as you walk right along with me, you hear?"

"Where the hell would I bolt to?" Matt demanded angrily. He turned to stare at Jon, venom in his eyes. "I wanted to show her a lousy grave!"

Kylie followed Ben and Matt.

Jon kept a small distance behind them, calling Rocky to let him know what was going on.

"This has already turned into one wicked mess," Rocky said. "We'll head back to the hotel and get Kylie's things. Sorry, my friend. Truly sorry. Then again, do you think you just might have stopped a killer?"

"He claims he's totally innocent, and he just had a knife to cut away the weeds on a grave."

"Don't they all claim they're innocent?" Rocky asked.

"But he's not who Kylie saw."

"He had Kylie, and he had a knife," Rocky said. "And..."

"And?"

"Maybe you should find out if the man knows Michael Westerly. Maybe he's the man's biggest supporter."

Maybe... He'd had a knife. He'd had Kylie.

That was enough for a trip to the station, at the very least.

Kylie sat in the reception area at the police station, not sure at all what she was feeling.

Matt could just be a good guy, a great bartender, a fun pirate, and an amateur actor. His story was true—he'd been telling her about the grave. And weeds did grow over the stones in the cemetery quicker than caretakers could keep up.

She sat alone at first; both Jon and Detective Ben Miller were in an interrogation room with Matt Hudson. She'd been told not to leave. And while the officers working the desks were all polite, she had a feeling she'd be stopped quickly if she tried to move.

Where was she going to go anyway?

She should call Corrine and tell her to drive back from however far she had gotten, Kylie was going home, back to New York City, a place that now seemed bizarrely tame and quiet.

But that wouldn't change anything. Not her fear.

And yet these people who were supposedly her saviors were talking about dead people. Dead people, who were their friends and even lived with them. She didn't know what to make of it, but she couldn't accept it.

She was staring down at her lap and didn't see Devin Lyle until she took the seat next to her. Startled, Kylie looked up. Rocky was there, too, hovering a distance away.

Devin's eyes were filled with sorrow and worry as she sat. "Kylie, I am so, so sorry. You might have been hurt and it was all my fault."

"And they might be questioning an innocent man who was just sharing an exciting discovery," Kylie said.

Devin nodded, not denying that it was true.

Another man came in, this one in seventeenth century dress. He took the seat next to Devin, but she didn't seem to notice him. Neither did the officers; no one came forward to ask if they could help him.

"Is it so hard to believe that we see the dead when you had a vision where you felt yourself killed as another woman?" Devin asked softly.

"Yes, actually," Kylie said weakly.

"Jon would have told you, explained the special unit," Devin said, "but you've been having difficulty dealing with what happened, and in our experience, we've learned… Well, it hasn't been that long for me. With these guys, Rocky and Jon, it's been a little longer."

Kylie didn't know what disturbed her so much about the older man in the seventeenth-century costume. She was usually polite and kind and not at all mean to people. But he was clearly listening to their private conversation.

"Sir, do you mind?" she said, leaning past Devin.

Devin turned, frowning slightly as she looked at the man.

"Obadiah Jones," he told Devin. "Old friend of Jon's."

Devin nodded an acknowledgment to him and turned to Kylie, a curious expression on her face. "You see that gentleman?" she asked.

"How could I not? He's dressed up for a show!"

"I should go," the man said. "I didn't know that…"

"She doesn't know," Devin finished for him.

Kylie froze, staring at the man. And then at the officers, all walking around, ignoring him completely. A fellow dressed up in Puritan attire. Extremely authentic-looking Puritan attire.

For a moment, she did nothing. She closed her eyes, took a deep breath and opened them.

Obadiah Jones got to his feet and said something to Rocky, who didn't look at him but nodded the barest of acknowledgments. Something no one else would notice.

Kylie wanted to scream—and bolt all over again. There had to be a conspiracy going on in Salem. Everyone—from the locals to law enforcement to the tourists—was involved in a conspiracy to make her think she had entirely lost her grip on reality. Should she run? Seriously, what could they do? Tackle her and arrest her, too?

"Why are you doing this to me?" she whispered to Devin.

"I was also terrified at first. Except that… I heard a woman screaming. She needed help, even though she was dead. Kylie, it's so frightening—it defies the mind and the heart and the senses. But it can be a good thing. The Krewe have solved more of their cases than any other unit in the Bureau. More than any other unit anywhere in the country, I daresay. Because we see the dead. Sometimes the victims. Sometimes others who have stuck around for one reason or another, to help."

"You're telling me that the gentleman in the bizarre dress is dead? And that when he was alive, it was 1692?"

"Yes," Devin said simply.

Scream, bolt—fall to the floor in a dead faint. These all seemed like good options to Kylie.

"And you live with a ghost," she said dryly.

"When we're here," Devin said. "My Auntie Mina. She's…" She paused, looking at Kylie with a wince. "She's lovely, I swear."

At that moment, Jon came out to the front of the station. Kylie stared at him, torn. She'd grown close to him quickly; she'd felt an incredible attraction. And now…everything was too confusing.

"They're holding him," Jon said.

Kylie stood. "I really don't understand. He might have been about to cut weeds, like he said. We were looking for a tombstone he'd told me about, of a girl whose mother had been arrested but survived the witch trials. I believe he was telling me the truth."

Jon looked from her to Devin and Rocky. "Matt Hudson travels for his different theater and pirate gigs. The dates of his different shows happen to align with the dates that the women were killed in other states." He looked at Kylie. "Maybe he's innocent, but because of what we've discovered about his schedule and the fact that he was standing over you with a knife, he'll be held overnight while his movements during those times are thoroughly checked out and verified."

★ ★ ★

Despite the conversation Kylie had evidently overheard between Devin and Rocky, she seemed more disposed to being with them than she was with him.

Which was fine by Jon. He needed to get over the feeling of desperation and rage he'd had when he saw Matt with the knife. Whatever the man had intended, he'd been holding it in a stabbing position right over her back.

He couldn't tell if Matt was genuine. He was just glad that they had gotten out of the cemetery with only a few tourists seeing the activity—and no media showing up.

But he was still worried about the woman who would sit in the park with Jimmy Marino. Mrs. Martinelli just might have talked to Jimmy about whatever it was he wanted to say to the police. Ben had sent officers out to find her; hopefully, she'd be found quickly.

Kylie stood tall and rigid in the station's waiting area. Jon thought she was going to tell them that she was going home—she trusted no one in Salem anymore. But when Devin said that they should head out so that Kylie could see where she'd be staying, Kylie didn't protest.

"We'll meet back at the Cauldron for dinner," Jon told Rocky.

"Really. You think they'll still let you in there?" Kylie asked him.

He didn't reply to that. "Excuse me. I have to call back to headquarters—Angela is doing research on Matt Hudson. We know he was close to the murder sites in the other states, but he may have alibis for the times of the murders. I hope so. I liked Matt."

He turned away. Behind him, he heard Devin speaking softly and Kylie agreeing that she'd like to see the cottage.

Breathing a sigh of relief, he returned to Ben's small office.

Ben looked up as Jon walked in. "We've had people out to

her house, but she wasn't there. The woman's name is Marla Martinelli, by the way, sixty-six years young, they say, feisty and fun. One of my men talked to Jimmy's sons at the hospital—he has two, Anthony and Frank—and they are both fond of Mrs. Martinelli. Apparently, Jimmy deeply loved his deceased wife and gave up everything to care for her when she was ill, and he mourned her loss horribly. Now, his sons want him to move on, and apparently, Marla Martinelli makes him happy."

"Nice to hear," Jon said. "But she's out there somewhere and could be in danger."

"We're on it," Ben assured him. "I thought you might want to go to the hospital with me and check on Jimmy. He's nearly stable, they tell me, though he's still unconscious. The sons are there, so you can talk to them yourself."

"Sounds good. Thank you."

When they reached the hospital, Frank greeted them. The younger of Jimmy's sons, he was a man of about twenty-five with dark hair and eyes. He expressed sincere appreciation when Ben introduced Jon as one of the men who had gotten his father out of the car.

"I am in your debt, sir," Frank said. "I believe you saved his life. Anthony and I are both in your debt. Anthony's in with my dad. Right now, they want just one of us in there—they're still monitoring Dad big-time. Which is good. They haven't given us guarantees, but the doctors are encouraged this morning."

"I wasn't alone," Jon assured him. "Great paramedics were on hand."

"Of course, but thank you," Frank said. He looked a little perplexed. "It's nice of you to come by. But I don't believe that you knew my father before this. So I guess your visit is for more than checking on his condition. You could have done that over the phone."

Jon glanced at Ben.

"He knows his dad called the station," Ben said.

"We're trying to find out why he wanted to come in," Jon told Frank. "He was evidently worried about something that he felt was important to report. Also, we know he was seeing Mrs. Marla Martinelli, and I'm afraid she hasn't been located yet."

"Marla was driving down to Revere yesterday to spend the night with her daughter," Frank said. "My dad mentioned it—said he was a bit lonely with her gone. I'm not sure when she's due back. I think she left just a few hours before the accident. We should have called her by now, but I don't have her number."

"Should have asked you and your brother about that right away," Ben said ruefully. He excused himself, heading over to a corner of the waiting room to put his officers on the hunt for either Marla's cell phone or her daughter's home.

"Do you know what your father was worried about?" Jon asked Frank.

Frank hesitated. "I'm not really sure," he said at last. "He called us after the murder was committed. I think it was disturbing to anyone in Salem, anyone who came from Salem. Not that any murder isn't horrible, but Annie Hampton was a good person. I never had her in school—she came in after I left—but I had friends a few years younger than me who adored her."

"I understand that she was well regarded," Jon said.

"Yeah. So Dad didn't say exactly what he was worried about. Just that he thought he might know something important. But he felt it would be wrong to cast aspersions on someone—especially someone in the public light—if he wasn't completely sure about it. He thought that talking to the police might ease his mind, and he'd either feel more strongly about something he'd seen, or he could dismiss it. He said he'd talk to me again after he spoke with the police."

"He said 'someone in the public light'?"

"Yes, those were his exact words." Frank was quiet for a minute, then he said passionately, "I'm hoping really badly that he'll be able to tell you himself in a few days. They have his heart stabilized, if that's the right terminology—I'm in finance, not medicine. He took a really good whack to the head despite the airbags."

"I understand. And we don't want to do anything to endanger him, please believe that," Jon said.

"Of course not. But anything at all that we can do, we're happy to do it."

"Let me give you my cell number," Jon told him. "And if he comes to and says anything, please call me right away. Or if your brother has any information, we'd appreciate it."

Frank studied him. He swallowed hard. "You don't think that what my father knew caused someone to... I mean, how can you force a heart attack? And what would that prove? I mean, a heart attack isn't necessarily fatal. Thank God. But do you think..."

"We're concerned, that's all," Jon said.

"Is that why there's been an officer in the hall since my dad came in?" Frank asked.

"There's never harm in taking precautions." Jon glanced across the room. Ben was talking with one of Jimmy's doctors. Jon thanked Frank once again, and hurried over to Ben.

"Dr. Allen, Jon Dickson with the FBI," Ben introduced them quietly.

Dr. Allen had a professional air about him—his trim white hair contrasted with his dark skin, and he stood tall and straight, and seemed suitably grave as he nodded at Jon.

"I was just telling Detective Miller what I could about our findings," Dr. Allen said. "Nothing like poison or heroin, but then the body is all about levels. Arsenic can kill, for example, but we also have arsenic occurring naturally in our bodies."

"And?" Jon asked.

"Naproxen and sodium," the doctor said. "There were high levels in Mr. Marino's system."

"Enough to bring on a heart attack?" Jon asked.

The doctor inclined his head to the side and answered carefully. "In my mind, yes, but all manner of over-the-counter drugs can be factors. Mr. Marino might have been taking something, thinking he had a cold. And sodium… Well, we all spend time warning people about the dangers of a high-salt diet."

"I see," Jon said.

"I don't know what he ate," Dr. Allen continued. "Whatever it was, it was absolutely filled with salt. Now I'm not sure how someone else can make a man eat too much salt, but…" His voice trailed. "I wish I could be more helpful. I understand that Mr. Marino meant to report something to you. It's still a stretch, in my mind, to believe that someone managed to get salt and naproxen into his system to this degree, but I'm not a detective."

"And I'm not a doctor," Ben said easily. "Thank you, sir, for the information."

"Thank you," Jon said as well.

"You're still keeping a guard on him?" Dr. Allen asked.

"Oh, you bet," Jon said. "You bet."

Devin's cottage was charming, and fascinating. A little like something out of a fantasy novel.

The first thing Kylie noticed on entering actually noticed her first—she heard a loud squawk and saw a handmade wooden cage. Inside was a large black raven.

"Hey, Poe!" Devin called to the bird as they entered.

The raven squawked again, a happy greeting. The bird fit right in to the overall feel of the cottage, decorated as it was with rich paintings and dangling crystals. A large stone mantel contrasted with a cozy gathering of furniture around the fireplace. A desk held a handsomely carved head of a woman with a kerchief over a thick head of curling hair—Madame Tussaud, Kylie thought. A large bookshelf displayed elves and gargoyles as bookends and charming little dragons dangled from the light cords.

"I inherited the place from my great-aunt Mina," Devin explained. "Adorable and wonderful and respectful of everyone. She was a Wiccan. She loved the unusual—and Poe, of course. He's the raven."

"He's...an unusual pet," Kylie said. "Beautiful bird, though!"

Poe seemed to understand. He flapped his wings and let out a caw as if in approval.

"Yeah, he always gives our neighbors in Northern Virginia a jolt, too," Rocky muttered.

"The cottage is from the early 1700s," Devin added.

"Just six rooms," Rocky told her. "The living room with that little dining area, the kitchen behind, and we've revamped a bit, two bedrooms to the left of the entry, one to the right."

"We're in Mina's old room," Devin said quickly. "Rocky and I take that room when we're here."

"Because she comes back, right? Mina is dead, but she comes back?" Kylie asked. She couldn't believe she even voiced the question. She couldn't believe that she had seen a man in Puritan dress sitting beside Devin at the police station. She had heard him speak.

But then again, she knew without doubt that she had been in another woman's mind—and felt her murder.

Devin and Rocky looked at one another. Rocky shrugged and folded his arms over his chest. "Here it is, plain and simple. We're with a special unit. You know that. We have the highest solve rate out there because we get unusual help. For some people—as apparently with you—the ability comes later in life."

"It did for me," Devin said helpfully.

"I heard a dead friend calling me for help when I was still in high school," Rocky said. "I came back here a few years ago when a similar murder had occurred. That's when Devin and I met. Case was sad as hell, but it was solved, with help from some spirits in the woods around Devin's cottage. So that's the gist of it—and the truth of it. We can talk to the dead."

"Some of the dead. Sometimes they've gone on. Sometimes they stay behind. When they've stayed behind, it's for different reasons," Devin said.

"Usually to help," Rocky said.

"I don't see the dead," Kylie protested weakly.

"You saw Obadiah," Rocky said with certainty.

"Obadiah?"

"The Puritan gentleman. Matt wanted to show you a grave? Well, we can show you Obadiah's. He's buried at the Howard Street Cemetery but hangs around the Old Burying Point a lot—more tourists, I believe. He likes when there's life going on around him. And you saw, in some manner, a woman as she died. Whatever this is—a gift, a curse, a genetic anomaly—you have it. And in this case, you need to accept it and use it. Four women are dead, that we know about. There might have been others before. And if so, the killer is speeding up his time line."

Kylie stared back at him. She wondered again how she'd gotten into this mess. Better to focus on something small and within her control. "So...where am I staying?" she asked.

Rocky nodded toward the rooms to the left.

"The house has an alarm system," Devin added.

"And Poe is the best alarm I've ever seen," Rocky said. "Jon will come out at night and take the sofa there in front of the hearth. He'll be watching the door and the front of the house. You'll be in good hands, I swear it."

She should thank them. They were doing this to keep her safe. But she couldn't seem to get over the chill she was feeling—as if she had stepped into one of Devin Lyle's fantasies for children and couldn't quite get out.

"Thank you," she managed. "Um, where would Auntie Mina be now? Is she here? I don't see her."

"She's not always here." Devin tried a smile. "She's still very social."

"Out carousing with the other ghosts?" Kylie said, sighing inwardly at the bitter and sarcastic sound of her own words.

"I'll bring your bag into your room," Rocky said. "Make yourself at home. We'll go meet up for dinner in about an hour."

He carried her overnight bag into the bedroom, then went to the desk near the wonderful hearth at the front of the cabin. A computer sat just in front of the bust of Madam Tussaud.

He had explained that they see the dead. She was sure that in his mind, he had done his best and had now dismissed her. She could accept his words or not.

"Can I get you anything?" Devin asked her anxiously.

"No, I'm fine, thank you."

"Tea, coffee, soft drinks… Anything you want, please, just help yourself," Devin said, gesturing to the little kitchen.

"Thank you," Kylie said, and then she hurried over to the bedroom assigned to her, closing the door and leaning against it.

She was shaking. She was terrified.

Despite her relief that they believed her about what she'd seen, she was also very afraid that they were telling the truth. Because that meant she had seen a murder—and a murderer. No matter if it turned out Matt Hudson had spent his time out of state, the murderer she had seen was still out there, walking free.

CHAPTER TEN

Jon returned to his office space on Essex Street. He hoped the police were able to reach Marla Martinelli soon. He hoped she had information. He was even more hopeful she was safe and well and just unaware her friend had been in an accident and was in the hospital.

He pulled out the crime scene photos again, pouring over them.

The way the victims had been attacked and then left was alike—as much as a set of perfectly crossed T's. The knife patterns, according to the different medical examiners who'd checked each other's files, were almost exact as well. In every murder, the killer had been right-handed. That in itself was nothing. Only about ten percent of people in the world were left-handed, and perhaps thirty percent were ambidextrous in certain ways.

He was getting nowhere.

He went over his notes again. No matter how he looked at it, no matter how many times he read over the information, he came out with the same conclusion. The killer appeared to be the same: a serial killer with a specific method.

Except that Kylie had seen Michael Westerly kill Annie Hampton.

His phone rang—it was Ben. Jon was certain by then that they should have managed to find and speak with Mrs. Martinelli.

"You found Marla?" Jon asked.

"Yes, and no," Ben said.

"How so?"

"We contacted her daughter. Marla left her house earlier this afternoon, but she left her phone at her daughter's place and didn't drive back for it."

Jon swore softly. "You've got to get people out looking for her."

"Every cop from here to Boston is on it, trust me. But she may just not realize she left the phone. Believe it or not, there are people who actually drive without playing with their phones."

"Not many."

"We'll find her, Jon."

"I have no doubt we'll find her. I'm hoping we find her alive."

"Yeah. Ditto," Ben said.

"Anything else on Matt Hudson?"

"He's biding his time. He knows that his every alibi is being thoroughly investigated. He doesn't seem disturbed by that fact. I don't know, Jon. On this one…he may be an innocent man."

"He might be."

"Better safe than sorry, especially with a knife-wielding man."

"That's my motto."

"I was a bit surprised today when you asked him about Michael Westerly. What did you think about his answers?" Ben asked.

"It was interesting that he admitted that the politician had been in the Cauldron several times, and that Matt knew him."

"I don't understand why you're so convinced that Westerly murdered Annie Hampton."

"I think he was her mysterious lover," Jon said. "And if Jimmy wakes up, I'm willing to bet that he'll tell us that he saw the two of them together. Or," he added quietly, "if we find Marla Martinelli, and she's fine and able to talk, she might be able to tell us. Maybe Jimmy told her something. She should be home by now. It's just not that long a drive."

"No, and every cop out there—"

"Is looking for her, I know."

"All right," Ben said with a sigh. "We'll stay in touch."

They rang off and Jon drummed his fingers on his desk for a moment. Then he stood up. He was going to look for Marla himself.

It was late Monday afternoon, and the weekend tourists had gone home, but Esscx Street still held an attraction for those who lingered through the weekdays, and some of the shops also managed to maintain local clientele. There were those on the street who practiced Wicca and met as friends or stopped to buy trinkets, books, and other paraphernalia from one another. The museums were also continually popular, offering much that went beyond the witchcraft craze and into the history of whaling and seafaring. Except for late at night, Jon had seldom seen the street empty.

He wandered awhile, then found himself heading back to the Old Burying Point.

It didn't close until sundown, and while the sun was setting, the gates had yet to be closed. He walked through, back to the place where he saw Matt Hudson with Kylie. Kneeling down, he saw that there was an old grave, one that, despite the best efforts of the caretakers, was crisscrossed with weeds.

Matt's story could have been true.

Jon was bent over the grave when Obadiah approached him.

"Have you found her?" Obadiah asked anxiously.

Jon looked up.

"Mrs. Martinelli. Have you found her?" Obadiah asked again.

"She was out of the city, at her daughter's," Jon said. He hesitated. "But she left there and forgot her cell phone and started to drive home. And she hasn't been located yet."

"Why aren't you looking for her?"

"Obadiah, I'm out here, hoping somehow… I don't know. Believe me, Ben Miller has every cop in the state looking for her car."

"Cars can be sunk in ponds and rivers and hidden in many places."

"I know that, Obadiah. But I can't just drive around pointlessly. I have to have faith in my fellow law enforcement officers. Ben is a good cop. You know that." Jon stood and dusted his hands. "There's a possibility we haven't considered yet. We're so afraid something might have happened to her."

"What's that?"

"She may be hiding. She may have heard about Jimmy's accident on the local news. Let's say she was already driving home when she found out. If she was aware that someone might be after her, she'd know they would probably find her daughter's place, so she wouldn't go back there. She'd hide—carefully."

Obadiah weighed his words. "Perhaps," he said.

"If so, maybe you could find her," Jon said. "You have other friends."

"Dead ones, you mean," Obadiah said.

"Maybe someone out there knows something," Jon said softly.

Obadiah turned and walked away.

Jon prayed Marla was just hiding; he wasn't at all sure of his theory. If someone believed she and Jimmy knew something about the murder, they were both in grave danger.

As Kylie would be, if Westerly knew she had somehow seen him.

He glanced at his watch, then back at the grave. It was an absurd thought that Westerly might hire a local bartender as a killer.

Absurd. Yet, Jon couldn't discount the possibility. And if not Matt Hudson, maybe someone else. Someone who had seen to it that Jimmy Marino had a system filled with chemicals that would bring on a heart attack and an almost-deadly accident.

"I don't think they're going to be happy to see us at the Cauldron," Kylie noted as they left the cottage to drive back into the historic district.

"I don't think they'll know anything at the Cauldron," Rocky said. "There are other bartenders. One has been called in to take Matt's shift. Some passersby saw what was going on in the cemetery, but we were out of there before any media showed up."

"We don't try to ruin lives. We try to save them," Devin told her.

They arrived early. Rocky parked in one of the garages off Essex Street and they headed for the restaurant. They passed a year-round horror mansion on their way.

Kylie knew she'd walked by the attraction before, but she'd never gone in. Today, she found herself pausing. The fake skeletal remains in the window had never bothered her before; the foam gravestones had been just that. The floating ghosts had seemed silly. Now they were macabre and frightening.

Her world had changed.

Inside the Cauldron, Kylie saw that Cindy was behind the bar, joined by another young woman. They were moving quickly, filling orders. To her surprise, Cindy waved cheerfully when she saw Kylie.

Curious, Kylie left her escorts behind and strode to the bar, though she assumed they were getting a table for dinner.

"Cindy, hey, how are you doing?" she asked when the young woman turned to her.

"Great!"

"You have a new coworker."

"Mariah—a friend. Yeah, she needs the work. She goes to Salem College and is trying to pick up a little extra money. And it worked out perfectly. Matt asked for the night off to help the police!"

"Ah, well, that was good of him. How is he...helping the police?" If that was the story Matt had chosen to tell, it was fine with Kylie.

"We're one of the most popular places in town," Cindy explained. "Matt is going through all kinds of information about people. Suspicious characters, all that."

"Ah, I see."

"What can I get you?"

"I'm fine. Having dinner with...friends. I just wanted to say hello."

"Well, have a nice dinner!" Cindy said.

Kylie turned to go back to Rocky and Devin, and bumped right into Carl Fisher. He was dressed in a Victorian frock coat and top hat.

"Kylie," he greeted her, "you're here."

"Carl...great costume," she told him enthusiastically. She was relieved that she knew for sure this was a man dressed in period clothing, and not a ghost from another time.

"Sometimes I dress up for the tours." He shrugged. "Depends on my mood. Some nights, I feel like being a complete professor—the facts and just the facts, you know. Then, especially on a Monday night, I might be just a wee bit bored, so I kind of play up the dark Victorian alley kind of a thing. Even though we don't have any dark Victorian alleys." He grinned.

She found herself smiling in return. He was, for all that she could see, a nice human being. Just making his living. And he shared her passion for history. "Well, you look great," she said.

"Thank you, my dear." He gave her a sweeping bow. "You've looked great every time I've seen you." Before the compliment could become something more, he added, "So, I'm hearing you had a strange run-in with Matt at the cemetery today."

"Pardon?"

"He was showing you something and had a knife out and freaked out the cops or whoever. They say he's trying to help with Annie Hampton's murder investigation."

"Ah, yeah," Kylie said.

"Matt is a good guy."

"I believe you."

He was still looking at her. "He thinks you know something about the murder."

Kylie shrugged uncomfortably, glancing over his shoulder to the booth where Devin and Rocky were waiting. "I wish—like everyone, I'm sure—that I could help the police in any way. But my friends and I were just a few blocks away from here when it happened. No idea what went on…"

She was babbling, wondering just how many people had seen her when she'd nearly passed out in the bar after seeing Michael Westerly's picture.

Anyone who supported Westerly—to death?

"Hi!"

Kylie didn't need to fear being put on the spot by Carl any further—Devin was there, smiling, and ready to meet the man.

"Carl," Kylie said, relieved, "my friend Devin. We were about to have dinner."

Carl looked at Devin with surprise. "The kid's book queen!" he said.

"I don't know about that, but I write books for children, yes. Nice to meet you, Carl."

"Can I interest you in signing up for a ghost tour?" he asked her, a crooked smile on his lips. "But then you're from here—you're even part of one of our tours, because of your connection to those murders a few years back."

Devin managed to keep her smile in place. "That's all in the past. Anyway, truly a pleasure—you look great, by the way—but may I steal Kylie back? My husband is starving."

Before Carl could say more, Devin linked Kylie's arm and led her to the table. Kylie sat gratefully, facing Rocky and then Devin who slid in beside him.

"Is it just me or is everyone looking at me suspiciously?" Kylie asked quietly. "Carl knows that Matt is at the station. Cindy knows that Matt is at the station. They were here when I nearly passed out seeing Westerly on TV. But why do I feel as though other people are staring at me?"

She broke off, frowning, and leaned forward. "I *know* that Michael Westerly killed Annie Hampton. Why would anyone else worry about that? Why would I have to be worried about anyone other than Westerly?"

Just then Jon Dickson slid into the booth beside her. She jumped—she hadn't seen him come in. Clearly he'd heard her, even though she'd almost whispered.

"You'd be worried because you're smart," he said. "Because we have absolutely no idea what is really going on here, or with the other murders. And Marla Martinelli is still missing while Jimmy Marino remains unconscious. So—" He turned to the others. "Did anyone ask about the special tonight?"

The world was upside down. She had visions of murder. Ghosts were walking the streets. And Jon wanted to know the dinner special. At least he didn't enter the restaurant with a ghost—his "friend" Obadiah wasn't with him.

Nor did he mention a ghost.

None of them mentioned ghosts!

Their waitress came to the table and Jon politely ordered. Then he excused himself and walked over to the bar, chatted with Cindy and her friend, and then Carl. As casually as if he'd never tackled Carl's friend in a cemetery and then had him arrested.

Kylie knew that he was casually watching everyone and everything there, certain that something might be gained from being in the Caldron.

Of course, she realized. The matchbox advertising the Cauldron. They still didn't know what it meant.

They were all observing, Kylie thought. Jon, Devin, and Rocky. At first glance, they all looked like they were enjoying a casual dinner; light conversation, no talk of the dead. But still watching.

After noting that his scrod dinner was excellent, fresh and perfectly cooked, Rocky spoke quietly to Jon. "All parties of interest are here. I believe that's the past-life-regression therapist, Dr. Sayers, who just walked in. He's with a young lady."

Dr. Sayers had a pretty brunette on his arm. He headed to the bar, chatted with Cindy, and thanked her when she pointed out a booth about to empty.

Jon turned to Kylie. "I know you found it really hard to experience, but do you think you could you do it again? Could you let him hypnotize you again?"

"No."

"If it meant finding a way to get evidence against Michael Westerly?"

"No."

"If it meant justice for Annie?"

Kylie wrapped her arms tightly around herself. She wished

they weren't seated at a booth, that they weren't so close their legs were touching—that she didn't feel torn in dozens of ways.

"Of course I want her killer caught. And if what I saw was real, good lord, I don't want the man holding any kind of public office. I don't want him walking the streets. But...it was really horrible. And disorienting."

"I'd be there. By your side. I swear to you, I wouldn't step aside a second. I'd have your hand."

Finally, Kylie nodded. "You're right. I can do this for Annie. If it will help bring her justice."

Jon immediately stood and walked over to Sayers's table. The two greeted each other cordially; Kylie saw that Sayers introduced Jon to his brunette companion.

Then Jon must have asked him about another regression.

Sayers looked back at her. She felt a chill. Sayers couldn't have been the killer, she knew, he was the one who had been with her in person when she'd entered another woman's mind and body.

Sayers smiled at her across the crowded restaurant.

She managed a determined smile back.

The doctor turned and nodded to Jon. They spoke for another few minutes, and then Jon returned to the table.

"We're on," he said. "Tomorrow morning at ten."

"Great," Kylie said without enthusiasm.

"Thank you," Jon said simply. He looked straight in her eyes. "We don't like putting you in this position. But when a killer like this is on the loose—"

"Yes, I get it. I understand."

"Dessert?" Devin asked.

"God no. Please, let's just get out of here," Kylie said. "Please. I just need some time...alone."

When they returned to Devin's cottage, Kylie felt she had to escape them, to make sense of what was happening in her own mind. She immediately made her way into the room that had been assigned to her.

She remembered to call Corrine—and say nothing about talking to the dead, though she did tell her about what had happened in the cemetery with Matt and Jon.

Corrine again told her to come home.

Kylie wanted to, but no, she shouldn't. Whatever had started here had to end here. She had to see it through.

Jon lay awake, staring at the ceiling. He was growing more and more worried about Marla Martinelli. With every cop in the state looking for her, how had she managed to elude them all? At least, her car should have been found.

He heard someone come into the parlor; he eased up on the couch, frowning, wondering if something had happened.

He didn't at all expect to see Kylie standing above him. She looked ridiculously dignified, even wearing only a long sleep T-shirt. Her arms were crossed over her chest, and she seemed to look down at him with incredible scorn.

"You bastard," she said quietly. "You…absolute bastard. I'm thinking I'm the most demented person in the world, seeing someone else as they're being murdered, wondering just how far my grip on reality has slipped. And all the while, you're the…weird one! Seeing ghosts, talking to them, getting your mysterious help from the dead! You said not one word about your 'special skill.' You practically accused me of horrible things the night we met, when all the while, you… You could have said something!"

He was so startled, he didn't answer for a moment.

That was long enough for her to grab the pillow he'd been using and slam it down over his head.

"Hey!" He jerked up, grabbing the pillow and then catching her arm when she would have stormed away. He didn't use force, but the way she had been turning sent her spinning back around so she landed on the couch next to him. They both looked at each other with surprise.

Flashes of heat seemed to arise—attraction. Anger.

Neither of them moved for a minute; they stared at each other.

She started to rise. He caught her arm again, but gently. Her skin was soft and slightly cool in the night air.

"Please," he said.

She looked at him but didn't relax her posture.

"It's not something you bring up in casual conversation when you just meet someone," he began.

"We didn't meet casually!"

"No, you were passing out. And talking about a murderer."

"That was...that was just at first. You dragged us all down to your office and put us through an interrogation. I felt like a victim, and a criminal...and an idiot! And all the while—"

He sighed when she broke off, looking out into the room, so aware of her warmth, her eyes, the feel of her by him.

"I'm sorry," he said softly. "I needed your help. I still need your help. I just didn't find the time in there with everything else to mention that... I have dead friends. Who still talk to me."

She stared a moment longer and he realized she was trembling. She lowered her head. "Dead people," she said. She shook her head. "Even then, it doesn't explain what happened to me during that hypnotism. Jon, I know you believe you saw Matt about to stab me, but he's not the one who killed Annie Hampton."

"I know. I believe you."

She looked up. "How can any of this be? I mean, I saw that ghost today—"

"Obadiah Jones."

"I saw him. He wasn't a dark shadow, he wasn't a blast of

cold on my arm. I thought he was real. Well, I mean I thought he was flesh and blood sitting there."

"I'll tell you the story," Jon said quietly. "Years and years ago, I saw Obadiah for the first time. I think we were both surprised. I thought he was flesh and blood, too. He'd never had anyone see or hear him before then. But because of him, someone *didn't* die. I don't have all the answers—none of us do. I think Obadiah just lived a very, very bad life, and so he stays to try to make life better for others. He died in jail during the trials—the executed weren't the only ones to die or have their lives ruined, but you know that. He...tries to help."

She nodded, still shivering. Jon wanted to put an arm around her. It really wouldn't be appropriate. Of course, he was still holding on to her. That wasn't really appropriate, either.

"I'm sorry," he said again.

"I still just can't believe any of it," she whispered.

"It's never easy. I think it is easier for those of us who had experiences when we were very young. Before logic and the learned order of things and real life set in. But I know it will get easier for you. Um, acceptable at least. You just learn to live with it."

"So walking down the street on any day at any time, a dead person might pop up and decide to talk to you?"

"Not that often. No. Not that many spirits stay. And if they do, they may choose not to communicate."

"And when the dead do try talking to you on the street, what do you do?"

He smiled. "You can ignore them. Or you can engage with them. Maybe learn something. If you're worried about seeming strange in public, pretend you're on the phone. That's easy these days. People are always walking around and talking."

She cracked a small, weak smile at last. She seemed to settle back into the couch; her shivering was easing. "I'm telling you, Matt didn't kill Annie," she said. "There was no reason for you to have him taken in. Why did you insist on that?"

"He had a knife over you."

"But—"

"Kylie, I do believe you that Michael Westerly killed Annie. But he knows he's a suspect. And many people, including Matt, saw what happened with you in the restaurant. I heard you from several seats away. It's possible Westerly might try to get someone to—"

"Murder me? He might hire someone to murder me?"

"I'm badly hoping Matt's as innocent as can be. But he had a knife. He was standing over you. And he was in every city where a murder from this case took place. That proves nothing, but it is something that has to be checked out."

She nodded. "He seems decent. I don't want to believe it."

"Like I said, *I* don't even want to believe it. There's no evidence against him, unless you file charges for assault."

"I honestly don't think he meant to assault me."

"He will be back out on the streets tomorrow night, so we'll hope you're right."

"I won't spend time with him in a cemetery again," Kylie said.

"Good call. You won't be alone again. As strange as you find us, please, put some faith in us," he said. "Don't go off on your own. Let one of us be with you." He hesitated. "Just believe in us. I'm begging you."

She nodded, lightly biting on her lower lip. "You believed in me. I'll believe in you. And I'll try not to fall to the ground screaming if a ghost decides to join in when I'm having a conversation with someone else. Or just walks up to me. Or..." Her voice trailed. "Or tomorrow. Seeing Sayers again. Trying to relive what happened." She shook her head. "I don't really understand. If I just see and feel the same thing again—"

"You may see and feel more. There may be something you

see him drop, something he says, something about his clothing... We need evidence. We can't arrest the man because of what you saw under hypnotism. But being hypnotized again just might give us something we desperately need."

"I'm going to try very hard to accept that I can inhabit another person's thoughts, but also accept that I am still perfectly sane." She was almost relaxed then, sitting at his side. No longer trembling.

"You are sane," he assured her. "Well, as sane as you ever were."

His joke was weak. She accepted it and looked at him with what was almost a smile. "And I'm going to try to think of you as perfectly sane, too. Well, as sane as you ever were, I assume."

He smiled. A real smile. He thought she might be about to smile as well, but instead she stood quickly. His hand trailed over her arm, and she stood there a moment.

"Well...good night."

"Good night," he said.

She started toward the little hallway to the two bedrooms, but paused. "You will get him, right? Somehow, some way?"

"We will get him," he promised, and prayed they would.

She went into the bedroom.

Jon stayed awake a long, long time, staring at the ceiling. Yes, they would get Michael Westerly.

They had to.

CHAPTER ELEVEN

"When we go in—" Jon began.

"Don't mention anything about Michael Westerly," Kylie finished. "I know. I'll be careful. I mean, I'll try. Jon, I've never felt anything like what I felt when he hypnotized me the first time. I don't think I have a lot of control over my reactions."

He had just shifted his car into a space on the street near the Salem Witch Museum, an easy walking distance to Dr. Sayers's office. They left the car and started walking.

Kylie couldn't help but notice people on the street. With a bit of dry wonder, she tried to determine if they were all living. She still had a bad time accepting that Obadiah Jones was a dead man.

They passed the magnificent and sweeping life-size statue of Roger Conant, founder of Salem, in his flowing cape. A group of young women were laughing nearby and talking about heading to one of the stores for love potions later.

Definitely alive.

Obadiah wasn't around, and to the best of her knowledge, they passed no one dead. Thankfully, she had yet to meet

Aunt Mina, Devin's personal haunt. And yet, despite Kylie's unease and fear, she was growing curious.

Jon seemed introspective. He was frowning. "You're going to be all right. I'm going to be right there. And Sayers will be able to get you out if I ask him to."

She nodded. She knew Jon was worried, too. She also knew that without actual evidence, Michael Westerly was going to get away with murder. She couldn't let that happen.

It seemed to her that Jon's footsteps slowed slightly as they neared the office. She looked at him.

"I'm second-guessing our decision to do this," he told her.

"Hey, I'm the one who is supposed to be protesting. You're supposed to be telling me about getting justice and stopping a killer."

He nodded. "I know. I still don't like it."

"Neither do I. But I'm fully committed to trying for something more," she added softly.

"All right, here we are," he said, walking up the few steps to the door and opening it for her.

Kylie thought about making some kind of joke regarding the spider and the fly. She didn't.

They were greeted by Dr. Sayers's cordial receptionist and quickly sent on in to his office.

Sayers was waiting for them. He stood from behind his desk, enthusiastically shaking their hands. "Welcome, both of you. Kylie, I'm honored that you've come back. I've never had anyone react the way you did, and frankly, we were all worried about you. But I think this is a fascinating opportunity. We'll take it very slow and carefully."

"That's good to hear, Dr. Sayers," Jon said. "Because if I say she has to come out of it, she has to come out of it. Right then. Not in a few minutes. That second."

"Well, of course," Sayers said, as if the very suggestion he would do otherwise was insulting.

"Thank you," Kylie murmured.

Sayers brightened again. "Tea? I always find it so relaxing to start with the tea. Chat a few minutes, relax. Sure, it has some caffeine, but millions of Irish throughout history can't be all wrong, huh?"

"Or the Chinese," Jon murmured.

"Pardon?" Sayers asked.

Jon shook his head. "Never mind."

"I'm sorry. I really don't feel like tea," Kylie told him.

"Well, then, there's the sofa. Lie down and get comfortable."

She glanced at Jon, who nodded, extending a hand toward the sofa as he went to bring one of the upholstered chairs right up beside it.

"You're going to be right by her?" Sayers asked. He didn't seem to mind; in fact, he wanted Jon there. That was encouraging.

Kylie lay on the sofa, one of the throw pillows behind her head; she realized she had been keyed up so long that she was tired. Lying down felt good.

Jon was by her side, sitting near her head. He held her hand between his.

"All right," Dr. Sayers began, "just lie there and breathe and think about nothing, nothing at all, Kylie. Think about the breeze and the blue of the sky. Ah, the air is so soft and sweet, gentle, just touching you. Count with me, we'll go backward from a hundred..."

He began to count; she counted with him.

"One hundred, ninety-nine, ninety-eight..."

She couldn't really feel a breeze; the day had been somewhat overcast. But then it seemed she was relaxed, that reality was slipping away.

"Ninety-two, ninety-one..."

She was somewhere else; she could still hear Dr. Sayers talking to her, guiding her, as he would continue to do even after the countdown, but she felt as if she was floating through the sky, moving to a different place.

"Eighty-seven, eighty-six…"

She was back at the old cemetery, a place natural to her. And her mind was racing—she was thinking about some of the tests that were coming up, and one of the teenagers, who was really a great kid, just torn down by the fact his parents were both out of work. She planned to help him all she could.

The man she was meeting would help her, too. When they were together at last, really together, she could tell him unreservedly about what was needed in the school system, what was needed to help children who were in problem situations, how to help those children become responsible, successful adults.

He was wonderful. She smiled, glancing around, knowing he would be there soon. She remembered the times they had been together before, sweet if secretive. Even the way she ran into him in the historic district after a special performance by one of the local theater groups at the memorial. The way he looked at her, even in public, even with his wife—the monster, clinging to him, horrible, always trying to ruin his career and destroy his dreams—there with him. She thought about the feel of his fingers on her flesh, and the way they had dreamed about the day they could be together without hiding.

Then she saw him.

She was excited, and she raced to him. But he wanted to get in deep, deep into the old cemetery where they wouldn't be seen. She went along. She understood, she loved him, she knew what he needed to do.

Then the fear set in. There was something different about him. His hold on her was harsh—cruel. And he wasn't leading her, he was dragging her.

She drew back, confused at first, hurt.

She saw his face and…knew.

He wasn't the same man he had been; he was the monster, and she had been a fool all along.

All that had been love turned to ice. She despised him.

She turned to flee.

He caught hold of her and spun her around. And despite her hatred for him, she wanted to live. She begged, she pleaded, she cried. She would do anything, say anything, to stop him. And yet she knew, even as he held her there among the tomb-stones, there was no chance for her

The knife fell, and she looked into the rage in his dark eyes. As he brought that blade down, ripping into her flesh again and again, she knew he would want her to suffer even past death…

Yes, she felt it, again and again!

First, the terror. Then, a strange numbness, the pain less-ening, fading, like the light before her eyes…

"Kylie!"

She heard her name called out.

She was no longer lying on the sofa. She was in Jon's arms. He'd pulled her from the sofa and on to his lap and he was holding her, rocking with her slightly, as if she was a child.

She blinked, realizing her position, and drew back a bit.

Yes, it had been terrifying.

But now she was fine. This time, reality came back to her like a gigantic cool wave. What had happened hadn't hap-pened to her.

"You're all right?" Dr. Sayers asked anxiously.

She nodded. Jon was easing his hold on her. She looked at him a little awkwardly and managed to stand up without the least wobble. He came to his feet beside her.

"Thank you, Dr. Sayers," Jon told him.

"I told you I'd bring her right out when you wanted," Dr.

Sayers said. "I have to say again, this is the strangest thing I've ever seen. Kylie, you are the only person I've ever had anything even remotely like this happen to. But are you really all right? Last time we did this, you were terribly shaken."

"I believe I'm fine, thank you. This time, it was as if stepped through a door. From the darkness to the light, kind of. I'm really fine."

"Scary again, though," Dr. Sayers said. He looked at Jon. "Can this help you? I mean, I can't imagine anyone accepting a regression as evidence in a court of law."

"No, our courts today don't put stock in any kind of paranormal activity," Jon said.

"But you're here and you asked me to do this...and you are FBI," Dr. Sayers said. "Do you really believe in this? Do you have a suspect?"

Kylie shook her head, surprised at her own ability to purse her lips sorrowfully and appear lost.

"But this may just help us," Jon said. "With a murder so horrible, we have to try anything."

"Of course," Dr. Sayers said. He smiled at them both, and Kylie had the feeling he didn't believe them. He thought they had a suspect. And that pleased him.

Why not? He would naturally be glad if he helped to bring a murderer in. She couldn't blame him. And it validated his work. Something like this was far more than just showing tourists what fun they could have with past-life regressions.

"You've been great, Dr. Sayers," Jon assured him. "We're truly appreciative and we'll let you know if we're able to discover anything from here."

"Thank you—I'll be anxious for updates," Dr. Sayers said.

They both thanked him again and headed out. In the reception area, Jon paused to pay for the session. The receptionist didn't accept his credit card, but rather smoothed back a strand of gray hair and smiled warmly. "No charge," she said.

"Oh no, really, we must—"

"No, no, sir, you really can't. Dr. Sayers would have me by the throat!" she said. "He said this appointment was important and that it was, frankly, a fascinating study for him, too. I'm just thanking you for coming."

"Well, thank you," Jon said. "And Dr. Sayers."

She nodded and then gushed, "Dr. Sayers is so wonderful! He is definitely worth seeing again and again."

Kylie nodded vaguely and started for the door to the street. Before she could get to it, the door swung wide and a group of young women came in. It was the same group she had seen earlier by the Roger Conant statue.

They were talking loudly, boisterous, and while not rude, it was immediately evident the receptionist found them annoying.

"Please," she began, "if you could—"

One of the young women, a slender redhead of about twenty, almost crashed into Kylie. She apologized quickly. "I'm so sorry— Oh, you must have just seen Dr. Sayers! Was it great? I've been trying to see him forever! He was great, right? I've heard it's so great!"

"He was great," Kylie said.

The girl smiled and moved past her.

Kylie and Jon continued out to the street. She knew he was patiently watching her—and watching her hopefully. "Where and when do you want me to talk?" she asked quietly.

"We can go to my office," he said.

She nodded and started walking down Essex, trying to hold on to everything she'd felt, remembered—and seen.

It didn't take them long to reach the empty shop space. Jon held the door open for her, and then he locked it behind them. She watched as he hurried over to his desk and picked up pictures, quickly putting them into a file. Then he looked at her and indicated the cluster of folding chairs.

"You good to do this?" he asked her.

She nodded gravely. He sat down opposite her.

"If that automobile accident was in any way connected to what happened," she began, "I believe I know what it was Jimmy might have seen."

"Oh?"

Kylie nodded. "This time, it was strange, I was with her while she was waiting for him. Just for a few minutes. Her mind was going in a few directions—the same way all our minds wander. She was thinking about her students and school. And then she was getting excited because she was going to see him." She looked away for a minute, flushing slightly. "She was thinking about being with him. Physically."

"Yeah, I got that," Jon said.

"What?" Kylie demanded, horrified.

He quickly shook his head. "You didn't do anything. During your regression, you just...moved."

"Oh, great!"

"Honestly, it was nothing. I swear, I wouldn't have let you put on a strip show on Sayers's desk," he promised her.

"I'm sorry, I'd be bothered by a lot less—"

"Kylie," he said, growing serious, "I swear to you, I would have stopped everything if I'd been worried your actions would make you uncomfortable afterward in any way."

"Not much choice but to believe you," she said.

He was quiet.

"Hey, I'm the one who...who really doesn't know what I did!" she protested.

"And I'm disappointed you still have no faith in me. Kylie, at this point, you have to believe in me," he said.

She sighed softly. "Sorry. I'm touchy on being out of control, you have to understand."

"I do. Please, go on."

"A memory came to me. There was a performance at the

memorial and Annie was there—and Westerly was there with his wife. Annie believed that even with his wife there, he looked at her in a way that showed her he wanted to be with her. He was planning to extricate himself from his marriage in the most amiable way possible."

"Or the most politically acceptable," Jon said.

"When she saw him at the cemetery, she wasn't afraid at first to go with him deeper into the tombstones. She believed in him, and accepted that their love had to stay hidden. But then he jerked her around and she protested—and then she knew he meant to hurt her. Everything had been a lie. He wasn't in love with her. He'd been using her. And she had become a political liability. She'd wanted to believe him, but she was smart beneath the longing for love, and she knew she was going to die. He couldn't afford to have her in the picture, not with the future he wanted for himself."

"So, Jimmy possibly saw something," Jon mused. "He saw them together at the performance. And that's what he meant to tell the police."

"That's what I believe. I'm not sure how it helps."

Jon sat back in his chair and Kylie knew he was thinking. They still needed evidence.

"Angela," he said suddenly.

"Pardon?"

"Angela Hawkins. Jackson Crow's wife. He's the field head for our unit and she's our office…magician. Angela can find almost anything. She's the one who's had a small army checking out Matt's activities. Her team leaves no digital stone unturned. If there were email communications or text messages between Annie Hampton and Michael Westerly, she'll find them."

"Do you really think Matt meant to hurt me yesterday?" Kylie asked.

He hesitated. "I couldn't take the chance that he didn't. I

mean that seriously. He had a knife in his hand, and he was standing over you."

"I believe that. But today reinforced what I know," Kylie said firmly. "Michael Westerly killed Annie. He did it himself, and he did viciously. He didn't kill her with sorrow. Or in a fit of passionate rage. It was calculated."

"Yes, he killed Annie. But that doesn't mean he wouldn't use other means to get rid of anyone else he thought to be in his way."

"All right. So what now?"

He was hesitant.

"What?" she pressed.

"I want to see Obadiah."

"I'm not afraid," she said.

"No?"

"No." Kylie sighed softly. "Okay, yes, I'm frightened and entirely freaked out. But feeling as if I was Annie... She was sweet, she was loved. She made a difference for a lot of young people. So, I'm stuck with this. And I'm not saying that in a good way. I think if I could run away from it, I would. But I don't believe running will do me any good. I'll spend the rest of my life terrified if I don't deal with this all now."

She shrugged. "So, I'm ready. I'm even ready for Auntie Mina. It all is what it is, I guess. I don't like it, I wish we'd never gone for that regression... No, that's not true. If it weren't for this, no one would suspect Michael Westerly. He's a horrible human being, and he would have gotten away with it. If I can stop him or help you stop him, then it's worth it."

"That's how we all see it," Jon said. "Come on, let's walk. Maybe Obadiah has found something out. After we see him, we'll take a cruise by the station."

"Oh?"

"I'll make my peace with Matt."

"You've decided he's innocent?"

"Nope. But I'll make my peace with him anyway. When you're the one hunting the monsters, you have to believe in guilty first, and all must be proven innocent. If not..."

"If not?"

"Then you can fall prey to the monsters. Come on. Let's go speak with the dead. It'll be great. I'll give you a formal introduction."

"It was in January, 2016, that the Gallows Hill Project determined it was Proctor's Ledge, and not Gallows Hill as had long been the general thought, where the victims of the witch trials were brought to be executed. They were brought by cart, and it was expected that the populace would witness the executions. This was not because the people were a vicious group relishing the agony of others. They came out to see the devil could be beaten, that evil could be put down. Perhaps it was also a warning, lest others fall in with the devil, who meant to seduce them and bring them into his nefarious fold."

Carl Fisher's clear voice rose above the noise of the street as Jon and Kylie walked toward the Old Burying Point.

There were several tour groups gathered by their guides in the area by the cemetery. It was midday, and Salem was alive with the business of tourism. Carl went on, informing his group they could look at the stones in the memorial to see the dates that claimed the lives of each of the victims.

"Bridget Bishop!" he announced. "She was the first to be executed, alone, on June 10, 1692, while the others were executed in groups. Bridget was a bit on the outside—she dressed in a red tunic. She owned property, inherited from her deceased husband. An apple orchard, right where one of our popular restaurants stands today." He winked at his group. "Haunted, of course. But the point remains she was a natural target—an outspoken woman, and one who denied to the end she had cavorted with the devil, signed a book, or practiced witchcraft in any way. Today, she might have run for Congress!"

His group laughed softly.

Carl saw Jon and Kylie watching him. He smiled and lifted a hand in greeting and then continued to tell his group about the accused honored at the Witch Trials Memorial by the Old Burying Point.

"Is Obadiah here?" Kylie whispered to Jon.

"I don't see him yet," Jon said. "But we'll wait a bit."

At his side, she nodded.

"We'll wander into the cemetery, look at the Hathorne grave…act like interested tourists," he said.

As they walked into the cemetery, Kylie asked him, "Do you think we'll find Mrs. Martinelli? I mean, the police haven't found her car. Not that there aren't dozens of ponds and marshes… I pray she's all right."

"Me, too." He paused, wondering if she thought he was wasting time. Perhaps she thought he should be out driving up and down the highways, looking for her. "I learned a long time ago that an agent—a cop, any kind of law enforcement officer—needs to be a team player. I've known Ben Miller a long time. Our other agents who know this area well have worked with the police, too. I'm having faith in my fellows. They're checking the roads. If something else is going on, well… I'm using that talent you hate so much. I'm hoping Obadiah, or one of his dead friends, can give us some insight."

She smiled. "I think you're right where you should be— keeping me alive!" she said lightly.

They came to the gravestone of Judge William Hathorne, a stone persevered within another stone.

"It's so incredibly hard to imagine what this man was thinking and feeling," she said, looking at the grave. "They called him the 'hanging judge.' It's said he behaved far more like a prosecutor than a judge, that he assumed people were guilty without giving them a chance, and demanded they speak against their neighbors. I've always tried to reconcile this history—how people could be so cruel to other people. But I guess nothing really changes..."

"Westerly," Jon said quietly. "His political career meaning more to him than the life of an innocent woman."

He noticed Carl had finished with his group, smiling as he collected tips. As the crowd dwindled, he walked into the cemetery toward Jon and Kylie.

"Hey, you two," he said cheerfully. "I'd have thought you both know this place backward and forward already."

"We do," Kylie said brightly. "I mean, I do. But it's still an interesting place to come. You must know that."

"I do," Carl said, then he looked at Jon. "Any news on poor Annie Hampton? Was Matt able to help in any way?"

"No news yet," Jon said. "We will find the truth. We're just hoping it's sooner and not later."

Carl let out a breath, shaking his head. "And Annie becomes another ghost story," he said quietly.

"Is that another tour group looking for you?" Kylie asked, pointing to people gathering by the memorial.

"Yeah, that's my next tour. Well, see you all," Carl said, and walked off.

Jon felt his phone vibrating. He quickly answered it, and immediately Ben spoke, "We've found Marla Martinelli's car."

Jon glanced at Kylie, who was watching him anxiously.

"Just the car. No sign of Marla, no sign of blood."

Jon let out a silent breath of relief. "Where was the car?"

"Near Salem Woods, just off the street."

"And officers are—"

"Looking for her. But I'm assuming you're getting out there."

"Good assumption," Jon said. He hung up and looked at Kylie. "I think she's hiding."

"Marla Martinelli?"

He nodded. "I need to take a walk. In the woods." He was already dialing Rocky.

She reached out, touching his hand. "I'd love to take a walk in the woods."

"We're worried about your safety."

"Then bring Devin and Rocky with us, instead of leaving the three of us here doing nothing," she said.

He hesitated.

She stared at him with her green eyes wide and certain.

Rocky answered the phone.

Jon looked at Kylie. Then he told Rocky, "It looks as if we're all taking a walk in the woods."

In Colonial times, Salem Woods had been pastureland. It was still a common area, but now it was filled with jogging paths, picnic areas, and more. A beautiful place to be used and enjoyed.

Kylie was glad the sun was out. Today, the trees seemed heavy and thick, and where they grew dense, it seemed they covered the paths in a strange, green darkness. The place seemed ominous, even as she looked on from the road.

She didn't have to be here; Jon would have left her with Rocky and Devin. Instead, they were gathered off the road with a group of police cars. Local officers were also searching for Marla Martinelli.

"We're operating under the belief Westerly did kill Annie," Jon told Kylie as they exited his car. "Whether he was able to get near Jimmy or not, we don't know. And whether he's hiring people to make hits or create chaos, we don't know. We do know Jimmy is in the hospital and Marla has disappeared." He was quiet a minute. "We're going to find her, dead or alive. We can still have you wait in the car. One of us can stay with you, or we can have an officer watch the car."

Kylie just walked into the woods—not looking for a trail, but simply stepping over a large tree root. Jon scrambled after her, followed by Rocky and Devin.

She immediately came up to a trail and then a little clearing in the dense woods. She stood for a moment, surprised by the soft, cool breeze that touched her face. She felt as if she'd stepped not just a few feet into the trees, but into a different world.

"What is it?" Jon asked quietly.

"I don't know," she said.

She took a step into the center of the clearing and closed her eyes, not understanding the strange, almost enveloping feeling that seemed to take her to a new realm. Nothing had moved; the trees were there, and the others were there—but there was something else.

She felt fear. Trembling, shaking fear seemed to send rivulets of cold through her limbs and into her blood. She saw herself hiding, terrified to come forward—and lost as well, aware she was not equipped to hide in the woods forever.

"Kylie?" Jon said.

"She's here," Kylie said. "Marla Martinelli is here, and she's afraid. She doesn't trust anyone." She started to move down the path. "Marla!" she called out. "We're here to help you. We'll get you safely to the police and to see Jimmy. Please! I swear, we'll protect you!" She wasn't sure she could protect a fly herself, but she was with people who could. "Mrs. Martinelli, please, trust us, trust us..."

She was running then, with Jon and Rocky and Devin right behind her. She wasn't sure how she knew which way to go, but she could envision the woman deserting her car and racing into the woods, desperate for cover.

Kylie came to another clearing and paused. This one was surrounded by thick bushes with small scrub trees growing between the more towering pines and oaks. She stood still, the others all but piling up behind her, and then she heard a rustling in the brush.

"Marla, on my life! I swear to you, it's all right. These are FBI agents, special agents. They're here to help you. Please."

The bushes parted.

Marla Martinelli made her appearance.

Under most circumstances, she would have been an attractive woman. She had smoothly cut silver hair with a contemporary swatch of indigo racing through it right at the temple while little wings of the silver framed her face—interspersed with a few pine needles and leaves—and large, beautiful, almond-shaped dark eyes. The lines on her face suggested that she smiled a lot. She was dressed in jeans and a tailored blue shirt, rumpled now at the sleeves and hem, also covered with bits of leaves, moss, and dirt.

"If you're going to kill me—kill me!" she said, standing in the center of the trail, hands on her hips, chin high.

Kylie didn't get a chance to speak. Jon went past her with his badge out. "Mrs. Martinelli, you're safe. I'm Special Agent Jon Dickson. This is Special Agent Craig Rockwell. You heard Kylie Connelly calling to you and Devin Lyle is one of our consultants. We're incredibly grateful to find you. We heard you were a savvy woman and might have decided to hide if you thought you were in danger."

Marla stood still, looking at them with some doubt still.

Devin pulled a bottle of water from her bag and walked forward to give it to her.

For a moment, Marla looked at Devin suspiciously, though it was painfully clear just how badly she wanted the water. And just how scared she was.

Kylie came to life. She hurried forward and took the bottle from Devin, broke the seal, and lifted the bottle so that it wasn't touching her lips, and let the water flow into her own mouth. If Marla feared that they'd spiked the water, she had proof otherwise now.

She was also thirsty. She grabbed the bottle from Kylie and drank several deep swallows, paused, and drank several more.

"Slow… It must be hard, but drink slowly," Devin warned her. She looked at Kylie, who nodded solemnly.

Marla studied them both. Perhaps making sure Kylie wasn't going to drop dead after drinking the water. Marla drank again, more slowly, pausing between swallows. When she finished, she looked at them all.

"So, I was afraid you might be about to poison me. Dumb, right? Those are guns you're carrying. You could just shoot me. Or…" she paused, looking the two men up and down "…strangle me. But then again, a poison that's slow-acting and undetectable…" She grimaced and glanced down, then up at them again. "Jimmy and I were talking about belonging to this mystery club. People like us who love mysteries and thrillers and true crime. Oh lord, it's fun when it's someone else. When it might be you, it's different. It isn't fun at all. It's terrifying."

She suddenly looked as if she was going to collapse into a dead faint. Jon moved forward, offering her an arm. She sagged.

"We may need an ambulance," Jon said quietly to Rocky.

"No, no, no… People can't see me," Marla said. "Jimmy— oh, my God, Jimmy. He was just at his cardiologist's… His heart was good. Passed the stress test with flying colors. We were talking about a trip to the Blue Ridge Mountains, hiking and enjoying nature."

"How did you know he was in the hospital? You left your cell phone at your daughter's house," Jon asked her.

"I had the news on in the car, and a reporter announced the accident. It was important because of the hotel, I guess, and they were saying that Mr. James Marino of Salem had evidently experienced a heart attack. And I don't know how—I mean, sure. It's possible. But I don't believe it. No, it's just not *probable*." She stopped and looked anxiously into the woods. "They could be out there," she said in a hushed voice.

"Who, Mrs. Martinelli?" Jon asked.

"*His* people," she said.

"Who?" Jon repeated gently.

"That slime… That Michael Westerly!" she whispered.

Jon looked over at Kylie for a second, but spoke softly to Mrs. Martinelli. "We're going to get you out of here. And we'll make sure you're safe."

She smiled slowly, nodding at him. "And Jimmy? Can you get me to see Jimmy?"

"Yes," Jon promised her. "Let's get you out of here."

CHAPTER TWELVE

Jon was impressed with Marla Martinelli. She seemed to be a remarkable woman. There was nothing wrong with her other than a little dehydration; she had simply hidden in the woods. When she had heard about the accident, she had immediately become suspicious. She and Jimmy had talked about speaking with the police. They kept telling themselves that, no, there was no way a man like Michael Westerly could be involved with murder.

"Jimmy and I were at the memorial one day when an open-air theater performance was going on. And we saw Annie there."

"You knew her?" Jon asked.

He was driving them to the hospital. Kylie was at his side, and Marla was in the back seat between Rocky and Devin. He glanced into the rearview mirror. Marla met his gaze and nodded gravely.

"I volunteered at her school sometimes. She would talk about being incredibly happy. She was with someone, but for the time, she was just going to wait and see where it all went. At the show, I saw her with friends. But I noticed the way she looked at Westerly—and the way he looked at her. They weren't as subtle as they might have liked to think. I also saw the way his wife looked at him, but I always considered her to be a prudish battle-ax. Oh, not that anyone should have an affair behind anyone's back," she clarified in a rush.

"But…anyway, Jimmy and I talked about it. At the time, it was just an observation. Maybe a little gossip. But when we heard that Annie had been killed…it was devastating. So bright, so lovely, so full of a goodness she wanted to share with everyone around her. Jimmy was a little worried," Marla admitted. "He told me he thought Westerly might have done it. I told him he couldn't hate the man just for being a politician, but the more we talked about it… Well, Jimmy told me he'd seen Westerly watching us when we were laughing and remarking on the way he and Annie were looking at one another. I guess we weren't subtle."

She paused. "I think Jimmy was concerned, but he wouldn't let me stress about it. He said, 'Hey, if he did or didn't do it, we didn't see it, we can't prove anything, so he wouldn't need to worry about us.'"

She paused, then said softly, "And we still can't prove anything. But I believe with my whole heart that Westerly is worried about us. And that he did something to Jimmy."

"Would Jimmy have been anywhere around Westerly?" Kylie asked. "If he was afraid of him—"

"Well, I don't think he'd have wandered down a dark alley with him," Marla said flatly. "Westerly couldn't just kill a man like Jimmy with a knife. He'd have had to think of another way to get rid of him. Like bringing on a heart attack."

"How would he have known that Jimmy was coming to the police station?" Jon asked her.

"I don't know. We had dinner at the Cauldron that night. We like it—we have dinner there together at least once a week. And…" she lowered her voice as if she might be overheard "...and we were talking about what we'd seen. Someone might have overheard us."

"Someone... Do you know who was at the Cauldron that night?"

"Battle-ax, for one."

"Who?" Rocky asked.

Marla made a dismissive gesture. "Battle-ax. Westerly's wife. She was with a few women from one of her posh garden clubs. And the usual crowd was there as well. Tour guides like to hang out there. The pretty bartender and the cute one. Matt. Who knows? The place was full, like usual—some locals and a horde of tourists. It's got the best location."

When they reached the hospital, they entered with Marla surrounded by the four of them. They moved swiftly through the corridors, bringing her up to Jimmy's floor. Jon noted that Jimmy's sons greeted Marla with affection, clearly happy that she had been found. Marla, in turn, was visibly relieved to see that Jimmy was doing better. He was in a private room, both sons could stay with him now, and Marla was welcome to be there, too.

Jimmy's sons made it clear they wanted Marla to stay, for her safety. It would be easy to get her clothing, and there was a shower in the room. Frank and Anthony would happily get her anything she might want to eat. They were glad of the police guard, but both men vowed no one would be getting past them, in any case, to hurt Marla or their father.

Thankfully, Jimmy was very much on the right side of stable. His doctors believed he would make a full recovery, and they expected him to awaken and talk at any time.

Jon stepped out into the hall and called Ben to make sure the police guard was made aware there was a chance there might be trouble, though none of them knew in what form.

Watching from just outside the hospital room, Jon noted that Kylie was sitting next to Marla, who was holding her hand tightly and leaning toward her. She had slid amazingly well into her accidental role, working with him and his fellow Krewe members. She had an innate inner light, he thought. An understanding of human suffering, an ability to care for what others were feeling.

With Marla safely at the hospital with Jimmy, and the staff and police aware of the danger the two might be in, Jon knew he had to hurry to the jail.

Matt would be released shortly, and Jon needed to talk to him one more time.

"I'm amazed at how easily you found Marla," Devin said, pressing the button on the hospital floor's coffee machine. "I thought that we'd be combing the woods forever. Obviously, I'm grateful we did find her easily. And very grateful that she was hiding and that we didn't discover..."

"A body in the trees," Kylie said. "Me, too. She was smart. Unless I'm way off track, and we're thinking about this all the wrong way."

"I think you nailed it as it was happening," Devin said sadly.

"Too bad it wasn't a precognition or an early vision or something that would have saved Annie," Kylie said. She put in another cup and Devin hit the button again.

"You've never had anything like that happen to you before?"

Kylie shook her head.

"And you never spoke to anyone who was...deceased? Never had a feeling, or anything that might suggest that you had a different perception?"

"Never," Kylie said. "And I didn't want to accept or believe any of it. But I saw that old guy sitting next to you. Obadiah. And... I want justice for Annie."

Devin studied her. "I believe that Westerly is our killer.

Still, finding the proof for a search or even putting him under arrest is going to be the trick. So far, we don't have much."

"So far, you have a woman claiming she was in another woman's body as she was being murdered," Kylie said wryly. "And two people convinced he was Annie's secret lover. And a wife who will swear she was with him at the time of the murder."

"If we went to court with that, it would be like setting the country back three hundred years." Devin shook her head. "Setting a precedent that would allow for all kinds of fabricated evidence. Still, knowing that Westerly is a killer is half the battle. We're on to the other half. That's something."

They had filled six coffee cups, one for everyone except Jimmy. He wasn't up for coffee yet—he had to open his eyes for that. But his nurses were confident, as was the doctor who had made rounds that night, that it was just a matter of time. He was well on his way to a full recovery.

"Wasn't there a case somewhere along the line where a ghost's testimony was allowed?" Kylie asked. "I saw it on one of the travel or science channels."

Devin looked at her curiously. "Yes, a real case. But it was in 1897. A young woman named Zona Shue was reported dead by her husband. When the doctor came to the house, he had her in bed, and he cried and carried on, and the doctor wrote a death certificate. She was buried. The woman's mother claimed in the weeks to come that Zona was appearing at the foot of her bed, claiming that her husband had murdered her.

"If I remember correctly, a prosecutor discovered that Zona had been the man's third wife—and another of his wives had died under suspicious circumstances. Stranger still, the husband, Trout Shue, had been heard mumbling that it could never be proven. Anyway, the young woman was exhumed, and a real autopsy was done. And just as the ghost had claimed to her mother, the autopsy proved she'd been strangled. The mother did testify in court about the visit from her daughter, the ghost. Trout Shue was convicted and sentenced to life in prison but died within three years of a disease. The prosecutor hadn't wanted to use the ghost testimony, though. The defense brought it in to try to make the case ridiculous."

"Interesting—and scary," Kylie said.

"It could never happen again," Devin pointed out. "The doctor in that case felt sorry for Trout, who was crying so much over his wife, and didn't complete a real autopsy. In that case, it did prove to be a good thing, but…if testimonies like that were allowed, God knows how many bitter or deluded people might like to see others imprisoned for life or facing a death sentence."

Devin shook her head. "We are incredibly lucky to have our strange form of guidance, but hard, physical evidence is crucial. Eyewitness accounts can even be questioned. Witnesses often see what they want to, or don't see people or events in context. But we will find what we need—I believe that with my whole heart. Sometimes, even fearing that the truth is known causes a suspect to make the mistake that finally allows the courts to put him away."

Kylie nodded. "I'm going to have faith," she said. "In you guys. Not that I don't have faith, but we all know that having faith hasn't always made the world right. Still, I can't believe that I saw what I saw during the regression for nothing. Or that I felt the pull into the forest." She shrugged and grinned. "I'm going to run with the notion that we don't use all of our brain's capacity, and I've managed to tap into one of the unused bits for a reason."

"There you go," Devin told her.

They carried the coffee carefully back to Jimmy's room.

Anthony was reading on his phone, Frank was in a chair at the foot of his dad's bed, and Marla was right next to Jimmy.

She'd showered and changed, but her night in the woods must have been taking its toll—she held Jimmy's hand but slouched in her chair, her head to the side as she dozed.

"Thanks," Frank said in a whisper, rising to take one of the cups. Anthony rose as well, smiling as he accepted a cup. Both brothers were dark-haired, handsome young men and evidently close as a family.

"Coffee."

They all heard the word at the same time and, startled, turned to the bed. Kylie caught Anthony's cup before it could fall; his father had spoken.

There was nothing like it—watching Jimmy open his eyes, seeing Marla rouse and then let out a sob as she held his hand, the love in her eyes, in his eyes, and then the love of his sons as they took their turn with their father, sobbing as well.

It was a good feeling. They'd found Marla, and so far, kept her and Marino safe. He'd be with his family, hopefully for years to come.

Kylie sank into a chair.

There was still no way to prove that Westerly was a murderer. And that meant that even now, no one even remotely involved was safe.

Unsurprisingly, Matt watched Jon as if he were the devil himself. He had spent a night in jail—and possibly was entirely innocent.

"You're all right talking to me again?" Jon asked him.

They sat across from each other in an interrogation room. Matt wasn't cuffed, as he was due to leave.

"If talking to you is going to get me out of here faster, I'll talk. The problem is that I have absolutely no idea what you want me to say."

"Matt, I'm not sure how to explain this any more clearly.

You were in a cemetery, in a secluded spot with a young woman. You were standing behind her with a knife."

Matt sounded a little desperate as he replied, "Okay. That's what you saw. What I saw was a young woman I met at a bar where I work, a woman who's from the area and interested in local history. Look," he said, frustrated, "I don't know what it appeared to be from your angle. I was focused on the stone. I can take you and show you."

"Just so you're aware, the story we told people for the time being is that you're helping the police," Jon said.

Matt lowered his head. "Thanks. I like you—you're a decent tipper. But I don't understand what you're thinking. You think that I…somehow managed to kill Annie Hampton, clean up, and start at work just minutes after she was murdered?"

"You're wrong. I don't think you murdered Annie."

"Then…what?"

"Annie's death is the fourth in a list of murders we've connected. You happened to be in the other locations at the times of those murders, too."

Hudson frowned and shook his head. "I travel! I'm an actor—a performer. Maybe they're not going to rush an Oscar to me anytime soon, but I do get gigs working on different projects. When I'm traveling, it's for work. Projects tend to go late into the night. You can check on my whereabouts anywhere that I've gone."

According to Angela's research, Matt had never missed one of his performances. There were also ample pictures of him with audience members after the performances, posted to his own and others' social media.

Alibis for every minute of his days couldn't be proven, but Angela had even had hotel managers checking the times when his keys had been used to enter the places he stayed. If he'd left his room at night, he'd either known how to trick a system or, in one case at least, leave safely out of a fourteenth-story window.

There was an air about Matt that made Jon believe him. But it wasn't the time to go by simple instinct. Psychopaths were often skilled at appearing charming.

Westerly had killed Annie; Jon didn't doubt Kylie's vision in the slightest. But Westerly also had solid alibis. So unless he had an accomplice, he couldn't have killed the other women. Which left Matt, someone who had been in the cities where murder victims had been found.

Just in case, Jon made a mental note to have other Cauldron regulars investigated, to see if anyone else had a history of traveling up and down the East Coast. He also needed to check out the men and women who worked for Westerly.

What were the motives behind the other murders, though? Had Westerly been having affairs with all of them? Not likely—the other women were suffering addiction and the hardships brought on by substance abuse. Their lives wouldn't have led them to a man like Michael Westerly.

Matt leaned forward. "I swear to you, I didn't kill anyone. I'm a bartender and an actor. I'm really good at the first, trying hard at the second. I see a lot in the restaurant—I hear a lot. Good bartenders are good listeners, and not just when people are talking." He paused, frowning. "I was at the Cauldron the other night... You were there, too, when Kylie had that bizarre reaction to Michael Westerly on the TV. Then the news about Annie Hampton broke..."

His voice trailed away, and his eyes widened as he looked at Jon. "Okay, I read in the news that Annie's friends were talking about a mystery lover. Why was it a secret affair? Maybe they were talking about someone with major league influence." He stared at Jon hard. "Michael Westerly. You all think that Senator Westerly was Annie's mystery lover, don't you? But you think that somehow I'm involved? I'm telling you, I wouldn't go out of my way to help him out of a puddle, much less commit a murder for the man. And that's what you're thinking."

"Matt, you're in here because you were standing over a woman with a knife. And because your schedule matches up with other murders."

"Hey, I'm not the only person who travels. Most people travel. Carl! Carl even does some of the same shows I do. I'm sure most college kids around here travel, too. And I didn't do anything. And you have nothing on me. I'm walking out of here."

"Yes. You can go right now."

"Really?"

"Yes."

"You mean I can just stand up and walk out—and I can go to work unembarrassed because the information out there was that I was trying to help the police?"

"Yes."

"Cool." Matt stood slowly, as if waiting for Jon to tell him it was a lie.

Jon stood as well, and Matt looked at him suspiciously.

"Matt, no one is going to jump you. You're free to leave."

Matt nodded and walked to the door of the interrogation room, opened it slowly, looked back, and walked out.

Jon started to shuffle through his notes. The door opened. Matt was back.

Jon looked at him questioningly.

"Nope. There's a brutal killer out there—a guy running around with a knife who's proven he can use it. And you think that Michael Westerly is involved—"

"I never said that to you," Jon interrupted.

"But you think he may have a partner," Matt went on. "You've told people I was helping the police, like maybe I know something. If I go out there, I'm liable to get a knife in my back!"

"This killer has never gone after a man," Jon said.

"There's a first time for everything." Matt seemed sincerely frightened. "Look, I don't think I'm a complete squawking chicken, but I'm not the bravest guy on the block, either. Hell yes, right now I'm scared."

"You want a police escort?"

"I can have a police escort?" Matt asked hopefully. "I need to go home and shower and then get to the bar. The actor thing only pays when I have an acting gig. I'm surviving by bartending, and I need to show up for work tonight. But I'm in a really bad position—you kept it from going around town that I was suspected of committing a heinous murder. But to the murderer, me 'helping' the police has to incite some not very happy feelings. *Can* you do something for me? I mean, who knows, maybe I'll realize something. You know, re- member something from the bar, from seeing people around town… Maybe, in the end, I could help."

"I think I can get you a police escort," Jon said. "Let me check on that. I can also call on some of our people out of Boston." He paused. It was difficult to think that this man could have been guilty of murder. He'd learned, however, that the friendliest face could mask a heart filled with hatred and evil.

If Matt was innocent, would he be seeking protection? Just how good of an actor was Matt Hudson? One way or the other, having him watched would be a good thing, Jon decided. It would keep him in line, and if he did need pro- tection… He was almost like bait.

Jon lifted a hand. "If you want someone watching over you, give me a minute."

He stepped out to talk to Ben and find out if the department could afford to put another officer on protection duty. They made arrangements for Matt to be covered.

Then his phone rang. It was Rocky. Jimmy Marino was conscious—and talking.

Jon spun on his heel and immediately left the police station so he could hurry to the hospital.

When he arrived, he nodded to the cop in the hall—a young man who was alert and stood when Jon approached—but who had been playing phone games, bored with a guard duty that didn't seem to require any real action.

Rocky came out into the hall just as Jon showed the young cop his credentials.

"He's up and talking," Rocky said. "And doesn't mind starting all over again. He was surprised to wake up and find more than just his sons in the room with him, but an FBI agent and friends, too. But he was quick to be grateful. Said he's only surprised because what he had to tell the police didn't seem worthy of a murder attempt on him. He's damned glad we're around."

"Does he know what happened to him?" Jon asked.

"He remembers leaving the restaurant to drive home. And then staggering pain—and nothing from there. Go on in. Devin and I will get some coffee. The hospital staff and the doctor are being very accommodating, but I don't want to push it with too many people in the room. His sons are down in the cafeteria. We'll keep them down there for a bit."

"Thanks," Jon said.

As Devin came out to join Rocky, she caught Jon's arm, looking at him gravely. "Everything corroborates what Kylie…experienced," she said.

"What's your plan from here?" Rocky asked him. "Anything on Matt Hudson?"

"I can't help but believe the guy. And I'm the one who suspected and tackled him," Jon said. "My instincts are usually good, but I don't discount anything. He asked for protection. Detective Miller had no problem providing it. Here's the thing—and it's not a bad thought on Matt's part. He's grateful that the story went around that he was helping the cops and not that he was a suspect. But if that's the word on the street, he could be in as much danger as anyone else. Anyway, I was thinking of hanging out at the Cauldron for a while. I'm not sure what we'll find there—"

"But a matchbox advertising the place was found near one of the previous victims," Rocky said.

"Right. And while I don't know how often Westerly is in there, we know that Matt will be bartending and Carl Fisher—someone else who has curiously traveled to the murder destinations—hangs out there doing what he can to gather clientele," Jon said. "It's a local hot spot. With no better plans for the night, I thought I'd see what I could see. Have dinner. Watch if anyone is watching Matt."

"It's so frustrating that no one has anything solid on Westerly," Devin said. "Except that now there are a couple of people who would testify that he *might* have been the man having an affair with Annie. That wouldn't prove murder."

"No," Jon said softly. "But it could ruin a political career."

"Exactly," Rocky said seriously. "All right, go talk to Jimmy. If Westerly did manage to do this to him, the man is afraid—and very dangerous."

Jon went in to the hospital room. Kylie was seated on one side of the bed in the large hospital chair that could be turned into a sleeper.

Marla was on the bed at Jimmy's side, avoiding the IV and heart monitor lines. She hopped up when Jon entered and hurried over to give him an unabashed hug.

"This is him, Jimmy—the man who was right there for you!" she said.

"Thank you, thank you," Jimmy told him. "And you ask

me anything." He was sitting up in his hospital bed and looked damned good for someone who had gone through a heart attack and a car accident to boot.

Jon glanced over at Kylie; she was looking at him expectantly. He offered her a quick smile and gave his attention back to Jimmy for the moment. "We've been worried about you."

"Thankfully, I'm doing fine," Jimmy said. "I woke up to all these fine folks around me. Grateful that Marla was okay and that you people—especially this young lady," Jimmy said, pausing to smile at Kylie, "made such an effort to keep Marla safe and bring her to me. I'll admit, too, that I'm feeling wicked angry. I mean, I'm no fool. I take my health seriously. There was no reason for what happened to me."

"Don't let him get started," Marla said. "This guy didn't slowly blink and come to. He opened his eyes and wanted to get out of bed right away. His sons managed to keep him in it, and his nurse and then his doctor arrived to explain his injuries and that they were monitoring his heart."

"I understand all that," Jimmy said testily. "I'll be careful. I'm in the bed, right? I listened to the doc. I know my ribs are fractured and they need to monitor my ticker. But I want to talk. This is important. And here's the thing—I'm naturally suspicious of politicians. I admit, I don't tend to like them. Maybe they can't help it, maybe lying is part of the game. But with this Westerly, it goes beyond that. There something behind that smile. Something wicked evil."

"Politicians tend to be...politicians," Kylie murmured.

"Didn't vote for the fellow. Oh, he's articulate, he talks a good talk," Jimmy said. "Everything about him is smooth, like he's playing a role all the time. He's well-spoken, and I bet people don't realize that most of the time it's double-talk. Of course, this means nothing. I mean, I can testify in court that I didn't like the way he looked at a woman—a sweet, giving young woman who's now dead. But I sincerely believe she's dead by his hand."

"I saw the way he looked at her, too," Marla said passionately. "Something was going on. On one hand, it was the look of longing. Lust, maybe. Then his wife was there—and I think there was a look of fear. Like he was worried about getting caught. I saw it all, too."

"Right," Jimmy said. "But it wouldn't prove anything against him." He paused, letting out a breath. He looked at Jon. "I do understand that you saved my life. For that, sir, I thank you sincerely. I'm pushing seventy and I've lost a lot. But I have wonderful sons and an amazing friend here... Marla makes these years very precious to me. And I know that this lovely young lady—" he nodded toward Kylie "—was her salvation. I would do anything to help you. I just don't know how I can."

"All our lives are precious, sir, as long as we have breath in us," Jon said. "And I appreciate your words. I'm not really the one who saved your life—doctors did that. I had the sense not to break your neck while getting you extracted from the car. You've been helpful. Anything you can tell me just may be the thing that gives us a direction to go in, Mr. Marino."

"Jimmy, please, call me Jimmy," Marino said. "Who has a name like Jimmy, and doesn't have people use it, huh?"

Jon smiled. "Okay—Jimmy. What we need to know is where you were before the accident that evening. There were high levels of salt and another chemical in your system. Could be natural, but that 'could be' isn't really probable. We believe someone may have tried to bring on your heart attack. I doubt they could have planned exactly when you'd have a heart attack and strike the hotel, but a heart attack while driving would certainly add to the possibility that it might kill you."

Jimmy nodded. He looked at Marla and squeezed her hand. "We were together until about noon. My lady was heading down to see her daughter. I was on my own. I puttered around the house a bit, and then headed to the Cauldron. There were tons of people there. I met up with a few fellows from my Masonic lodge. We were just talking, rehashing the good old days, Halloween nights with Wiccan friends, spooky old houses we put together ourselves for charity…" He took a breath, looking around the room. He shrugged.

"Do you remember specifically who was there that night?" Jon prompted.

Jimmy thought about it. "Matt and Cindy were working the bar, as usual. That tour guide, Carl Fisher, was in there— but he's always trolling for customers. Not that he's the only tour guide who does that. I just know and like him, so I noticed he was there." He glanced at Marla. She smiled encouragingly at him.

"But tell them… Westerly's wife was there, too," Marla said.

Jimmy nodded. "She and several women from one of her clubs had a little section in the back, next to the stained-glass windows that look out to the street. But she's way too high and mighty to socialize with the likes of us." He let out a sniffing sound. "We look like a pack of battered old dogs. Guess she wouldn't realize that Will Norman is an old computer genius, worth really big bucks. Or that Sammy Tyson writes one of the most influential political blogs out there."

"She's not a nice woman," Marla said. "Sandra Wasserman Westerly is her name. Her family comes from the right part of Rhode Island, if you know what I mean. She has a great political smile. On TV and at speeches and rallies, she looks like the nicest sweetest woman in the world. Except no equal rights for that woman, she's just her old man's big-time support, perfect little wife. If she kissed my baby, I'd halfway scrub the poor little tyke's skin away."

Jimmy grinned. "I like my women feisty," he said, looking tenderly at Marla.

Marla shook her head. "I'm sorry, I don't mean to sound like a terrible human being. It's just that, well, I think that woman uses her husband as a stepping stone. She likes being elite. I think he could do anything at all, and so long as it didn't interfere with her garden clubs or balls or ability to hobnob with the elegant people, she wouldn't care in the least. She'd defend him to the end."

Jon had to admit, it was natural to wonder if a wife was lying when she gave an alibi for her husband.

"Tomorrow, he has a speaking engagement in Boston," he said. "They'll both be away from Salem. I'm afraid we can't let down on our guard, though, just in case others are involved."

"We'll stay vigilant," Kylie said.

He smiled. Kylie had been so reluctant at first to believe any of it, or to be involved at all. Now, she was passionate and indignant, determined to have justice.

"Whatever caused this all to come about, I believe that someone thinks you know more than you really do," Jon told Jimmy, "not that you merely suspect Westerly is dangerous. I think that someone might have overheard you the night you were speaking with Marla. They might have planned to take advantage the next time you were out on your own."

"You have no evidence," Jimmy said, sadly shaking his head.

"Not yet. But if Westerly did something to you or had someone else act on his behalf, then he's nervous. For now, do what the doctors say and do your best to relax," Jon told him.

"You know, the cop outside is a nice kid, but..." Jimmy began softly.

"Rocky—Special Agent Craig Rockwell—and Devin will be here, too. You'll be safe," Jon assured him.

"What happens when I have to leave?"

"That won't be for a bit," Jon said.

"What are you going to do?" Jimmy asked.

"Find the truth—and a way to prove it."

CHAPTER THIRTEEN

Matt seemed to bear Kylie no ill will.

She and Jon were in seats at the Cauldron's bar while waiting for a table. Matt paused in front of Kylie, offering her a rueful smile. Jon was chatting with someone seated on his other side.

"So, you seem to be really friendly with the FBI guy, huh?" Matt asked her. "Maybe I'll get you both back to the Old Burying Point to show you the stone I was going to. I swear, Kylie, I meant you no ill will in any way, shape, or form."

She offered him a sincere smile. "I believe you. I'm sorry you spent a night in jail."

He shrugged. "It wasn't that bad, really. A lot of people around here are suddenly impressed with me. If the cops think I'm worthy, so do they!"

"Well, if anything good comes out of it, I'm glad," Kylie said.

Jon turned back to them.

Matt lifted his hands. "I'm innocent!"

Jon nodded. His smile was tight, but apparently, whatever he and Matt had shared, things were all right with them now.

"The guy closest to the tables at that end of the bar is my cop bodyguard," Matt said. "Nice guy, I like him. Midtwenties but looks like a wrestler."

"Good. So, you feel safe?" Jon asked him.

"He instills confidence, for sure. Excuse me—customer heading this way." Matt moved on.

"What are we looking for?" Kylie whispered.

"I'm not sure. Actually... I think maybe I am," Jon said softly.

"Oh?"

"The 'garden club' has arrived. Be nonchalant, but the perfectly dressed woman over there with the perfectly brushed hair is Sandra Westerly."

"Oh?" She started to turn to look.

"Hey! Don't be obvious."

"Sorry! I guess Westerly hasn't left for Boston yet. Or she isn't going with him."

"We're not that far from Boston. He could easily plan on leaving early in the morning."

"The ladies' room is right next to her. I think I'll wash my hands... You never know what germs you might pick up in a hospital." She stood and pretended to laugh casually at something he said. As she headed to the ladies' room, she allowed herself a good look at the woman in question.

Sandra was about her husband's age, an attractive woman, tall and slim. Her clothing was modest but excellently tailored, a skirt suit with a brocade vest and white tailored blouse. She had stopped at a table with two couples to offer them generous smiles and chat while she waved the friends who had arrived with her on to follow the hostess—they evidently had reserved tables toward the back of the restaurant.

Kylie went into the ladies' room, a place decked out with murals of various movie witches and sinks that resembled cauldrons.

She was washing her hands when Sandra came in behind her. Kylie pretended not to notice her, but as she glanced up into the mirror over the sink, it was impossible not to realize that the woman was staring at her.

"You're a witch," Sandra stated softly. "It's you—I know it's you. There are rumors going all around about my husband, and they are your fault. People talk, you know. You were here, and his picture came on the television and you made it seem as if you were terrified. As if he was some kind of a monster. Anyone who thinks my husband is guilty thinks so because of you! Witch. *Bitch.* What was it, your pathetic way of garnering attention?"

Sandra kept her distance, almost as if she was afraid she might fly at Kylie with claws bared if she came too close.

Kylie wasn't afraid of her—not that she was any kind of a fighter. But they were in a busy, public place. The door might open at any minute. And though she might not have taken any karate lessons, she was probably stronger than Sandra.

But the hatred in the woman's eyes was immobilizing. Did she not know her husband was a killer? Or did she not care? Were her garden parties and clubs more important than anything else? Or, more likely, was the prospect of being the wife of a US senator the most important thing?

"I don't know your husband, Mrs. Westerly," Kylie said. "And I could hardly be any threat to him. I wasn't anywhere near the cemetery where Annie Hampton was murdered." She started to walk out, but turned back. "I would think about it, though, Mrs. Westerly. Annie died a horrible death. I hear that killing gets easier and easier—once you've done it once."

"This is Salem," Sandra said. "It's hell on witches, even if they're modern-day bitches. They're known to meet with very bad ends here."

"As I said, Mrs. Westerly, I don't even know your husband. But you do. That's what you need to be thinking about."

Kylie turned for the door. Apparently, Sandra Westerly did fly at her—but too late. She heard a thud against the door as it closed behind her.

She hurried back to the bar. Jon was standing, looking anxious. He couldn't know what had happened, but maybe she had been gone too long.

"I was about to burst in there," he told her. "Did she speak to you? I saw Sandra walk in after you, and I was wishing to hell we'd brought Devin with us. I'd have gone inside in another sixty seconds." He studied her face. "Something did happen."

Kylie shrugged, not wanting to make more of the situation than it had been. "She accosted me, said it was all my fault."

"I guess a fair amount of people did see your reaction to the news about the murder that night. And to Michael Westerly. So, yes, talk could go around. Just as it apparently went around about Jimmy and Marla gossiping about Westerly having an affair with Annie." He shook his head. "I keep thinking we should be safe with him in Boston tomorrow, at least during his speech. Boston is too close to feel great about anything, but I've spoken with Jackson—he'll have an agent in Boston keeping tabs on the senator."

"That should make you relax," she said, "for a bit."

"Yes and no."

"Why the no?"

"Because he has alibis for when the other murders occurred. Film footage of speeches, events. So, someone might well be killing for him, or else he knew confidential information about the other murders and was able to copy them completely. It would be strange if he was best friends or partners with a sadistic killer, but stranger things have happened. And maybe not so strange, since he was able to commit such a brutal murder himself." Jon hesitated. "I was thinking we should go back to the cemetery again tomorrow—the one where Annie was killed."

She couldn't help the chill that ran up her spine; she hoped she kept the eerie fear from showing. "You think I might be able to find out even more?" she asked.

"I think the crime scene people are good at what they do, but we have to have missed something," he said. "There has to be some strand of evidence against him somewhere. That was a bloody murder. How did he manage to stab her so many times, and then appear again elsewhere without any trace of blood? He had to have stripped in the cemetery or his car, with clean clothing stashed somewhere."

He shook his head. "We're at a dead end at the moment. I believe he killed Annie because news of their affair was going to get out. Maybe she was going to call his wife. Maybe his wife knew and wanted it stopped. From everything we've heard about her, Annie was a sweet and giving person. I don't have the impression Sandra Westerly is sweet or giving in any way."

"But she'll stand by her man," Kylie said.

"Exactly," Jon murmured softly. His attention turned toward the door.

Carl Fisher had just come in. It was his usual time, about forty-five minutes before one of his tours. He paused to chat with people on his way up to the bar, smiling and handing out postcards that advertised his tours.

He was good at what he did, Kylie thought. His was a no-pressure sell. "Charming," she murmured.

"What?"

"The kind of man who could get his victims into a cemetery would be charming. Someone who could make a woman think he meant nothing but kindness. Or genuine interest. Even if the other victims were kind of down-and-out... I mean, addiction makes people wary, but if you met someone handsome and charming who seems benign…"

"He's coming this way. And he's someone who does travel. We've been looking into him as well as others, but not that closely," Jon said lowly. "In fact, Matt mentioned that they did some of the same shows which would mean the same cities. Maybe Angela can find something deeper down than what we've discovered about him so far."

Kylie suddenly felt bad. She liked Carl. He gave a great ghost tour.

And he was charming.

Carl came up to them, wearing his frock coat and tall hat and wielding a gentleman's walking stick. He appeared truly pleased to see them. He nodded to Jon and looked at Kylie.

"Nice to see you still here," he said. "You guys have almost become regulars."

"There are a lot of the same people here all of the time," Jon agreed.

Carl nodded, then grew serious. "I heard you rescued a man—the guy who crashed into the hotel. He's in here often. Jimmy Marino, right? Nice guy. I do hope he's doing well. We all love him and Marla. She's a sweetie. It's adorable. A December-December romance! I really hope the old guy is going to make it. They are nice people."

"You saw him in here before the accident?" Jon asked.

Carl nodded. "Yep. He was with a group of guys." He waved a hand indicating the back tables where Sandra Westerly was holding court with her club. "Let's see… Yep. The same people are around here a lot. Sandra Westerly was here that night, the bartenders, of course—good to see that Matt's back! Oh, yeah, a few of my other guides who hang out kind of like I do, and Dr. Sayers. One day, I'm going to do that regression thing. For fun. I don't believe in it."

"Dr. Sayers is here tonight?" Kylie asked.

Carl pointed. The doctor was at the high bar where Kylie and her friends had been sitting the night after the ghost tour. He was with a young woman and another couple.

As if he had somehow heard Carl's words, Sayers looked over at them. He offered a smile and a nod, and apparently excused himself to come over and greet them.

"Hello, Carl—Jon and Kylie!"

"Hey," Carl said in response. "I was just telling them… One day, I'm making an appointment with you."

Dr. Sayers laughed. "For psychiatric help? Carl, based on your apparel, I think you do your own regression in your mind."

"I think I'm just fine as far as psychiatry goes," Carl said. "But some people believe you're the real deal."

"Let's hope so, or they wouldn't come," Dr. Sayers said. "But I don't guarantee good experiences. Ask Kylie here. She had a bit of a bumpy time."

"Strange regression," she agreed quietly.

"Oh, I'm willing to take a chance," Carl said. "It all goes into history and mystery, right? It might make me an even better guide. Hey, you can ask Kylie—I'm a great guide!"

"I'm sure you are," Dr. Sayers said.

"He's a great guide," Kylie said.

"And what do you think, Mr. Dickson?" Dr. Sayers asked.

"I haven't had the chance to take the tour, but if Kylie says he gives a great tour, I believe that he must."

"He really loves and knows the city's history—all of it, not just the witch trials," Kylie said.

"Which is good. Salem has been filled with all kinds of characters through the years," Jon noted.

"Hey, Doctor." Carl lowered his voice. "Have you ever regressed the ice queen over there?" He inclined his head toward Sandra Westerly's table.

Dr. Sayers grinned. "Ice queen? Not a good description for a politician's wife."

Carl shrugged. "She had plenty of smiles for the TV cameras. But I heard her husband took off for this leg of his campaign without her. Think there might be troubled waters there, Doc?"

"Either that, or she just didn't feel like the drive to Boston. Who knows?" Dr. Sayers shrugged. "Anyway, that's between them. Doesn't matter to me. He wouldn't be my choice for any office, so whatever he's up to wouldn't sway my vote."

"What do you think?" Carl asked, turning to Kylie and Jon.

"I think I'm a resident of Virginia," Jon said, "and we have enough going on with local politics to last a lifetime."

"New York resident at the moment," Kylie said.

"So, Carl, what do you think of him?" Jon asked.

Carl laughed and looked a little uncomfortable. "I think she's an ice queen, like I said. And he's very smooth. But there's something about him... Oh, well, it's time I get back out on the street. People will start grouping up and I need to be there. Photo ops for my group, you know?"

He grinned and left them, pausing just a second to tell Cindy to hold his tab—he'd be back after his tour.

"They say he's one of the best in the city," Dr. Sayers noted. "Now if you'll excuse me, I'm on a first date. I should get back if I'm hoping there's a second."

"Probably," Jon said. "By the way, thanks for all the help you've given us."

Dr. Sayers grinned. "If I was any help to you, I'm truly glad."

Jon nodded to him. When the doctor had returned to his group, Kylie murmured, "What now?"

"Bed."

"Pardon?"

"I think we're done here for the night. I say we call it quits and start fresh in the morning."

"And you want to go back to the cemetery," Kylie said.

"Something has to have been overlooked," Jon said. "We need a piece of solid evidence. At least something that would allow for a search warrant. We're dealing with a public figure who has hoodwinked tens of thousands of people. If we're not careful, he'll get away with it. Worse, he'll turn his supposed persecution into something he can use in his career. Our case must be real and solid. Now, you don't have to go this time. You can stay at the hospital with Rocky and Devin to be safe."

"What about Rocky and Devin? Can they just stay there all this time? Won't they need a break? Showers, changes of clothing—"

"We'll see to it they get a break. I believe Jackson is going to come up. The possibilities here call for a stronger Krewe presence."

She smiled grimly. "I want to go with you."

"You're not frightened anymore?"

"Oh, hell yes. But as I've said, I don't want to be frightened all my life. And I'm not worried about going to the cemetery with you."

Jon lowered his head and she wondered if he appreciated her words or doubted them.

Whatever his thoughts, she knew her own. From their strange meeting through the intense hours they had spent together, she'd come to admire him tremendously.

As she and her friends had all noted from the beginning, Jon was a compelling man. Awkwardly, she realized she'd been attracted from the first time she'd opened her eyes in his arms. Furious and terrified—but attracted, which seemed at odds. Or maybe the feeling had grown. She knew his face fascinated her. It was a combination of a certain matured ruggedness and classical strength. And now...

Would it be so bad? Was it wrong? In the world they lived in, was stealing a few moments of simple longing and pleasure a bad thing?

It would be—if he wasn't attracted to her in the least and she made an absolute fool of herself.

He looked up then, right into her gaze, and she didn't know exactly how she knew, but there was something deep in his ice-blue eyes, maybe, or his manner.

But she knew.

He'd been thinking the same thing.

It wasn't her usual behavior, but her eyes held his, and she spoke very quietly.

"Well, then, let's go to bed."

Jon wasn't sure if he decided they should just head down the street to his office space because he didn't want to return to Devin's and run into Auntie Mina or any other possible ghostly presence, or if it was just the fact the office was very close.

And the moment seemed to demand immediate attention.

Her simple words created an amazing hunger in him. Maybe it was natural instinct, or a fascination with the woman he had come to know.

But even then, he steeled himself from stupidity; as soon as they were inside, he locked the door. He laid his Glock and holster within easy reach of the bed, and then turned back to the woman who had so enchanted him.

She stood before him, smiling, a slightly rueful smile, and he returned it, pulling her into his arms. Logic went out of his thoughts. She felt like sweet, molten fire against him as they frantically shed their clothing, laughing between searing wet kisses as he nearly tripped over his trousers.

"So much for a smooth striptease," he murmured.

"Hey!" she protested, and he realized she'd gotten her shirt stuck coming over her head.

He helped, the shirt went flying, and they were tangled together again. They stumbled to the bed, getting onto it a bit awkwardly and ungracefully, since his bed was an air mattress on the floor. It didn't matter in the least. The last of their clothing went, and the feel of that fire of her body against his own was even greater.

He was captivated by the scent and warmth of her, of the look in her eyes, crystal pools of honesty and sensuality. They locked in a deep kiss again, tongues stroking one another, as if that simple exploration was the greatest and most arousing adventure known to man.

Her lips moved against his throat and down his chest. He rolled her over to her back, touching her with his lips and tongue. They caressed, ever more intimate, until there could be no more play, and they came together in a moment of searing pleasure, holding tight for seconds that were a beautiful eternity. Then their bodies turned to writhing, arching, twisting, thundering…and soaring. Climax roared within them, explosive and sweet.

They lay back, exhausted—panting, hearts pounding, still wrapped in each other's arms.

Ridiculous as it might have been, he found himself wondering what it would be like to lie so every night, to wake, to laugh…to find time that was really theirs, on an island somewhere, with the sun above them and the sea glistening before them.

And suddenly he was worried that maybe for her it had been…just sex. The intensity of the situation, a release from fear… Lesser things had brought people together for a moment of pleasure.

She was curled against him. They didn't speak for several

minutes, just breathing. Then she rose halfway, hands resting on his chest. He wasn't sure what he was expecting.

"Thank you," she said softly.

He had to smile. "No, thank you," he said.

She smiled. "I mean, I never do things like this… I feel as if I was ridiculously forward, but you didn't make me feel awkward in any way. I know it's a little bit crazy. And it's probably against your rules, but…"

"There's something special, something right, about it, though," he said softly.

She rested her cheek against his chest once again. He moved his fingers gently through her hair. He decided he'd be honest, too.

"We could have gone back to Devin's, you know. You have all your things there now. But once you looked at me, I couldn't wait that long."

She twisted in his arms again, facing him. He loved her eyes and wondered if people fell into whatever this feeling was just because of someone's eyes.

"You know I have absolute faith in you," she said, "but I'm not sure I'd have been comfortable at Devin's."

"Well, Auntie Mina is a lovely ghost. She was a lovely woman, I'm certain, and is very discreet. She'd never show up where she knew she shouldn't be."

"Well, that is one aspect, but honestly, Devin's cottage is in the middle of the woods."

"You underestimate Poe—that bird is an incredible watchdog. And the cabin is wired for security. It would take a genius to break through Devin's system."

"That's good to know."

He nodded. "Devin once found a body in the woods. That tends to make you want some good security. But she loves the cottage. A good friend in town watches the place for her when she's gone—and cares for Poe."

They were both silent for a few minutes.

"Kylie," he began.

She eased up again, over his chest, her hair teasing his skin. She pressed a finger to his lips and lowered her face to his.

It would be rude to refuse her kiss...

Or all else that followed.

In the end, they slept curled together, flesh to flesh, and bizarrely comfortable.

It was the best sleep he'd had in forever.

When Kylie woke, Jon was already up, showered, and dressed for the day. He had coffee for her and brought it to her in bed.

He sat by her side. "I'm sorry—none of your things are here."

"You have soap and water, right?"

"I do."

"I should be fine. I'll be wearing the same clothes, but if I leave off the jacket, maybe no one will notice."

"I have spare T-shirts."

"Hmm. Might be a bit big, but...do they say FBI?"

He shook his head. "I've got a few rock bands. And *Star Wars*."

She smiled. It was nice to realize that he was just a man, with likes and dislikes and a touch of whimsy in him.

"Oh!" he said suddenly. "I have one that I didn't realize would shrink so much. Didn't notice until I got here. It may work for you. I'll get it. Then, you should shower and dress, and we should get moving. And keep your distance, okay?"

She laughed. "Keep my distance?"

He nodded with a slight grin on his lips. "Yeah. You're too tempting. So I'm heading to my desk now."

"Too tempting?"

"You know what I mean."

"I think it's one of the best compliments I've ever received."

They bantered, but she knew he was serious. When he stood and went to his desk, she leaped up and headed for the bathroom. After she showered, she saw that he'd left the T-shirt in question on the bed. It made her smile, because it had a cartoon image of Chewbacca. He did love *Star Wars*.

She dressed quickly, and they left his office right away.

It wasn't easy, returning to the cemetery. But believing she could make a difference made it better. What was frightening was just how well she remembered every step that another woman had taken. She remembered her feelings. The excitement at first, growing into confusion—then the realization and pure terror.

Jon let her lead the way.

For a moment, Kylie closed her eyes. She remembered where she had been and where they had walked, behind the tiny church.

Annie had first begun to feel uneasy when she had seen his face. And then he'd pulled her along with such force, away from the street and far into the forgotten privacy of the old cemetery.

Kylie opened her eyes and looked at Jon. "Blood flew—how did he get rid of the blood on his clothing?"

"They installed water spigots here about thirty years ago, when people gained real interest into their pasts and ancestry and all that," Jon said thoughtfully. "That would allow him to wash his hands, at least. For his clothing, I don't know."

"This isn't nineteenth-century London," Kylie said.

"Pardon?"

"Jack the Ripper—he had to walk through the streets covered with blood. But dozens upon dozens of people worked in slaughterhouses. Of course, that makes me think that it wasn't any of the upper echelon who committed the murders, though I suppose a killer could get away in a carriage if the driver was an accomplice, but…"

She stopped speaking. It wasn't going to help, bringing up unsolved murders from well over a hundred years ago.

And yet something in his face had changed.

"What?" Kylie murmured.

"An accomplice," Jon said. "I had thought maybe he was working with partners. That's why we've been looking into regulars at the Cauldron. An accomplice might hope to gain from his success, someone with a very sick mind as well. But one way to get rid of everything would be to have someone waiting for him. Someone who knew what he was going to do and was ready to get him and his blood-spattered clothing far from the scene."

"I know that what we see isn't always what's really there," Kylie said, "but I just don't see Carl Fisher or Matt Hudson being a vicious killer. Or even an accomplice."

"I don't see it, either. That doesn't mean we can discount it."

He walked past her, moving quickly, covering a great deal of ground in a short time. Then he turned back, as if kicking himself, and walked to the outer wall of the church.

He hunkered down near a far corner of the wall, and Kylie hurried over to him. She saw he had found a water spigot. He was keeping his distance, not touching it. The ground around it was damp and trampled down.

"You see any blood?" she whispered.

"I don't see any. Which again, doesn't mean it doesn't exist. I'm going to call Ben and have him get his people back out here. I'm willing to bet that forensic experts will find blood. Annie's blood, washed off by her killer. But you never know. They just may find something else."

He rose and then frowned, walking just a step away to squat down again.

"Didn't crime scene investigators go over this place?" Kylie asked.

He nodded. "They might not have investigated this far. They might not have tested by the spigot since the main scene was elsewhere. They would have been in the church and around the church. I could be wrong. But..."

He reached down.

He'd found something.

It was a tiny object, smashed and covered in dirt. He didn't try to clean it; he put his other hand into a pocket of his jacket, producing an evidence bag.

"They cleared this area. Other people have been here since the murder. Still..."

"What is it? All I see is a lump of dirt."

He shook his head, looking up at her. "It's covered in dirt, yes. And it may mean nothing. But it could give us something."

"Jon, what is it?"

"A matchbox," he said. "From our favorite watering hole—the Cauldron."

CHAPTER FOURTEEN

On their way back from the cemetery, Jon first drove to Devin's cottage. Jackson had called to say he was coming to relieve Rocky and Devin at the hospital, but Jon was fond of Poe and figured the cottage was on the way to the hospital, so he and Kylie could stop and make sure his food and water bowls were filled. Kylie could also change out of his T-shirt and into her own clothing, if she wished.

He could see her frowning at the cabin as they drove along the dirt-and-gravel driveway. The whole place, nestled into the forest with its solitude and charm, was picture-perfect. So long as you were comfortable with a bit of isolation.

"I don't see this security system," she said.

He laughed. "If you saw it, the system wouldn't be that great."

"Ah. So, how do you plan to get in?"

He smiled at her. "Key."

"You all have keys to one another's houses?"

He shook his head. "No. In a real emergency, we'd know how to get in. But I have Devin's key right now because we're all working this crime."

He paused at the end of the driveway; there were fresh tire tracks along it.

"Stay here," he told Kylie.

"What is it?"

"Tracks," he said simply.

"If you're out of the car, I'm out of the car—and close," she told him.

He didn't really think any danger might befall her when she was just feet away, but he smiled. "Watch out for the tracks," he said.

"I'll stay over on the grass at the side. No problem."

The tracks didn't go all way to the house. In fact, they led just a few feet up the drive, as if someone didn't want to be seen from the house. He thought the tracks were from a car, rather than a truck or SUV. Whoever it was might have gotten out of the car and walked to the house. Perhaps they'd realized there was an alarm system.

It was possible a friend had heard that Devin was in town and just drove up to see if she was in. But why leave a car so far away from the front door?

"It could have been someone just turning around, right?" Kylie asked.

"Yes. But I'm going to give Ben a call anyway and get someone out here to take a cast of these tracks—just in case."

He walked up to the house and Kylie followed carefully in his footsteps. He used Devin's key, and once they were in the house, he tapped in the security code he'd been given, setting the alarm once again.

A loud screech sounded. "Blessed be, blessed be, and Holy Mary, too!"

It was the raven, of course, but at Jon's side, Kylie jumped a mile high.

"Poe, hey, yes, give it a rest," Jon called out. "We all know you're here!"

Even as he spoke, Devin's Auntie Mina slipped out of the kitchen, eager to greet him. "Jon! Thank goodness—this was beginning to feel like a ghost town."

He smiled. "Technically, Mina, when you're alone, it might be something like a ghost town—or ghost house at the very least."

Behind him, Kylie let out a breath.

The ghost drew closer, her face beaming. "Another! Miss Connelly! I was told you'd be coming. What a pleasure." She glanced at Jon, then back at Kylie. "You do see me quite clearly, don't you, dear?"

Kylie nodded.

Jon set an arm around her shoulders. "She's a little new to all this, Mina."

"Dear, dear, I didn't frighten you, did I?" Mina asked.

Kylie solemnly shook her head. "I've already been frightened. I just… Well, it's still new, seeing…"

Jon lowered his head, smiling. Kylie was trying not to use the word *dead*. She was surely certain that it would be painful or offensive.

"Oh yes, I'm dead," Mina said. "Which sometimes has its benefits. I always listen to what's going on. Jon, I don't know what went on last night. Someone was here. I tried to see who it was and what was going on, but I wasn't in the right place at the right time. And I believe they were here for no good reason, prowling around the house. To my deepest dismay, I realized too late they were even here. I don't know who it was…"

A worried expression worked its way into her face. "The alarm system is brilliant, but it's quite sad, you know—it wasn't needed in all the time I was living here. Ah, not that evil didn't exist, just not in the way it did when my sweet Devin came. I'm babbling! But you need to know, someone was prowling around the house last night."

"I believe you're right," Jon told her.

"Poe was having a fit," Mina said.

"He's a great watchbird," Jon commented.

Mina nodded and looked at Kylie. "You're doing okay?"

"I am," Kylie said. She was staring at Mina, still probably not quite believing they were having a full conversation with a dead woman.

"I wanted to check on the bird," Jon explained, "and let Kylie get a few of her things."

"Did you want to watch Westerly on the set?" Mina asked.

"What?" Kylie asked, frowning. She shook her head with an almost imperceptible movement. She'd probably just forgotten for a moment that Michael Westerly was in Boston for a campaign speech, which would be televised on local news channels. She looked at Jon. "I really don't want to watch."

"You don't have to," he told her. "I'll watch. Why don't you see if you want to change, gather a few things just in case we stay in town? You don't need to watch."

Kylie nodded and went into the bedroom.

Jon turned on the TV. The announcers were going through the usual discussions that preceded such a speech, talking about Westerly's possibilities and so on. A few of them compared him to some of the truly ethical, dignified men who had entered the political arena before.

No, politicians weren't always on the up-and-up. But Jon liked to think very few people who rose to political power were cold-blooded killers.

Westerly came to the podium, smiling as he raised his hands to his adoring fans. His speech was much the same as any other political monologue. He talked about how he would fight, always fight, for the Commonwealth of Massachusetts. There was truly nothing of interest in the material. The most interesting thing about the entire performance had to do with the people surrounding him.

And the closest to him was…his wife. Sandra was smiling. Applauding her husband's words to encourage the audience to do the same.

Yet, when the speech was over and both Sandra and Westerly turned to the crowd, something seemed off to Jon.

"Body language," Aunt Mina said.

He turned to look at her. He'd almost forgotten she was watching with him.

She nodded gravely. "Look at the way she took his hand. There's no warmth in the hold." She sniffed. "Reminds me of a few other things I've seen through the years. You forgive all kinds of things in a man—or a woman—if it fits your personal agenda. Doesn't mean that touching them doesn't rather make you want to gag."

Jon turned back to the screen. Mina was right—Sandra Westerly's smile was there. The movements were all just right. But something else was very, very wrong.

If the two of them didn't hate each other, they sure as hell weren't deeply in love. Could Westerly's wife be his accomplice?

Kylie didn't realize how distracted she was until they were several miles down the road, and Jon finally asked, "Kylie, what's wrong?"

She smiled and looked at him. "What's wrong? What's right at this moment?" She winced at how she sounded. "Oh, Jon, I'm sorry. I mean, you're all right—far more than all right. But my world, or what I knew as my world, has changed completely. We just said goodbye to a ghost. As if it was normal. We have conversations with the dead, as if they were flesh and blood standing before us and not…dead."

"It's a lot to get used to," he agreed softly.

"What scares me is that I am getting used to it. Will they start popping up all over?" she asked.

He hesitated before answering and then said, "Yes, and no. Some wish to be seen, some don't. And only some stay. It's sad sometimes. I have friends, co-agents, who never get to see the people they've lost, those with whom they'd love just a chance to whisper goodbye. But we believe they're happy when they've gone on. Spirits often stay because of something traumatic—but then again, there are others who stay because they want to guard a place or a family or even one special person."

"Obadiah," she said thoughtfully.

"He is a tiger against injustice," Jon said, casting a quick smile her way.

"And Mina watches over Devin," she said.

He nodded. "Obadiah was my first. He told me where to find a kidnapping victim. I was able to lead the police to her." He was quiet a minute and reached out with one hand to squeeze hers. "And whatever it is that has happened with you, we may well catch a killer."

"I hope so," she said passionately. "I truly hope so. I think... yes, I think I am getting used to this. At least I get to learn with you. I mean, when the whole thing began, my friends had to be afraid I was going to need serious therapy. Maybe I do need serious therapy!"

He shook his head and squeezed her hand again. "I think you're okay." He laughed suddenly, looking her way. "No, I think you're way better than okay. You're amazing."

"Thanks," she said. "So what now?"

"I already called Ben. He's going to send someone to take an impression of those tire tracks. It may mean nothing, but we'll have them if something does come up where we can make a comparison on a suspicious car. We'll head to the hospital. Jackson should be there by now."

"Jackson Crow—your director."

"Field director," he said. "We have a great founding father, you might say. Adam Harrison, a philanthropist. But he also has a strange knack for finding people who have what it takes to be in the Krewe—like me, Rocky, and now many more. His work and philanthropy allow him to be friends with many people in law enforcement and the government, which led him to create the Krewe. Jackson was his first choice to lead the fieldwork."

Jon paused as he changed lanes for their exit. "Jackson is a very interesting man. His wife was also one of the first Krewe members and she's pretty much our guru now. She chooses the right cases to take, assigns the right agents. Along with a growing roster of agents, we also have a whole floor of various techs now, too. We're a mini office on our own."

"In Washington."

"Technically, Virginia."

"I see. I think. There's a major unit of agents…who speak with the dead."

"Right. Agents, first. Everyone goes through the Bureau."

"But Devin is still writing children's books."

"Yes. She comes on as a consultant when geography or some other factor influences the situation."

"As in, she knows Salem very well. And happens to own a cottage in the woods. A haunted cottage in the woods."

"That's about it."

They arrived back at the hospital. When they reached Jimmy's room, Marla and the boys weren't there. They were fine, Rocky assured them, meeting Jon and Kylie at the door. They were down in the cafeteria, taking some quiet time.

Jackson Crow had arrived. He was a tall man with black hair and light eyes, a striking combination of both Native American and Anglo features. He greeted Kylie almost as if he knew her, and then she realized that he probably did—he would have been briefed on everything that had happened.

"A pleasure to meet you," he told her sincerely, his hand-shake firm. "And you're doing all right?"

He was good; she knew he looked slightly over her head at Jon, but somehow, he also kept his focus on her.

She was surprised she meant it when she said, "I am doing very well."

"She's more than well," Jimmy said from his hospital bed. "She's amazing! She found Marla when my poor girl was scared right to pieces."

Jackson grinned, turning to speak to the man. "Mr. Marino, you seem to be doing darned well yourself."

"They need to let me out of here," Jimmy said.

"The doctors want one more night," Jackson told them "And Detective Miller has been very helpful. We have two men heading in from the Boston office to watch over the family for the next few days along with the cops, so every-thing is moving along."

"Ah, excellent," Jon said. "We can discuss the case to-gether."

Jackson nodded. "When the men from Boston arrive, we'll head out."

"Back to Devin's," Jon said, glancing over at Devin. "Poe is fine, by the way."

Kylie noted that he didn't mention the tire tracks. Maybe he'd called Rocky or Jackson while watching Westerly's speech.

She hadn't wanted to see the politician, speaking or not speaking. It would simply make her furious. She had seen him kill Annie. She had *felt* him kill Annie.

That almost felt like a normal thing now, after chatting with Auntie Mina and Obadiah Jones.

Marla, Anthony, and Frank returned to the room. Marla hugged Kylie as if they'd been best friends forever and Kylie naturally returned the hug. There was a bit of chaos in the room—and far too many people in it for a sick man—so Jackson excused himself, stepping out.

Moments later, he poked his head back in to say that the agents from Boston had arrived—the rest of them needed to clear out before the hospital threw them out. And the group said their goodbyes to Marla, Frank, Anthony, and Jimmy.

Jimmy caught Jon's hand. "Thank you," he said quietly. "For my life and…for believing us. Many people might have thought I was just paranoid. Or making up dangerous gossip. They'd have never investigated what was going on. Most people would have accepted that an old dude had a heart attack. You've believed in me. And you've protected Marla and my boys. Thank you."

"We'll make it safe for you," Jon promised him. He looked at Kylie. "We'll find a way to bring an end to this."

Marla hugged Kylie again, and once again, Kylie hugged her back.

She briefly met the two agents in the hallway, solid, serious men who were also polite and quick to smile. They had made friends with the police officer on duty; it appeared that all would go well at the hospital.

Out on the street, Jackson, Rocky, Devin, and Jon decided that they'd go first to Jon's office on Essex Street; his work and notes were there.

Jackson got in the car with Jon and Kylie and got straight to business on the drive, asking Kylie questions about the past few days. He was curious about the regression, listening intently as Kylie told her story again, from the time she had arrived in Salem for Corrine's bachelor party up to the present with a little help here and there from Jon.

"I want to meet this Dr. Sayers," Jackson said.

"We could go tomorrow morning," Jon suggested.

"Maybe tonight?" Jackson said.

"Maybe. He and others you might want to meet usually hang out at the Cauldron."

"And none of us have had dinner. Perfect combo—food and people to assess," Jackson said approvingly. He glanced at his watch. "And I imagine that Michael Westerly is back in the area by now."

"He's back here already? His speech was just this afternoon—" Kylie said.

"We have sources," Jackson said. "He didn't stay in Boston. He headed straight back."

"Wonderful," Kylie muttered.

"In truth," Jackson told her, "we need him here. We need him to give himself away."

"How is he going to do that?" Kylie asked. "I sincerely doubt he's the kind of man who is suddenly going to be overcome with guilt."

"No. He'll slip up, though," Jackson said confidently.

Jon drove into the municipal garage near his office, and in a matter of minutes, they met up with Rocky and Devin at his front door. When they were inside, Jackson went through the crime scene photos on Jon's desk, glancing over notes he had taken, and Jon informed them about the second matchbox that was discovered.

Jackson shook his head. "Damn, the crime scenes make it look like one killer. Westerly was one damned good copycat." He looked up at them all. "Or he has a partner. Or we're still looking for another killer who has nothing to do with Westerly."

"You don't question that Westerly killed Annie Hampton?" Kylie asked.

Jackson studied her, smiled slightly, and shook his head. "No. Jon believed in what you saw from the start. So do we all. Not to mention that Jimmy Marino was heading into the police to tell them what he'd seen when he—a man recently checked out by a cardiologist—mysteriously had a heart attack and crashed into a building."

Kylie nodded slowly; they appeared to be a truly tight-knit group. Jackson Crow might be the field director for the group, but he apparently trusted his agents.

"Thank you," she said. "I still have moments when I feel the way Jimmy does. There are far too many people who might believe, and with some reason, that I'm just losing my mind or seeking attention."

"You're not crazy," Jackson assured her. "You're different. The good thing is, there's a percentage of the population—small, maybe—who are different as well. I must admit, you've brought *different* to a new level, though. A fascinating and incredibly useful level." He stood up straight and clapped his hands together. "And for now, I haven't eaten in a very long time. Dinner sounds like a fine plan. Is this place close?"

"Just down at the end of Essex, across from the Clue house," Devin murmured.

"The Clue house—I think I heard something about that," Jackson said. "Let's get going and you Salemites can fill me in."

They headed out, with Devin pointing out the grand old mansion with its redbrick facade and handsome white portico that was now part of the Peabody Essex Museum. "There was a horrible murder here," she explained. "You'll hear about it on any tour."

"The Parker Brothers had their business here," Kylie put in. "The house might well figure into their game."

"Yes, in 1830, Captain White, an old seafarer who owned the place, was bludgeoned to death one night. It was a very complicated investigation," Devin said. "There were family members who might inherit his riches, and then there was the theory that a stranger had broken in. Massachusetts had many abolitionists at the time, and White had been involved in the slave trade. Could it have been such an enemy?" Devin smiled as she spoke dramatically.

"White had no children of his own," Kylie went on, "but he had a niece, and also a more distant relative working for him."

"In the end," Devin continued, "it was an imprisoned convict who came forward with information. It was murder for hire."

"Then one of the alleged killers committed suicide," Rocky put in.

"Daniel Webster gave an amazing oratory as the prosecutor," Jon said, "and many people believe that several famous writers took inspiration from him—authors such as Nathaniel Hawthorne and Edgar Alan Poe, among others. Also, the name White remained in the American version of the game, along with something like a cudgel."

"So, tell me justice was found," Jackson said.

"Well, it did all tie together," Rocky said. "Captain White's niece Mary had a daughter named Mary as well. Against the captain's wishes, she married one Joseph Knapp. Knapp's brother suggested to some men in a bar that Joseph would gladly part with a thousand dollars to see the old man gone.

"The killers were the Crowninshield brothers," he went on. "Richard Crowninshield was indicted for the murder and his brother and two others were brought in for abetting the crime. Eventually, it came out that Joseph and his brother and the two Crowninshield brothers had met and planned the crime. Richard tried to save the others by committing suicide—unless he was found guilty of a crime, as the law read, his brother couldn't be prosecuted for abetting."

"Eventually, though," Jon added, "the Knapp brothers were both hanged. The remaining Crowninshield was released. He had witnesses swear he was with them on the night of the murder, a few 'ladies of the evening,' and the authorities couldn't connect him to the murder weapon or to anything other than having participated in a few conversations.

"Interesting, though. Daniel Webster usually fought hard for defendants, but he was also a drinker, in debt, and when he died due to an accident, they discovered he might not have had long anyway. The very brilliant orator was suffering from cirrhosis of the liver."

Jon paused and frowned. He looked around at the others. "Sorry, I was just thinking. White was rich, so members of his family were immediately suspect. Knapp was married to White's great niece, and bitter that she'd been disinherited, but he was still easily familiar enough with the house to create the murder weapon and unscrew the window screens for the killer. It relates to what we're dealing with now."

They were all silent, waiting.

"Um, Annie Hampton wasn't rich," Rocky reminded him.

Jon shook his head. "I'm talking about family motives. I may be way off on this, but I watched Sandra Westerly today at her husband's side during his speech. I can't help but believe she hates the man but likes what he offers far too much to distance herself from him. She wants to be a Washington wife. She wants the society and the prestige."

"You think she killed Annie?" Rocky asked skeptically.

"No, but I do think she might well have been Westerly's accomplice when he killed her."

They were now across from the Clue house and right by the Cauldron.

"Maybe she's a loose link," Jackson said quietly. He looked away from the house and across to the restaurant. "It will bear investigation."

Jon nodded. Kylie could tell he was already thinking about ways to trip up Sandra Westerly. Could she be involved?

As they headed into the Cauldron, Jackson asked Jon, "There's still a cop watching out for Matt Hudson, correct?"

"Oh, yeah. He claims absolute terror."

"And what do you think?"

"I think he's telling the truth or he's such a good liar that my radar is off entirely."

Inside the restaurant, a hostess caught them at the entry; it wasn't busy yet and they asked for a table for five. As she was showing them to their seats, Jon excused himself and Jackson, saying he wanted to see how Matt was doing and introduce him to Jackson.

As they sat, Devin whispered, "I don't believe it."

"What?" Kylie asked her.

"Speak of the devil," Devin said.

"It is Salem," Rocky murmured dryly.

"Sandra's here. Westerly just gave his speech with her at his side—and she's here!" Devin said.

"Where? We're in her usual spot," Kylie said.

"The four-top near the bar. She's with a young couple," Devin said. "Don't look now."

But Kylie was already staring. And Sandra looked right at her. The look she gave Kylie cast daggers of hatred across the room.

"She does not like you," Devin whispered.

"No," Kylie agreed.

She looked away from Sandra and over at the bar, where Jon and Jackson were speaking with Matt. They'd be back any minute, she was sure.

Rocky reached across and took Kylie's hand. "Are you afraid of her?"

Kylie grinned. "No. I'm not great at self-defense, but I think I could take her."

He leaned back. "You'd be surprised," he said. "The least dangerous-looking, smallest, skinniest person in the world can prove to be deadly. Keep your distance from her."

"She came at you in the ladies' room before, right?" Devin asked her.

Kylie hadn't told anyone else about the encounter, but she realized that Jon must have. This team was constantly communicating.

"Well, she said some nasty things," Kylie told them.

"But she didn't touch you." Devin confirmed.

"No…"

"I think we should see if she follows you in there again. You should go powder your nose, as the saying goes," Rocky said.

"And don't worry," Devin added quickly. "I'll be right behind her if she does follow you in."

Kylie looked at the two of them and then stood. She wasn't going to think about it. She was going to do it.

She walked to the ladies' room.

Once inside, she combed her hair, keeping an eye on the door through the mirror above one of the cauldron-like sinks.

Sure enough, within a minute, Sandra Westerly entered. Once again, she kept her distance but caught Kylie's eyes through the mirror.

Kylie turned to look at her.

"Now you've really entered dangerous territory," Sandra hissed. "Threatening my husband."

Kylie frowned. "I don't know what you're talking about."

"That message you sent him—telling him that you saw him. That you *saw* him!"

"Saw him doing what?"

"Oh, you bitch," Sandra Westerly said.

"I don't know what you're talking about."

"Kylie Connelly. You sent him a message."

"I did no such thing."

"Liar!"

"I'm telling you—"

"My husband is not without friends. You're going to jail!"

Sandra looked as if she might come forward. For a second, Kylie's heart thundered. She wasn't sure, but she thought Sandra whispered, "Or worse."

The door opened, and Devin stepped in. She smiled benignly at Sandra, saying to Kylie, "Hey! There you are. We've ordered drinks and appetizers. They're on the way."

"All set," Kylie said. She looked at Sandra. "Excuse me," she said, and hurried past her.

CHAPTER FIFTEEN

Matt was clearly glad to meet Jackson. He shook his hand energetically but kept his voice low—the bar was busy.

"Great. The more people who can protect me since I look like a snitch, the better." He leaned on the bar, smiling, as if discussing the bar's specialties. "Of course, I'm glad it didn't get around that I might be a heinous murderer, but with what's happened…"

"You mean beyond Annie's murder?" Jon asked.

Matt nodded gravely. "Poor Jimmy being in that automobile accident."

"I'm curious. Has anyone said anything to you?" Jackson inquired.

"Not really. I told my buddy Carl about what happened, and he agreed that I need protection." Matt sighed. "I miss Jimmy and Marla. They're class acts. Twenty percenters. Never stiff anyone. Not like Westerly's wife over there. Fake smiles and pathetic tips."

"Sandra stiffs the waitstaff?" Jon asked.

"Sandra Westerly almost never pays her own bill. I can't say that they *stiff* us. Her rich friends are more like ten percent—

a standard fifteen when we're really lucky. I guess that's why they have so much money. They don't part with more than they have to."

Being on the cheap side didn't make a person evil. But the woman obviously had an agenda of her own. And that agenda surpassed whatever morals or conscience she might have.

Or maybe she was simply evil. As evil as a man who would kill a woman rather than admit an affair—especially when an election was coming up.

Matt shook his head. "Carl says he's getting nervous. Every time he walks into the bar now, he's looking for customers and afraid of what he might find."

"What could he find?" Jackson asked.

"Someone who takes his tour, stays after for a photo op, and puts a knife in his side," Matt said with a shrug.

"I don't think Carl has much to worry about," Jackson told him. "Annie was a woman alone in a cemetery."

"Jimmy Marino is a big man. No knife in the side, but maybe something else. A friendly drink with something in it." Matt let out a sigh. "Jimmy was in here right before that accident. I know I did nothing, and I swear it, and I know you know that. But it's hard to think someone in here would do anything like that. I shouldn't be saying anything bad about Mrs. Westerly, just because she smiles drippy smiles and still manages to act like a queen on high. I don't like her. Doesn't mean I should be saying bad things."

Matt appeared to shiver. "That's what went on here in 1692, you know. People on the outskirts got accused first and that got the ball rolling. We should be more careful here than anywhere, one would think."

"Good thinking, Matt," Jackson said.

"And I think we should be getting back to the table," Jon said.

"Yes, I guess," Jackson said. He smiled and reached out to shake Matt's hand again. "Good to talk to you, Mr. Hudson."

"I'm a bartender—you have to call me Matt."

"Will do," Jackson promised.

Jon looked across the room to the table. He saw Kylie come out of the ladies' room. Her features were tight. Devin was right behind her.

"She's fine," Jackson assured him when he noticed Jon staring. "Devin knows when to scream bloody murder. And she's armed. I seriously doubt that the wife of a Senate hopeful would attempt anything in a public restroom in a busy restaurant."

"I don't think you ever know for sure," Jon said, watching the women take their seats.

Kylie looked up as Jon and Jackson rejoined them at the table. While they appeared casual as they took their seats, Jon quickly leaned in.

"What was it this time?" he asked tensely.

Sandra had yet to make an appearance back at her table, but that didn't matter; she would surely expect that Kylie would tell friends what she had said.

Kylie repeated the woman's words. She didn't mention Sandra's final threat—*or worse*. Kylie might have imagined it.

"She thinks I threatened her husband with a message," she said instead. "She knows my name, which isn't much of a shock. She seemed to know I believe her husband is a murderer. She didn't say what kind of a message. She didn't say if it was a letter, a text, or what. She just said I'd sent a message claiming that I saw him. I pled innocence—saw him *what*?"

"I should ask her," Jon said. He stood, walked over to the bar, and leaned against a wall, waiting for Sandra to leave the ladies' room.

"He's just going to ask her?" Kylie said.

"That's one way to get an answer," Jackson said.

Sandra exited the restroom. From the look on her face, she

knew exactly who Jon was, and she didn't appear pleased to see him. But she didn't try to walk by him—she stopped and answered his questions. She crossed her arms over her chest as she spoke. Her features were tense.

Jon seemed to be at ease, speaking naturally, betraying no emotion. He even smiled at the end, and while Kylie couldn't hear him, she was pretty sure he apologized for interrupting Sandra's dinner and indicated that she should rejoin her friends.

"Mr. and Mrs. Gerrit Northumberland," Rocky said, looking up from his phone as Jon rejoined them at the table. "I sent a pic to Angela—she got back to me already. Mrs. Westerly is dining with a lingerie heiress and her iron baron husband. Large contributors to any race in the state, I would imagine."

"She'll complain to the police that you harassed her in the middle of an important dinner," Kylie said.

"No, she said I could meet her at their suite in the morning and see the phone message for myself. Signed by Kylie Connelly," Jon said.

"I sent no such message," Kylie protested. "When was it supposedly sent?" She pulled out her phone, wondering if someone had sneaked it away from her to send a threat to Michael Westerly. As far as she could tell, no one had.

"In the middle of his speech today. You were packing—I was watching him on TV," Jon said.

It wasn't an accusation, but she nevertheless repeated herself furiously. "I didn't send any message! I just checked. Come to think of it, I wouldn't know a number to reach Michael Westerly."

"We know you didn't," Jon said. "But it's going to be interesting to see where that message came from."

"Burner phone. Untraceable," Jackson speculated.

"But it does mean someone is trying to cause trouble. And

knows that Kylie is somehow involved. Which brings us back here," Jon said.

"Matt?" Kylie asked.

"Not necessarily. At this moment, there are a dozen possibilities," Jon said.

"And there could be two murderers. We know one and not the other. One is possibly not even in Salem, and the other we can't touch. And they appear to know everything we know." Devin sounded exasperated.

"Yes, it looks bad, but we will discover the truth," Rocky assured Kylie. "First there's the possibility Mrs. Westerly is making it up to turn the tables on you. And us."

Jon added, "Then, of course, there are other people who have consistently been around this bar. And remember, Kylie, we did find another matchbox at the cemetery. It's been sent in for testing, and it may or may not give us anything." He looked over at Jackson. "This is getting worse if Westerly is gunning for Kylie."

"Ah," Jackson said. "But he knows that she's surrounded by law enforcement. He knows Jimmy survived the accident and that Marla is just fine, too. He must know he'd have to kill a half dozen people to allay suspicions against him."

"Suspicion—that's still all we've got," Rocky muttered.

"Carl Fisher, the guide, knows everything, according to the notes you've accumulated so far. And his movements oddly match those of the sites where the other victims were found," Jackson said. "I talked to Angela, and she verified that he acted in the same shows as Matt, traveling to all the same cities where the victims were killed."

"We need to see Westerly's phone. The one that received the threat," Jackson said.

"I'm going to drop in on the Westerlys first thing tomorrow morning. I think Sandra actually wants to prove the message is real," Jon said.

"And just what does she believe about her husband?" Rocky asked. "Or is she just as guilty of heinous crime as he is?"

Jon was quiet a moment. "I think she's acting it all out. Maybe she sent the threat herself, trying to prove that her husband is the victim of a smear campaign. But while I don't believe another thing about her, I think Westerly did receive a threat from someone claiming to be Kylie. That puts us back to someone else being involved."

As he spoke, his gaze turned toward the front door.

Carl Fisher, tonight in a tailored shirt, vest, and hat, but no pretense at any particular historical era, walked cheerfully into the restaurant. He took the time to say a few words at the tables he passed and walked right up to the bar. Matt had seen him coming and already poured him a soda. Carl sat on one of the bar stools, leaning close to talk to Matt, and then glanced down the bar at the man Kylie assumed to be Matt's plainclothes policeman.

Then Matt indicated their group sitting at the table and Carl turned to look at them all. He waved cheerfully, his head angling to the side as he saw the newcomer—Jackson.

"I'll take you to meet him," Jon said, and once again, the two left the table.

"Hey, you guys are hanging around here as much as I am," said a voice by Kylie's shoulder.

Startled from watching Jon and Jackson head to the bar, Kylie turned to see Dr. Sayers at her side of the table. He was accompanied by an older man, slim with cheerful dark eyes and a deeply lined face.

"The food is good, and you can't beat the convenience," she said. "Dr. Sayers, you know Devin and Rocky."

"I do," Dr. Sayers said, shaking their hands. "And I'd like you meet Mr. Brendan Pitman—his family goes way back. All families go way back, of course, but he had an ancestor on the *Mayflower*."

"Wonderful," Kylie said.

"Did you go for a regression, Mr. Pitman?" Devin asked politely.

"I did!" he said with enthusiasm. "I was in medieval England. I could smell, touch, and feel the grass, and I was a young man again, in love. I was on a hill, waiting for my lady to slip away and join me. It was an absolutely unique experience in a long, long life, I do assure you!"

Jon and Jackson had returned in time to hear Brendan's last words. Introductions went around again.

Jackson turned to Dr. Sayers. "What you do, it's absolutely fascinating. I would love to find out if I've lived a previous life."

"I make no guarantees," Dr. Sayers said. "Most people find a place in time and space where there was something beautiful in life. Maybe that's the human spirit. But things can occasionally go…strangely. As they went with Kylie." He paused a minute, studying Jackson. "I imagine you've heard all about it."

Jackson just shrugged and said, "I'm willing to take my chances."

"Come in tomorrow. I'll squeeze you in during the morning. I'm not sure about my schedule, but I know you're a busy man. If you can make it, I promise you we'll have a go at it."

"Wonderful," Jackson said.

"Well, looks like your food is coming. We'll leave you to it," Dr. Sayers said. He grimaced. "I'm going to step outside for a minute for a smoke. Wish I had a cigar. A bummed cigarette will have to do."

"Did you eat already? I didn't see you in here," Kylie said.

"Oh, we were at that corner table. It's pretty dark over there. There's a reason they call this place the Cauldron. They like their spooky shadows!"

They said their goodbyes.

"You're really going to go through a regression?" Kylie asked Jackson.

"I'm curious," he said.

"Don't drink the tea," Kylie said. "Or maybe you should drink the tea. My friends did, and they had great experiences."

"I'm curious about the man," Jackson said. "He may create most of his 'regressions' through the art of suggestion, just leading people where they want to go. But what happened with you... That's new, even in my experience." He lowered his voice. "This happened, and then you saw Jon's friend, Obadiah Jones. It's as though your experience with Dr. Sayers opened a door for you. I don't know if I can learn anything new or not, but it will be very interesting to see just what this man does."

"Any hypnotism is scary to me," Kylie said. "I wouldn't have gone if I didn't go with all my friends."

"Not to worry," Jackson said. "I won't be going alone."

"I went back to him, you know," Kylie said, and then added, "Of course you know. The experience was still strange. Horrible, but better, I suppose? By that, I mean being murdered as Annie was still horrible, but going through it again... There was purpose. And maybe because the first time seemed to take place as it happened, and the second time was a memory, it was less intense."

She hesitated, not sure she should be saying what she intended to propose next, but she was also certain that she was right. While the second matchbox brought them back to the Cauldron, it wasn't definitive that any of it tied to Michael Westerly. In fact, of all those who frequented the place, Westerly was there the least of those they were coming to know.

"We need to use me," she said.

They all stared at her.

"As bait," she said.

Jon shook his head. "He's targeted you—obviously. Maybe

he sent the message to himself. One way or another, you're in the sights of both Michael and Sandra Westerly."

"And the five of you can spend the rest of your lives protecting me?" she asked. "You need to at least consider what I'm saying. You are all law enforcement officers, and you can surely come up with a foolproof plan."

"A foolproof plan doesn't exist. Ever," Jon said.

"Okay, ninety-nine percent foolproof?" she said softly. "Something has to break. The only way may be for us to force his hand."

"We'll get him," Jon said.

"We do have faith in you," Jackson told her.

"Then have faith in yourselves! You still have nothing except envisioned evidence from a hypnotized woman and the suspicions of two locals. That won't get you anywhere," she said. "Don't discount me, please. I know you always intend to get your man or woman. But we all know that we can't go on for weeks or months like this. The election will come up. He could win, if people aren't shown the truth about him. Please, at least think about it. I'm willing to be bait. I have infinite faith in you."

They were all silent, staring at her.

"Please."

"All right. We'll all work on it," Jackson said softly.

Jon stood impatiently and went to pay the check. At the table, there was silence. Jon returned and they headed out.

The decision had been made that they would all stay at Devin's cottage. Jackson rode with Jon and Kylie, and the silence that had begun in the restaurant seemed to permeate the car. Kylie was sure they were all thinking it probably wasn't protocol to allow civilians to risk themselves. But they weren't ordinary agents and she was a different type of civilian.

Auntie Mina was in the cabin when they arrived. She already knew Jackson and was happy to welcome him, and then she told Jon that crime scene technicians had been by. They had cast the tire tracks he had found earlier.

"Ben is a good man. He follows through every time," Jon said, pleased.

"What good will they do?" Kylie asked. "I mean, don't you have to compare them to other car tracks?"

"Technically, yes. But they will possibly give us the make and model of a car," Jon told her.

"Go to bed, people. I'm taking the sofa, and it's been a long day," Jackson said.

"I'll get you sheets," Devin said. "You know, there are other, perfectly good bedrooms."

"And you know that if Angela isn't with me, I'm a sofa man."

Poe let out a loud screech, as if agreeing. It was time to go to bed.

Kylie headed to the bedroom she'd been assigned. She wondered if Jon would come to her room; would it be awkward around the others?

She wondered if Jon knew that Jackson preferred the parlor sofa when he was overnight on a case when his wife wasn't with him.

Had Devin known that, leaving two rooms for her and Jon?

Or did these people—who could talk to ghosts—know what was going on in one another's lives as well? She showered, slid into a cotton nightdress, and wondered to herself just how she might be used to draw out Michael Westerly. He was back in Salem with his wife. He could have stayed in Boston. He could have moved on, headed to another city on his campaign trail.

He had not; he had come back here.

Why?

Because Krewe members were still here, searching for the murderer. Was he afraid of what they might find?

She didn't know.

Lying on the bed, she realized Jon wasn't coming to her. She stared at the ceiling. She thought about how she had instigated the intimacy of the night before, and doubts ran through her system. But she couldn't believe that there wasn't something between them deeper than just naturally falling in together at an opportune moment.

They'd been alone. Now they weren't.

But they were alone on the same side of the house.

She shouldn't get up, she thought. She really shouldn't.

When she walked the few feet of hallway from her room to the next, she saw that his door was ajar. She tentatively set her hand on it and pushed lightly.

He was lying in bed, a folder at his side, dozens of papers in his hands. He'd clearly heard her the second she pressed at the door. He'd showered, too, she thought. She could smell the fresh scent of soap that hung lightly in the room. It had been a very long day. Maybe they'd all needed to wash it off. He'd donned a pair of sweatpants, but his broad, muscled chest was bare.

He sheathed the papers in the folder and leaped up. "Kylie! Did something happen—are you all right?"

She opted for honesty. "Nothing is wrong. I just wanted to be with you. I don't mean to… I mean, if where we are means something, if…"

He walked over to her, pulled her tightly into his arms, and kissed her lips.

Damn, he had a good kiss. When his mouth touched her, when their lips parted, it seemed as if the whole of her was awakened in an instant. Searing warmth cascaded through her being.

When his mouth lifted, just inches above hers, and his eyes met hers, he smiled. "I was being circumspect on your behalf."

"Pardon?"

"I didn't want you to be uncomfortable."

She smiled. "I was only uncomfortable alone."

"Well, then." He closed and locked the door, swept her up, and moved toward the bed.

Sweatpants were easily discarded. So was her simple cotton nightdress. They fell together in a heated, liquid kiss, rolling, touching one another, stroking. Then she found herself prone and quickly discovered that his kiss had an even greater fire as he pressed his lips to her flesh, moving along her body, invoking a hunger and desire in her unlike anything she had ever known.

Then they were together again, moving like wildfire, and the world became a frantic but beautiful place, an astral feeling of wonder, of touching stars, all because of the very physical reality of the room and sheets and bed and the night and the man. Climax was a gift from above.

She lay beside him, and despite the wonder of their chemistry, she tried very hard to be rational. They'd been thrown together. He had helped her when she'd all but fallen apart.

Logic meant nothing. He was unique. In that moment, she couldn't conceive the time when they would part.

She realized that he was looking at her.

"I can't imagine being far from you now," he whispered.

"Let's not imagine," she said softly, curling against him, holding tight.

Early the next morning, Jon sat with Jackson at the island table in the center of the kitchen. They'd come up with something of a plan.

"Here's a point," Jackson said. "Kylie might be in danger forever if this isn't finished. Michael Westerly is a monster. Angela scoured back ten years to other, similar unsolved cases. A young woman had her throat slit in a cemetery near St. Louis, and Angela managed to dig up the fact that Westerly has a cousin there—and was visiting at the time. He was also in Broussard, Louisiana, when a woman was killed there in a like manner. That was six years ago. So we have visuals that prove he couldn't have committed the murders that we've grouped together now in what the FBI has accepted as serial killings, but that doesn't mean he hasn't killed before."

"He's a monster, we've all agreed on that," Jon said. "And if he is responsible for any of these other killings, he's controlled, he's careful. He can put time between his attacks, develop relationships, when he chooses. And he doesn't worry. He appears to be above reproach. He can bide his time. And that's what scares me. Kylie has a point. If he gets away with this, she could turn a corner three years from now, and he'd be there."

"Right. But he also knows that we're hanging around here, searching for a killer. And he knows that we have guards on Jimmy and Marla and his sons, and that Kylie is with us."

Jon nodded. "Okay, if we're going through with this, we need to throw him off. And the way I see it, there's only one way to make him think that it would be possible to find Kylie alone."

"And that would be?"

"To arrest someone else for the crime."

Jackson sat back, staring at him. "We have no solid evidence against Westerly. Or anyone else."

"I know," Jon said quietly. "We'd need to convince someone that they were doing an incredible service to the community—to the country—by agreeing to a sham."

"Ah. Allowing themselves to be arrested as a heinous and detestable murderer? Jon, where are we going to find someone to fit that bill?"

"No one like an actor," Jon said.

"And that actor would be… Matt?"

"He is an actor, as you know. That's why he travels so much—and why he showed up on our radar in the first place."

"But we still don't know that he didn't commit the other murders," Jackson said. "We'd have to be really careful. Double jeopardy could be a factor—"

Jon shook his head. "Not if we say that he's only being held for the murder of Annie Hampton. We know he didn't commit that one. And my instincts could be off, but I don't think he committed any murder ever, anywhere. But don't go by that... He'll stay on our radar."

"And you're going to talk to him and find out if he'd be willing to accept this?"

"Yes. There's a lot to promise him. When we catch Westerly, Matt will get tremendous publicity for helping in an incredibly important sting. He's an actor who bartends—he'll thrive on the publicity. He could get on a dozen talk shows. I think I can do it."

"And as for Kylie?"

Jon let out another breath. "Well, it's still frightening as hell—and there is no foolproof plan. But logistically, we would have every advantage. So long as we pull off Matt's arrest convincingly. Kylie will slip at the Cauldron that she plans on visiting an out-of-the-way cemetery near here. And we'll have that cemetery so laced with agents and cops that we can take him down before any harm is done to her."

"What if he doesn't offer her any harm?"

"We could fail. But I think we have to try."

"Try what?" Devin came into the kitchen. Poe let out a squawk.

"Let's wait for Rocky and Kylie and then go through this," Jon said. "Then I'll go see Ben and lay it all out for him."

"Rocky's awake. I'll get him moving," Devin said.

Kylie came into the kitchen, smiling and saying, "I smell coffee! Great." She paused, looking from Jon to Jackson.

"We have a plan," Jon told her.

"Oh?"

"We're just waiting on Rocky."

"Rocky is here," he announced, appearing in the kitchen as well.

They were all assembled, and Jon outlined his plan.

"You really think that Matt will agree to this?" Rocky asked.

"I do. I'm going to dangle an incredible carrot—national celebrity," Jon said.

"Bad publicity?" Rocky said doubtfully.

"Yes, at first. But so noble once it all comes out."

"He'll do it," Kylie said. "I really think that Matt's a good guy. Even if there are risks involved, I believe he'll do it."

"I have to see Ben, and then talk to Matt," Jon said, finishing his coffee.

"I think that Rocky, Devin, Kylie, and I will head off to see Dr. Sayers," Jackson said cheerfully.

"I have to say, I don't believe in regression. That's me. But hypnotism is possible," Rocky said, "and though they claim no hypnotist can make anyone do what they wouldn't do, the concept of that lack of control isn't a good one."

"That's why we're going together," Jackson said. "So, let's move!"

Kylie went back to her room for her purse. Jon followed her and pulled her into his arms.

"You're okay with this?"

"Yes, definitely, yes. You're okay with it?"

"No, but I don't see anything ending here anytime soon. All we need is Matt on board with the plan."

"I know he'll agree."

"Yeah. I'm on my way out to talk to him now. Until we have this down…stay with Jackson, okay? Jackson, Rocky, and Devin. Always, one of them, like glue."

"I promise," she told him.

He kissed her lips and then hurried out. He wanted to see Sandra Westerly about the threatening text message, and then a visit to Ben, and then Matt.

He had to hope that everything would come together.

CHAPTER SIXTEEN

The friendly receptionist greeted them cheerfully when Kylie entered Dr. Sayers's office with Jackson, Rocky, and Devin.

"The doctor told me that I should be expecting you," she said. "And your timing is perfect. He's just finishing up a session. He'll be right with you."

Kylie introduced the others to the receptionist, who introduced herself as Cathy.

"Who is doing the regression?" Cathy asked.

"I am," Jackson said.

"Wonderful!" she said. "While you're waiting…coffee? Water? Tea?"

"Oh, we're fine, we just had a big breakfast," Devin said. "I can't wait to see this… I'm tempted to try, but I want to see Jackson go through it first."

"I'm a skeptic," Rocky said.

"You won't be when you leave," Cathy assured them. "Just have a seat, and you'll be in there in just a few."

They sat. Kylie's stomach tightened and she hoped no one heard it growl. Devin had lied. They hadn't eaten—they'd filled up with coffee, determining to move quickly. They'd find someplace for a meal as soon as they finished Jackson's "regression."

They certainly weren't going to have anything here.

In a minute, Dr. Sayers came out to the reception area, dressed in a handsome leisure suit. He smoothed back his unruly blond hair as he escorted his last client out.

"Thank you, thank you, it was wonderful," the young woman was saying. "I knew that my family hailed from London, but being there in the 1800s... Oh, it was amazing. I'm sure that I'm one of my ancestors, living again! And to think—we do get more than one chance at this craziness we call life. I can't thank you enough!"

"I'm delighted that it was a wonderful experience for you," Dr. Sayers said.

"Oh, people are waiting," the woman said, noting the foursome in the office. "It's amazing," she assured them.

Dr. Sayers looked at Kylie and grimaced behind the woman's back. Kylie just smiled and said, "Thanks!" To the woman, who seemed to float as she walked out of the office.

"So, Mr. Crow—but it really is Special Agent Crow, isn't it?" Dr. Sayers corrected himself. "After Jimmy's accident and Matt helping the police and all the questioning, you do know that everyone in town—other than tourists—knows who you all are."

"We are aware," Jackson assured him.

"Well, come in, come in. You're my first FBI agent," Dr. Sayers said happily.

"We're all coming, like when I did it with Corrine, Nancy, and Jenny, all right?" Kylie asked.

"Absolutely. There are no hidden lights or puppet strings," Dr. Sayers assured them. "Come in, come in."

He offered all of them his tea. "Chamomile, that's all," he assured them.

"We're really fine," Rocky said. "Big breakfast."

That lie again. Kylie hoped her stomach would be quiet.

"So, Jackson, where are you most comfortable? People usually take the sofa and rest their heads on the pillow there. But you're welcome to a chair, or, if it makes you happy, you're even welcome to stand. Now, I begin the regression by counting backward, so choose your seat, and we'll begin."

"Well, if the sofa tends to be the place, I'll take the sofa," Jackson said. He arranged himself comfortably. He didn't appear overly excited, but intrigued and ready for whatever the experience might be.

The others selected chairs nearby. Kylie noted that just as Jon had chosen to be very close to her head, Rocky did the same with Jackson. Ready to support his boss if needed.

"I'll start at one hundred and go backward, slowly," Dr. Sayers said. "You just need to listen to the sound of my voice as you count with me, and then it will seem distant, but my voice will be there, guiding you."

They began to count together, and for a while, Kylie thought that nothing would happen. They got to seventy-five and Jackson was still in tandem with Dr. Sayers.

Then, he stopped counting, and Dr. Sayers continued softly, "You're relaxed. You're seeing where you are, who you are, you are relaxed and comfortable with your being…"

"The grass…" Jackson murmured.

"Yes?" Dr. Sayers leaned closer.

"Is green," Jackson said. He did something with his hands in the air; with eyes closed, he smiled.

"It was a good time in life," Dr. Sayers said.

"The grass…"

This time, Dr. Sayers didn't say anything.

Jackson spoke again. "So green. The sky is bright blue. The day is beautiful. And yet…human beings can be so ugly. So much beauty given…and rejected for the cruelty of man."

Dr. Sayers seemed dumbfounded. Jackson suddenly appeared to be in distress, grabbing at his throat.

"Jackson!" Rocky snapped.

"Let me take him out—" Dr. Sayers began.

But he didn't need to. Jackson swung to a sitting position, eyes open. He looked at Dr. Sayers and finally nodded appreciation. "Doctor, you have a talent."

"Why, thank you…but what?"

"I'd love to keep the past to myself, Dr. Sayers, if you don't mind," Jackson said.

"I don't know why, but people usually regress to a happy time in life," the doctor said. "Kylie, of course, was different. And it did appear that you were in distress. I assure you, that is never the intent, and when someone is upset—"

"Not to worry, Dr. Sayers," Jackson said. "Rocky's voice brought me right out, and it was fine. We work closely together—always have one another's backs. But still I'd like to mull over my experience, if you don't mind."

"Of course, you're the client. And I was delighted to have you here. Please, any of you, come back any time," Dr. Sayers said weakly. "And, Kylie, you're doing all right? Whatever his experience, Special Agent Crow seems to be just fine. You, on the other hand—"

"I'm doing very, very well," Kylie assured him.

He beamed. "Of course. You are surrounded by our country's finest, after all! Seriously, you are welcome here any time, and for those defending our nation, no charge, of course."

"Dr. Sayers, it's illegal for us to take advantage. But thank you," Jackson said.

They shook hands, and Dr. Sayers opened the door to the reception area for them to leave.

Another group of young people—two women in their early twenties and a young man of about the same age—were waiting with cups of tea in hand.

After the new group moved into the doctor's office, Devin spoke with the receptionist, who once again told them that there was no charge, and Devin explained that it would be unethical, if not illegal, for them to accept the service for free a second time. She finally managed to pay.

When they were back out on the street, Rocky, Devin, and Kylie all stared at Jackson, waiting for him to say what he would not while he was in the office.

"That was actually rather amazing. He is an able hypnotist," Jackson said.

"You—you really were hypnotized?" Kylie asked. "I mean, I know I was, but..."

"There was a piece of me I held back," Jackson said. "But I allowed a part of my mind to go where it would in such a situation."

"Why did you become distressed?" Rocky asked.

"It was interesting. This is Salem, so easy enough to imagine that you were back in the midst of the witch trials. A part of me believed that I was John Proctor, the day before being hanged. That was the end. But there were other fleeting glimpses of something in there."

"And what were those glimpses?" Kylie asked anxiously.

"A cemetery," Jackson said. "A typical old cemetery. New England, somewhere. It must have been. There were crooked slate gravestones, a few aboveground tombs, a lot of trees, some newer graves. But none really recent."

"Was anyone in the cemetery?" Devin asked.

"Just me. I could hear my breath, feel my heartbeat, as I moved through it," Jackson said. "It was strange. At the same time, I was in a cart with other men and one woman. Someone said that it was 'the year of our Lord, 1692, August 19.' I knew others who were with me... George Burrows was one of them.

"I was looking at the sky, waiting for the drop in the noose and watching the sky while George said the Lord's Prayer and Cotton Mather said that the devil could play tricks or something like that…and then I'd see the cemetery again.

"I don't know the city the way the three of you do, but I know the crucial history of the witch trials. It was an easy enough route to take under suggestion," he mused, "not that Sayers spoke about Salem and history, just that it's where we are. As to the cemetery, I don't know. It was just something I kept seeing."

"So, now what?" Rocky asked.

"Lunch. I'm starving, as I imagine we all are. Then I'm going to find that cemetery."

Jon's first stop was to see Sandra Westerly.

It wasn't a long stop, but it more or less confirmed the text had been a fake. It was from an unknown or blocked number, and had been signed—too obviously—"from Kylie Connelly."

"I'm telling you, it's very disturbing," Sandra said.

He wasn't a tech, but it seemed obvious that the message could have come from anyone.

He was careful to sympathize with her before moving on; he didn't want his suspicion that Sandra had sent the text to herself known.

On to Ben Miller. And he wasn't surprised by Ben's initial comment to him.

"You believe that after everything we put him through, this man, Matt Hudson, is going to agree to your plan?" Ben asked Jon skeptically.

"I do. For a number of reasons," Jon said.

"Okay, well… I'll take part in your charade. But you do understand that we have nothing at all to bring him in on. We already dragged him in here once. I really need you to make sure that the man is completely on board with this."

Jon nodded. "I just need to find him. He doesn't start at the Cauldron until later in the day."

"That's easy enough. Officer Allen is with him. He's in his living room as we speak. They're watching a replay of a college game—they both happen to be basketball nuts. Whoever is watching him has to report to me on the hour, and the call just came in."

"Great. I'll go over," Jon said. "Hate to interrupt a replay, though."

"Thankfully, in this day and age, they can just put it on hold."

"If he's willing, we'll put out a press release as soon as possible. A suspect charged in the killing of Annie Hampton."

Ben nodded. "If he's willing."

"I have every confidence that he will be," Jon said. Well, he spoke with confidence. He hoped that he—and Kylie—were right.

"You think this will really bring the killer out?" Ben asked.

"I think that we try this, or we have to hope that a clue will suddenly appear, or that the killer will come running in to unburden his soul and confess."

Ben was silent a minute, then nodded. "Annie's parents were in. They're a mess. Her sister has come to be with her mother and is just about a basket case over this. Sure, go see Matt. Get him to agree. And pray that you're right."

Jon stood to leave.

"Hey, wait," Ben said, keying something into his computer.

"Yeah?"

"Got the make and model on the tire tracks at Devin's cottage."

"Yes?"

"They fit an SUV, this year's model, part of an upgrade package," Ben told him, reading his email. He looked at Jon. "I know of one locally."

"Yeah?"

Ben hesitated. "It belongs to Michael Westerly. He and Sandra have two cars—hers is a little Mustang, but it seems that they both drive the SUV everywhere. I wonder if they fight about who gets to use it when."

Jon nodded slowly. "Thanks," he said. "All right. I'm off to see Matt."

Matt's home wasn't far from the historic district. Jon knew he was being watched from the minute he parked his car and walked up the little path. He didn't get a chance to even knock at the door before it opened.

A young officer in plainclothes opened the door. "Jon Dickson?" he said.

Jon nodded, showing his credentials.

"Detective Miller said you were on your way. I'm Pete Allen," the young man said. "Come on in. Matt is right there on the sofa."

Matt's place was comfortably furnished with an old plump leather couch and a few matching chairs. A television against the wall had a large screen; it was frozen on an image of a young man leaping toward the basket, the ball flying to score.

Matt stood, looking at him curiously. "Is there a break in the case?"

Jon took a deep breath. He looked over at Pete Allen.

"Okay, okay, I'll, uh…be looking at the grass," Pete Allen said, exiting the house.

"What the hell is going on?" Matt asked Jon.

"We want to arrest you for the murder of Annie Hampton," Jon said.

"What—what the hell?" Matt repeated, incredulous.

"As a pretense. We know you didn't kill her."

"So, you're going to arrest me for killing her although you know I didn't? You're going to let the world believe that I'm a vicious killer?"

"Let me explain—the downside and the upside."

"Go ahead and try because all I'm seeing is a downside," Matt told him.

Jon indicated that Matt should sit. And he went through his arguments—what might be if they achieved their goal. He was honest, stating again what they all knew. No plan was foolproof.

Matt listened, still appearing to be somewhat shocked.

Jon finished and awaited Matt's answer.

They headed to Derby Street to find a lunch spot, opting for a place called Sunshine Café and Books, an establishment that made no mention of witches or any paranormal thing.

It was a pretty spot with a charming backyard patio. The lunch menu included almost anything anyone could want, from hot dogs to tacos to pasta. Jackson excused himself almost as soon as they were seated, asking Rocky just to order him sparkling water and a burger. A cheerful waiter quickly appeared, and they ordered, Devin taking care of ordering for the empty chair.

Jackson was back quickly with a book in his hands. He looked exceptionally pleased.

"This is an oddball you'd be lucky to find just about anywhere, even online," he said, showing them his purchase.

It was titled *Graveyards and Cemeteries of Olde New England*.

"Nice," Devin said.

"It's perfect. I'm going to find that damned cemetery."

"Just remember, Salem was more than the current city way back when," Kylie told him. "Salem Village is now Danvers, and Peabody was part of Salem Towne."

"Right," Jackson said. He was studying his book. "And back then, Salem Village was a parish of Salem Towne…" He paused in the midst of flipping pages. Without looking up, he told them, "Talked to Jon. He's on his way here."

Before they could ask him the outcome of Jon's visits, Jackson led out a triumphant cry. "Aha!" He pointed his finger on a photograph on the page. "That's it!"

Kylie reached for the book. "Not where Annie Hampton was murdered," she said quietly.

"Don't keep us waiting!" Devin said.

"It's in Danvers, old Salem Village," Kylie said, studying the cemetery. Many old local cemeteries were similar. This one had a stone wall about three feet high around it. Parts of the cemetery seemed to be filled with nothing but slate gravestones, weathered to a point they were probably unreadable. There were a few aboveground tombs, something that appeared to be a caretaker's shed, and the shell of what might have once been a chapel.

There was what looked like a marble arch at the entry to the cemetery, with iron lettering that read, The Resting Place.

Devin looked over Kylie's shoulder. "Nice name—it's rather gentle for the Puritans. They didn't say Place to Rot, or whatever. They did kind of belie the name by adding those death's-heads at either end, though." She peered closer. "I'm pretty sure I've been there. Auntie Mina used to belong to a group that preserved old cemeteries. I think I pulled weeds with her there once."

"It's not more than a twenty-minute drive from the heart of Salem," Rocky said.

"Curious," Jackson said, looking at Kylie. He smiled. "Maybe I'm filtering something of...you."

"Because that's it?" Kylie said, looking at him. "That's the cemetery I'm going to visit?"

She was startled when Jon spoke up; she hadn't realized he'd come to the café.

"It's as good as any," he said. "*After* we've checked it out thoroughly and made sure we can put our plan into action."

"Detective Miller has agreed to the plan?" Kylie asked. "And Matt?"

Jon nodded, taking a seat at the table and smiling at her. "You were right. All I have to say is we'd better catch Westerly and make damned sure Matt Hudson, actor, gets some great publicity when this is all over." He glanced at Jackson. "I think we're going to have to be careful doing this as well. I think someone keeps tabs on us in this city. Or at least, they're keeping tabs on Kylie."

"So, you two need to stay here and do touristy things and keep busy," Jackson said.

"And we need to head out to Danvers," Rocky agreed softly.

Kylie found they were all looking at her.

Jon reached across the table, taking her hand. "Kylie, this is still dangerous. It's your call. Nothing has been set into motion yet," he told her quietly.

She looked back at them one by one. She'd have been a liar to say a certain amount of fear wasn't burning in her heart. But she was equally sure she'd never be the same if they didn't stop Michael Westerly. Especially before he made his final political play.

She forced a smile. "I trust you all," she said sincerely. Then, determined, "We have to do this. Let's catch Michael Westerly."

"You really think that someone is aware of what we're doing—or I'm doing—all the time?" Kylie asked Jon. They had wandered back to the Witch Trials Memorial and were sitting on a patch of stone wall between the benches dedicated to the victims of the trials.

Jackson, Rocky, and Devin had gone to scope out the cemetery in Danvers. Rocky had slipped away first to get the car and swept around on a side street to pick up Jackson and

Devin. Jon and Kylie had split with them at the last minute, hoping anyone following or watching would give up on the others in their determination to keep an eye on Kylie.

The day was beautiful. Kylie told Jon it made her think of Jackson when he had been hypnotized and he'd been talking about the blue of the sky and the green of the grass.

When Jon looked to his left, he saw the crooked stones of the Old Burying Point, shaded by the trees. Beyond was the Grimshawe House, for a story by Nathaniel Hawthorne, published posthumously. The house looked as if it fit right in with the cemetery, old and faded, but it had a great history: Nathaniel Hawthorne had spent many a day there, when it was a warm and loving home owned by a man named Peabody with three daughters, one of whom would become Hawthorne's wife.

"Are you doing all right?" Jon asked Kylie. He wasn't sure how she could be, but he'd discovered—which he should have known from the get-go—she was extremely stubborn.

She smiled and nodded. "I'm fine. And by the way, I love the concern in your eyes, and the fact you can be watching everything and everyone around us and still have that care so intensely focused on me as well. Impressive."

"I aim to please," he said lightly.

"I was thinking there were good things that happened here, too. A horrible past could help forge such a fine author as Hawthorne."

"Hawthorne was brilliant. He used the power of stories to right the wrongs of the world, particularly his own ancestry." Jon lowered his voice. "And at this very minute, your friend, the excellent tour guide Mr. Carl Fisher, is doing a bit on that house."

Kylie hadn't seen him. She turned her head to note that Carl was in fact in the alley, about to bring a daytime group into the cemetery. They listened as he told the tale of the house and how Hawthorne courted his future wife there.

"Do you think Carl is watching us?" she asked Jon.

"Possibly," he said softly. "But I'm also pretty sure I know who drove to Devin's and stopped to check out the house on foot—trying to determine if we were there or not."

"Who?"

"Sandra Westerly. No solid proof. Many people own SUVs, but she does own a vehicle with tires like the tracks found at Devin's place. Well, she and Michael own it, but both drive it—they switch cars a lot. We could try to get casts of her tires when she parks in soft earth somewhere, but even then, it would prove she stopped at the cottage and nothing more."

"Do you really think she helped her husband?" Kylie asked.

He shrugged. "I think she might have even demanded he do something. At this point in his career, just breaking it off with a mistress wouldn't be good enough to salvage his reputation."

"Politicians have proven to be philanderers time and time again. Was that enough to kill?"

"For a woman like Sandra Westerly? Yes, I think so. Most of the time, a man or a woman rises to power before what they've been up to comes to light. And there's still a core group to whom decency matters, so…"

"That's horrible," Kylie murmured. "How can people be so horrible? Want something so badly that they ignore anything resembling human decency…and the law!"

"I still believe human beings are mostly good," Jon told her. "That's why it became so important for me to work on finding the ones who would hurt those who are decent," he added softly.

She reached out and squeezed his hand briefly.

He slipped off the wall, glancing toward Carl and his group. "Come on. Let's head to the Cauldron. The media has been informed that Matt Hudson has been arrested for the murder of Annie Hampton. I want to see what happens and who shows up—the bar will have to have the news on their TVs. I particularly want to see how soon Carl comes in once we're there."

"He can't abandon a tour group."

"No, but he can talk fast and end it quickly. Let's see if I'm right."

He offered her his hand; she smiled and took it and they wandered the block or so back to the Essex Street pedestrian mall and past various shops until they reached the restaurant.

Cindy was behind the bar with another young woman. It was evident she was trying to smile and be a good bartender—and equally evident she was having a hard time.

Especially since the conversation at the bar was all about Matt.

The man's arrest hadn't sent clientele flying away in horror. Indeed, it seemed to have drawn in every local Jon and Kylie had ever seen in the place.

And everyone had an opinion.

There was only standing room by the bar. Cindy and the other young woman—one they'd seen working with her there before, Mariah, Jon thought—were racing around. Jon was finally able to catch Cindy and order two soda waters with lime.

Cindy looked at him, accepting the order, but as she did so, her eyes filled with tears.

"Help Matt," she said urgently. "Help him!"

As she spoke, he heard a newscaster on the TV over the bar describing the murder—and showing Detective Ben Miller and the police as they arrived at Matt Hudson's house to arrest him.

"There you go," one man said at the bar. "I watch the crime shows all the time. We should have known it was the charming bartender."

"I can't believe it," whispered the woman on the stool next to his. She stared wide-eyed at the screen.

"You don't want to believe it because Hudson was so good-looking. Women fall for a good-looking face every time," the man said.

"I don't want to believe it, but there's no surprise he might have been the mystery lover," another man said.

"Well, everyone will be relieved," a young woman commented. She was probably right around Annie Hampton's age. She happened to glance Jon's way. "I'll be able to walk the streets here again without being terrified."

The conversations went on. Jon listened, giving his attention to the television screen and to those coming and going.

As he expected, Carl arrived shortly. He wedged his way up to the bar to stand beside Jon. He shook his head. "They're wrong," he said at once. "Matt may be under arrest, but when he goes to trial—and thank God we have laws and lawyers, and this can't be turned into a witch hunt—his innocence will be proven."

"You know he's innocent?" Jon asked Carl.

He thought the man hesitated.

Do you know he's innocent of this, Jon wondered, *because you're guilty yourself?*

Carl traveled to the same cities as Matt—the same cities where victims had been found. Angela had verified it, and now Carl seemed a bit more suspicious to Jon all the time.

It also seemed to Jon, now that he was right beside him, that Carl smelled like cigarette smoke. He might have been imagining it, looking for some reason for having found the matchboxes. Then again, he'd had an aunt who collected matchbooks and matchboxes everywhere she went as cheap souvenirs—and she'd never smoked a cigarette in her life.

His suspects didn't seem like the souvenir-collecting types.

There was another question. Did Carl know Matt Hudson

was innocent because he knew Michael Westerly was guilty? Perhaps Carl had been the one following them, trying to turn the tables. He had been in the Cauldron the night Jimmy Marino had his accident.

"Apparently the local police have something that's real evidence," Jon said.

"They can't," Carl said, and then looked at Jon, a new hostility in him. "But then you would know, wouldn't you?"

"At the moment, it's the police. We'll see if there's anything for the Bureau to do later. I'll be down at the station tomorrow," he said.

A table for two emptied in the center of the restaurant area, and Jon and Kylie leaped on it before it was even fully cleared of dirty dishes.

Jon pulled out the book on cemeteries Jackson had purchased. They spoke loudly to one another— easy enough to pull off because there was so much chatter in the bar and restaurant.

"I never knew about some of these, can you believe it?" Kylie asked. "So fascinating. Especially when the engraving is deep and you can really read the old stones. In some of the well-documented cemeteries, the older engravings have been re-chiseled or redone...repaired? I'm not sure what they call it. But some of the not-so-well-known places are amazing, too."

"I know. I love the old stones that tell stories like, 'Here lies Peter Stone, a mammoth fall did crush his bone.'"

Kylie laughed. "I never saw one exactly like that. But I did read one about a Charles Allen, and the headstone listed all his wives, all his children, and talked about his voyage from England, how he became a farmer and then a Revolutionary War hero."

"Speaking of Charles," Jon said, "there's a great story about Dickens. He was visiting a cemetery in Edinburgh, and he misread a tombstone. The fellow who died had sold various food products, and it was on his stone that he was a 'meal' man. Dickens read it as 'mean' man. When he wrote *A Christmas Carol*, he even used part of the name of the man on the stone—Ebenezer Lennox Scroggie. Of course, there was more to it. Dickens was appalled by some of the conditions around him at the time, but he did visit the Canongate Cemetery. It's presumed that Ebenezer Scrooge's creation was influenced by the misreading of *meal* as *mean*."

"This one," Kylie said, and she pointed at the book. "It's called the Resting Place. Well, yes, I'm going to guess it's restful. I have to visit this one—it's not far, just in Danvers. I'm going first thing tomorrow. Would you be able to come with me?"

"I'm afraid not." He made a show of looking disappointed. "We'll be at the station being briefed by the police. Matt Hudson has already demanded an attorney, but maybe he'll speak with me. Even with an attorney present, I believe it will help me."

Kylie kept the book out, studying pictures of old, broken, and decaying gravestones, the trees and the tombs, and information on those who were buried there. "Oh, Jon, this is so sad! Behind this big vault there's a group of graves. Several of the people buried there were accused of witchcraft and languished in jail for months before it was all ended. Many died from illnesses they contracted there." She looked up at him. "I can't wait to see this place. I can't believe I've never visited it before."

He caught her hand, smiling at her across the table.

They could all be wrong on this. They could plant themselves and more police officers in and around the cemetery, Kylie could walk all over it, and nothing could happen.

But it wouldn't be for lack of trying if the Cauldron did have ears. His smile deepened. Adam Harrison ran a theater and many of Jon's coworkers had spouses who were renowned thespians.

Kylie's performance here could rival any.

He was still holding her hand when the restaurant's door opened and Sandra Westerly swept in, her head high, her manner triumphant.

She spoke to a few people as she entered and made her way through the tables. Her pasted-on smile deepened into something real when she saw Jon and Kylie. She strode straight to their table and leaned on it.

"You see, you horrid witch. My husband is innocent! Trust me, you'll be hearing from my lawyer. You will pay for your lies and your harassment."

They both just stared at her.

She didn't expect an answer. Her smile was terrifying in its malicious pleasure. She looked down, as if she were too delighted to look straight at them while she relished the moment.

The book on cemeteries was on the table, open to the page that showed the Resting Place and its address in Danvers.

Sandra looked up again. "You should have never messed with us, little girl," she told Kylie. "What, were you hoping to sleep with him? There will be consequences. And you—" she turned to Jon "—big, strong agent man. You wait. Your superiors will have you writing traffic tickets."

Jon did reply then. "Sorry, Mrs. Westerly, agents don't work traffic. That would be the police."

"Fine. I believe having you fired will work just as well."

Apparently, Kylie was unable to keep quiet a minute longer. "Good lord, why on earth would I want to sleep with your creepy husband when I'm with a 'big, strong agent man'?" she asked.

Sandra looked as if she could explode. She pointed a finger at Kylie. "You'll pay," she whispered. Her hands fell on the book. "You will pay," she repeated, her words almost a growl. She spun around, leaving them.

Jon realized some of the talk in the room had quieted—others had heard her. They were staring at Jon and Kylie. He was glad to see most of them looked surprised and uncomfortable.

Sandra had allowed her politician's-perfect-wife mask to slip. And while people might know she wore a mask, they were nonetheless stunned by what they had seen.

"I think you really pissed her off," Jon told Kylie quietly.

"If we're doing this, we might as well go all out," Kylie said. She let out a shaky breath. Then she said, a little too loudly for regular conversation, enough to be heard by anyone near her, "Annie Hampton was nothing but happy and excited—nothing that would make anyone angry at all. Westerly didn't have to be angry, but he tore into her as viciously as his strength could allow."

Jon nodded, feeling tension grip his gut. *No plan was foolproof.* He knew Kylie was unwavering and the machinations had been set into motion. But that didn't matter. "We can still stop this," he said softly.

She shook her head. "No. I will not live my life in fear of that kind of monster. You will take him down. I know you will."

"Kylie, you're risking your life."

She smiled grimly. "If you don't take him down, Jon, I'm not going to have much of a life. You heard his lovely wife. Please. I have faith in you. Have faith in me."

CHAPTER SEVENTEEN

At Devin's cottage that night, Kylie was nervous.

It had been her idea to be bait. She wanted Westerly taken down. She had never been so sure of anything in her life than that Michael Westerly had killed Annie Hampton.

She didn't know what was going on with Sandra, and she didn't know who else might be helping him. Maybe not with murder, but with information. But she did know Westerly was a killer. And hopefully, if he was caught threatening her, the rest would fall into place. Maybe not easily, but bit by bit.

Still, when Jackson drew out the map of the cemetery, she kept looking around. Someone seemed to have eyes and ears everywhere.

Devin saw her and smiled. "I have special windows here now—we can see out, no one can see in."

"Like an interrogation room," Kylie said.

"Hopefully not quite," Devin said, and hesitated. "I met Rocky because a horrible murder had taken place when we were young—and then another here, and another. But I couldn't give up this cottage."

"I should hope not!" Auntie Mina called from the kitchen.

Devin smiled. "I couldn't give it up, but I couldn't stay here without being certain I was safe at all times. It is, in a way, a tech fortress."

"Not to mention Poe," Rocky said.

"And Mina!" came another call from the kitchen.

"And Mina!" Devin said.

"What is she doing in the kitchen?" Kylie whispered.

"Supervising. I put some muffins in the oven for later. She's convinced I'm going to burn them," Devin said.

The two of them realized Jon, Jackson, and Rocky were waiting for them to give their undivided attention to the map.

"All right," Jackson said. "The archway is the obvious access. The wall is fairly high, but it can be climbed over. If Westerly does show up, he could hop the wall. We also believe he comes with an accomplice—most probably his wife. She'll be in the car, and I believe he'll just come through the archway. But we'll be stationed all about—Devin watching the archway from behind this tomb, Rocky here by this massive oak, I'll be back closer to the old holding house, and Jon will be on that side of it. We're going to have to hope stray civilians don't wander over to the cemetery, but it's unlikely. We did manage to find a truly-out-of-the-way place."

"Ben has four of his best men who will be taking positions behind ours. Two of his guys were army sharpshooters. I don't believe we can be any more prepared," Jon said.

"My plan is to get dropped off by a ridesharing service—" Kylie began.

"Which will really be an officer of Ben's," Jon put in.

She nodded. "And I'll make my way casually through the graves and around behind the holding house."

Jon nodded. "The view from the street and even the front of the cemetery is obstructed. The holding house is pretty large. When the cemetery was laid out, the ground would freeze too hard for burial in the winter, and they needed enough space for their dead until the earth thawed."

"And that's it," Kylie said. "I guess I just wait to be attacked."

"We believe he'll approach you there," Jackson said. "We can't be certain. Until we see what he does, we'll be close enough to move in no matter what's happening. Once we see him head in your direction, we'll follow. Carefully and discreetly, of course. We have to keep him from suspecting anything."

"To that end, we'll have you come to the police station with us at first," Jon said. "We'll leave our cars there. Ben has it set up for us to exit out back with his officers. You'll come out of the station alone, pull out your phone, and pretend to call a ride."

Kylie nodded. She tried to summon a bright smile. "I like it." She glanced at Jon and then looked around at the others. "She threatened me today—outright threatened me! Sandra Westerly is almost as scary as her husband. I believe she might well have put him up to it. Except that..."

"That what?" Devin asked.

"He enjoyed it," Kylie said. "He liked killing Annie."

Auntie Mina appeared in the parlor. "Muffins," she said firmly. "I understand you're saving Kylie and that's all important, but you can do so without burned muffins."

Kylie was grateful for the woman; she made Kylie smile and forget just how nervous she was—and how her anxiety was growing, even as she tried to hide it from the others.

The muffins were delicious. They had them with a hearty soup. Devin turned on the television while they were eating.

The arrest of Matt Hudson still filled the media.

Watching, Kylie asked, "If Westerly kills me now, won't he worry that they'll let Matt Hudson go?" she asked.

Jon shook his head. "Police evidence is going to prove

sketchy, at best. The rumor will have surfaced by now that his lawyer will be arguing first thing tomorrow, and Matt just might be out on bail sometime by then."

He nodded at the television. "And in Westerly's own mind, he's beloved—which he really is by many people who see his public persona. Those people won't want to believe he could have possibly done this. His spin would be the horrible injustice of a system that lets a heinous murderer back out on the streets. Or, if he can't make it appear that Matt really is the murderer, he can blame the FBI. We haven't caught this atrocious serial killer and he's struck twice in Salem. Remember, Westerly can prove he wasn't in the places where at least two of the other murders took place."

Kylie nodded grimly. She arched a brow at him. "We're all right, legally, doing this?"

He nodded, reassuring her.

They talked a while longer with Jackson, Rocky, and Devin, pointing out specifics of the cemetery. They were prepared to go.

Everyone stayed up late, too keyed up to sleep. When they finally went to bed, Jon asked Kylie again if she was sure she wanted to go through with the plan.

"I do." She slipped her arms around him and said, "I may not be physically trained to kick butt, but I'm mentally a tiger!"

He laughed softly. She kissed his lips, sliding against him.

"I can just hold you tonight," he told her. "I know you're nervous… I'm all right with that."

"That's great, but I'm not. I need you to keep this kick-butt mind of mine occupied," she said.

"Oh? Okay, sure, I can do that!"

And he was very good at keeping her mind occupied.

Morning came, and Jon was up first; he showered and woke

Kylie. She should have been tired, considering how little they both slept, but she was anxious and ready to move.

When she was dressed and ready, she found she was the last to arrive in the kitchen for coffee. There wasn't a lot of conversation. It was time to head to the police station.

As she headed toward the door, Kylie felt a strange mix of cold and warmth behind her. She turned. Auntie Mina was there. She gave her a strong, ghostly hug—one Kylie was certain Mina could feel.

"Get him, young lady. Get that monster!" Auntie Mina said.

Kylie nodded, a small smile curling her lips. Somehow, the sprightly little spirit gave her something she hadn't expected.

A true feeling of strength. Yes, she would be the best bait ever. They would get their man.

What could possibly go wrong?

There were always dozens of things, seen and unseen...

No law enforcement agency in the country was happy with using a civilian. Jon knew it had been done before, that it was sometimes the best way to proceed if the civilian and law enforcement were in agreement. And if it had been anyone other than Kylie, he wouldn't exactly be pleased with the arrangement, but he would see it as a solution.

But in this case, Kylie was insistent. And he understood.

He still held her for a moment, looking deep into her eyes before leaving with the others in police cars from the rear of the station. He wanted to be with her, but he couldn't be. He had to have faith in the ardent young officer who was acting as her driver. The car she would go to the cemetery in had been outfitted with stickers advertising several rideshare companies. Hopefully the disguise would help.

He held her tight, heedless of where they were. Then he

smiled and walked away. When he looked back briefly, she gave him a thumbs-up.

"I'm not worried about Kylie," Jackson said as Jon joined him in the back of one of the police cars. "Are you doing all right?"

Jon nodded. "We have to do this. I'll just be glad when it's over."

"I'll be glad if it's over. We could have this massive array of hidden agents and police, and still nothing might happen."

"I know," Jon said. "But I don't think so. Westerly himself hasn't made any direct threats, but his wife has."

"And if you watch her on TV at a rally or something, she seems so wholesome."

"The trick here," Jon said, "is to catch him in the act. Do you think that even that will be enough? We can't let him get far. He's a killer. If he gets too close to Kylie with a knife, she's dead."

"If he has the knife on him, even if he cleaned it after Annie's killing, it's the evidence we need. We'll find trace amounts of blood, or the size and shape will match the wounds on Annie's body," Jackson said with assurance.

"Maybe he'll use a new knife."

"Let's hope we know our killer as well as we think we do."

They arrived at the cemetery. An agile enough person could leap the stone wall surrounding the place, but it was high enough that someone not in decent shape wouldn't manage such a feat. The iron gates—with the arch reading The Resting Place above it—were open. Still, the cemetery seemed exceptionally forlorn.

There was obviously some maintenance done here; the place hadn't returned to the total wild. But there were weeds and scruffy grass growing everywhere, and several large trees grew through old stones. There were aboveground tombs and, down what remained of a path, the holding house.

Jon and Jackson arrived ahead of Rocky and Devin; they all knew their positions. Jon broke from Jackson, aware that police would be filtering in to surround the cemetery as well.

There were several monuments in the cemetery, created in the 1800s rather than the 1600s. Angels with broken wings rose above illegible slate stones and more recent markers hewn from marble.

"There's a large crying cherub holding a lamb right behind the holding house," Jackson told Jon.

"Great hiding place. We'll test our mics and earpieces as soon as we're in place."

Jon nodded and went to take up his position.

For some reason, a holding house seemed a sad place. He remembered when a family friend had died one bitter winter; they'd waited until spring to lay him next to his wife. And of course cemeteries—despite the Victorian effort to make them more beautiful—were always sad places. They held memories of the lives that had come and gone.

Yet, maybe the alternative was worse. Lives lived and lost... and not remembered.

The sun was rising overhead; the sky was blue. Jon realized the grass, even the weeds protruding through it all, were a bright, vibrant green.

Green grass, blue skies.

Maybe there was something to Dr. Sayers and his abilities after all. This was the cemetery Jackson had seen.

As Jon settled behind the large lamb-holding cherub, he realized it was a perfect place to wait, to watch—until the time came to act.

He heard Jackson's voice through his earpiece. "In position."

"In position, and you're right, it's perfect," Jon said.

"I saw Rocky wandering into place. The waiting begins."

The waiting was half of it. With the sun overhead, time ticked by as if each second lasted for minutes.

Jon didn't need to check for his Glock—he knew exactly where it was. And he was ready to use it.

Kylie didn't hear a word her driver said. The officer was a pleasant young man, speaking easily, not chatting incessantly.

He was from New Hampshire. "Live free or die," he told Kylie dryly when she asked if he was from the area. His name was Liam Decker. He assured her she was working with some of the finest officers to be found anywhere. And everything after that was lost in the blur of her nervousness.

When they arrived at the cemetery, she looked out at the archway and its sign that read The Resting Place for several seconds before reaching for the door.

Panic almost seized her. She tamped it down. The arguments she had made were real; if they didn't find a way to lock up Westerly, she might be looking over her shoulder for the rest of her life. She could topple into the subway, go flying over a high cliff...or be stabbed in cold blood when visiting St. Paul's or Trinity or another cemetery, anywhere, anytime.

"We've got your back," Decker told her. He gave her an encouraging grin. "And your front and sides, too."

She managed a smile in return and remembered she was giving a performance again—she was supposed to be excited to be there. She had Jackson's book in her hand, and she could study different parts of the cemetery as she wandered through it.

She'd been wired with a microphone, and as she left the car, gazing up at the archway, she heard Jackson's voice: "Kylie at the archway."

She heard an echo of voices assuring her agents and police were around. She knew she heard Jon's most firmly.

"Kylie, just be the historian-slash-tourist you are. Take your time. It could be a long wait," Jackson warned.

She had to remind herself not to nod. She pretended great interest in the archway; it was hard to take the first steps into the cemetery. Then she saw someone in front of her.

Not Michael Westerly.

And not anyone—solid.

It was Obadiah Jones. He looked at her, nodding acknowledgment and respect. "I'm here, too," he told her. "Walking with you every step of the way."

She managed not to say thank you, not to say anything at all until she had started down the rocky, overgrown path toward the holding house.

She stopped to study one of the oldest, broken slate stones and bent down, softly telling Obadiah, "Thank you!"

She knew Jon and the Krewe would know she wasn't speaking to them; she heard a few murmurs from police on the wire.

"Take your time, Kylie," Jackson said again. "Matt Hudson's lawyer just gave a statement in front of the courthouse. They did a damned good job, ripping into the FBI and the local police for hitting up a man with so little evidence because we're all inept at our jobs. But we could be sitting here another few hours—our 'acting' attorney is crowing because he's gotten his client out on bail."

Hours!

"I'll show you some intriguing graves," Obadiah offered, "introduce you to some friends. Okay, well, most have moved on, but they're still great history. Now, this section is all from the late 1600s and early 1700s…"

He led her to a chipped, moss-covered, aboveground tomb. "This was Ethan Hammersmith, a good man. He escaped arrest by fleeing the colony and returned to help those who were jailed. A great man. He helped me when I thought all was lost and continued to help my family when I died. He was distantly related to Rebecca Nurse—there were few women who so loved her church and led such a fine life! When she was accused, and convicted, Ethan became convinced the only devil in Massachusetts was in the power of suggestion and fear."

Obadiah sighed. "It's always difficult when people choose to stay blind to even the facts when they point to something they don't want to believe."

There were stones from all manner of graves that people had re-etched over the years. On one were sad words.

Goody Jane Purcell, beloved of her family, strong in spirit, loving only her God, resting now in his arms for keeping that faith.

"She was in jail a long time. Even when it was over, families struggled to pay the room and board for their loved ones' time in the old place. As with me," Obadiah said.

Even with her ghostly guide keeping her occupied, Kylie began to feel she'd been in the cemetery forever. They had known it might go this way, that they had taken tremendous resources to dangle a carrot…and their prey just might not bite.

She was making her way around the holding house when she heard the warning from Jackson.

"Westerly is in the cemetery." He was quiet for a beat and continued with, "He's wearing jeans and a dark hoodie."

A man in what he hoped was stereotypical criminal garb, a disguise that might make him invisible in plain sight if someone saw him?

The disguise didn't matter.

It was Westerly.

Jon never should have doubted Kylie.

He could see her easily, and he was grateful to see Obadiah

walking by her side. He could only provide moral strength, of course—Obadiah didn't have what it would take to stop a vicious assault by a knife. But Jon was nonetheless pleased that his strange but very good old friend was with her.

For Kylie's part, she kept referring to her book. She knelt by different stones, studying them, moving weeds aside, swearing softly as she knelt in a place just a little bit too rocky. She was playing the role of engaged researcher perfectly.

Then came the moment they'd all been waiting for.

Michael Westerly, in his jeans and hoodie, came around the holding house. Jon fought his instinct hard; he couldn't jump until he saw that Westerly was carrying a knife and going for Kylie.

Westerly walked straight toward her. She pretended to become aware of him and stood, turning to look at him.

"Miss Connelly, we meet alone, face-to-face," he said.

Kylie stared at him for a moment, as if she was equally curious. Her fear didn't show in her face. "Michael Westerly," she said at last, shaking her head. "I'm just at a loss."

"A loss?"

She shrugged. "You could have had the world at your feet."

"You weren't in that cemetery," he told her. "I kept telling Sandra there was no way you could know anything, that you couldn't have seen anything."

"But I did. I saw you do it."

Jon waited, certain Westerly would make his move.

There was a burst of static over his earpiece. Then he heard one of the officers say, "I don't see anyone else in Westerly's car. I never saw Sandra move, but she's not in there anymore."

"I see her," Jackson said heatedly. "She's moving into the cemetery."

They had waited forever. Then everything happened at once.

Kylie was facing Westerly. "I know what you did," she insisted. "I *was* there. Just in a very odd way, you see."

"Did you have a séance? Are you really a witch?" he mocked.

She shook her head. "No, something a bit different. But I saw you. I felt you. And I know you killed Annie Hampton. I guess that means you'll have to kill me."

Jon was ready to leap. He wanted an arrest, but he was willing to shoot.

Westerly shook his head. "Oh, no, I'm not going to kill you," he said.

"You're not?" Kylie asked.

"No. I left that for someone else. Someone who really hates you!"

It was then Sandra Westerly came racing across the cemetery, leaping over broken stones as if she'd memorized every one of them. She didn't trip or stumble—she moved with an ungodly speed, racing toward Kylie.

A large kitchen knife was in her hand, catching the brilliant rays of the sun, appearing as deadly and sharp as a razor.

Jon saw Obadiah warn Kylie.

A warning was good, but it couldn't stop a knife.

That was enough. Jon stepped from the cover of the cherub, shouting, "Stop!" He fired a warning shot.

Sandra either didn't hear his warning, or she didn't care. She let out a scream like a banshee. She was too close to Kylie. Jon lowered his gun and threw himself at the enraged woman, aware Jackson and the others were right behind. He tackled Sandra to the ground, slamming her arm against the earth so the knife went flying.

Jon heard shouts all around, but when he rolled off Sandra and looked up, Westerly stood above him, his rage so deep that his face had turned red.

And he carried his own knife.

Jon reached for his Glock.

Westerly suddenly looked shocked. And fell to the side.

It wasn't Jackson, Krewe, or the police who had come to his defense. Kylie stood above him, looking like an avenging angel.

She had felled Westerly with the book. The hardcover book. Not enough to knock a man out, but enough to surprise him, throw him off balance.

As Westerly staggered, spewing incoherent rage, Jackson, Rocky, Devin, and the officers arrived.

Jon came to his feet, his gun on Westerly, and he reached for Kylie. They stood holding each other, somehow both shaking and strong. They watched and listened as the couple was arrested: Westerly, the man who would be king in his own world, and Sandra, the woman who would be his queen at all costs.

The murderous pair was led away, still fighting, still swearing vociferously, crying entrapment and swearing they'd come to tell Kylie to stop spreading lies.

The day had felt like it lasted forever and ever.

Jackson came up to Jon and Kylie.

"That regression experience sure was something. The grass is green. The sky is blue...starting to darken just a hair, but still, even now, a beautiful blue. It worked," he added. "We have two knives. I feel certain we'll find proof on one of them. It worked."

Pleased, Jackson left them there, heading to the front of the cemetery.

"Let's get out of here. In fact, somewhere out of Salem," Jon said. "Somewhere..."

"Where no one has ever died?" Kylie teased.

"Somewhere...else," he said. His arm was around her. She fit there so well.

They started to walk out, but she stopped him. "Oba-diah!" she said.

The ghost appeared, looking as pleased as everyone else.

"Thank you," Kylie said.

He moved to lift her hand; she did it for him and Obadiah placed a spectral kiss upon her flesh. "My pleasure! Justice... It is my reason for being." He stepped back. "Get thee out of here!" he commanded.

"Indeed, good sir! As you command," Kylie promised.

Jon laughed, and they made their way out of the cemetery, moving quickly under the archway.

In the back of his head, he knew they had caught the copy-cat. There was still a serial killer out there.

But Kylie was safe; that was enough for the moment.

CHAPTER EIGHTEEN

They all convened at the Cauldron. Matt Hudson was back, except he wasn't working the bar that night, other than to show one of the reporters filming him how he made the restaurant's famed drink, the Witch's Brew. Matt was widely being hailed as a type of hero, willing to sacrifice his reputation for an important police and FBI operation. He'd definitely achieved some celebrity.

He had a chair at the table with their group, along with Detective Miller. They were also joined by Dr. Sayers and Carl Fisher, and in the middle of the evening, the owner of the place made sure another bartender came in so Cindy could join them as well.

It seemed she and Matt were a pair, something they'd kept quiet until now. Since Matt was on top of the world, he just didn't care who knew.

He excitedly told Kylie that it had all paid off—he'd been offered spots on half a dozen national news stations and one late-night show.

"And you—you were all right?" he asked her anxiously.

"Better than I thought I would be," she told him. "But I had a lot of help."

She was glad of the celebration; she was equally eager for the night to come. But dreading it as well.

She had worked long and hard and beaten out a lot of applicants for the job she was due to start on Monday in New York City. And however long Jon stayed here to clear up details and paperwork—though the FBI had given the arrest to the local police—he would eventually go back to Washington, DC. She'd never heard of a good long-distance relationship.

But food and a sense of satisfaction were being enjoyed by all. She could afford to not think about the future for a little while.

Devin sat by Rocky, hand in hand, and Kylie wondered if it got easier each time they went through something like this. Kylie sat between Jackson and Jon, her chair so close to Jon's that when she turned to talk to someone else, she was leaning against him.

It was a good place to be. And yet she hoped they'd leave soon.

Carl was talking about the difficulty of being a tour guide when something was close and emotional, yet also part of the city's history. And Jackson was talking to Dr. Sayers, probing into just what talent the doctor had and how he might control it.

Dr. Sayers lowered his voice. "I don't think the talent really lies with me. Let's face it, people are susceptible to suggestion. When clients come for a regression, they've been curious about past lives, and they've wondered if they were kings and queens, happy and triumphant, or if they were scullery maids and grooms. Most people want to believe in the beauty of the life they're living, and that there was beauty in the past as well. You were different. Kylie was different. I wish I could take the credit. I do make a nice income doing those regressions, but in all honesty, I believe it has more to do with the person being regressed."

"Still, quite an interesting talent," Jackson said.

That Jackson was intrigued impressed Kylie. She noticed Jon was listening in to the conversation as well.

"I love what I do," Dr. Sayers told them. "Most of the time, it's young women, and they're very seldom scullery maids! They're usually noble young ladies and the knight on the white stallion comes riding along to save them."

"Ah, well," Jon murmured, smiling at Kylie, "sometimes those damsels are darned good at saving themselves."

Dr. Sayers laughed. "I've never had a man come in and regress to being saved by a woman."

"Hey," Devin protested. "It happens."

"I'm sure it does," Dr. Sayers said. "It's just not most men's dream, to be rescued by the woman they love. Not macho enough, I guess." He shrugged.

He started to say more, but just then Cindy and Carl came back up to the table, bearing a cake alive with sparklers. It was in honor of Matt, and he was beaming.

They all lifted a glass in his honor, but eventually, it was time to leave.

Exhausted and back at Devin's, Kylie discovered her new friends had applause and honor for her as well.

"You, young lady, are amazing," Jackson said once they were in the door.

"Absolutely," Rocky agreed.

"It took you long enough to get here and tell me about it!" Auntie Mina said, arriving in the midst of the group, her hands on her hips. "Thank goodness for that lovely Obadiah Jones... You know, I had never met him before?" she said, shaking her head. "Anyway, he made sure I knew everything was all right!"

She chastised them again, but she, too, came to Kylie, giving her another ghostly hug. "This group… It's what they do. Well, Devin tells stories, but she's been in this with the group often enough. You, Miss Kylie Connelly, were amazing." She glanced at Devin. "The house phone has been ringing off the hook, people wanting interviews with Kylie."

Kylie grimaced. Matt wanted the exposure. She did not.

"We'll deal with it," Jon assured her.

"For now—" Jackson began.

"Bed!" Jon announced.

"Then get away from my couch, all of you," Jackson commanded.

Alone at last, Kylie meant to talk. Except that she and Jon fell together in a kiss almost as soon as the door closed. Fear could bring about passion. Relief could do the same.

They luxuriated in one another, savored each touch, each kiss, and made love a long, long time before lying together, awake but replete.

Then they both started to speak at once. Kylie laid her hand on his chest and said, "You first."

"I will never know anyone like you again," he began. "Our time together has been short, but I know there's no one else out there I could feel this intensely about. You are you, of course, but perfect for me, and I believe I'm perfect for you. I'd never want to change your life and what's good in it. Like your job." He stopped for a breath; she was going to speak, but he went on, "And there's nothing I can do. There's only one center for the Krewe."

"You have to do what you do!" Kylie exclaimed, sitting up on an elbow. "Not everyone can to it. And what you and the Krewe do is important. You have to stay with it."

"Can we stay together long distance?" he asked quietly.

Kylie was silent.

He smoothed her hair back. "Two hundred and twenty-five miles," he said. "Four hours or so to drive, depending on traffic. A quick hop on a train."

"I do have to report to work on Monday. But I can actually do that now. Because of you," she said.

He nodded. "Because of us all, including you, especially you." After a moment, he added, "We can't let this end."

"We can't," she agreed.

She curled against him. They wouldn't let it end. Because it was true. They couldn't. She'd known him just days, but that meant nothing. There was no going back.

She'd been "regressed" and been murdered in another woman's body by a heinous killer. She'd begun to see the dead. And she'd almost been murdered in the flesh.

Just days. And yet, they were days that changed her life.

Jon sat with Jackson and Rocky in his makeshift office on Essex Street. They'd come from the jail and an interesting session with Ben, who told them about the current state of affairs with Michael and Sandra Westerly.

"They turned on each other like pit bulls bred to fight, both of them blaming each other," Ben had said. "Westerly claimed he didn't kill anyone and Sandra was the killer. She went all teary, swearing that he was the murderer, she was just desperately trying to be a good wife and keep herself safe. Then they both claimed they didn't do it, they'd been framed by the FBI and the police. And then their lawyers shut them both up."

It wasn't a surprise to Jon the two had turned on one another; neither was a particularly good person, no matter what masks they had worn.

"What will happen with them both denying it? Westerly never touched Kylie in the cemetery, and the best against either of them might be attempted murder," Jon had said.

But Ben had grimly assured him someone would be going

down for murder. "There was trace blood on that knife Sandra had. I'm pretty darned sure it will prove to be Annie Hampton's. Her fingerprints will be on the knife now, but I'd be willing to bet that she'll turn on her husband and give us all the details of Annie's death for her own plea deal."

Back in the office with Jackson and Rocky, Jon found himself unhappy as the three of them went through the photos and notes he had there. It should have felt over. But he still had a sense they were missing something.

His phone rang; it was Kylie. He smiled. He'd left her soundly sleeping, safe in the cottage with its state-of-the-art alarm system, Devin, Auntie Mina, and Poe.

She was a little anxious at first, asking him if the Westerly couple was still locked up. He assured her they were.

"I talked to Corrine and then Jenny and Nancy," she told him. "They were thrilled to know the killer and his accomplice were caught and locked up. I obviously played down having too much to do with it. But I've thought of something, talking to them. It's a little mundane after all this, but… I do need a date for Corrine's wedding."

"I will be delighted," he told her. "It happens I'm hanging with my boss. I can make sure right away I have the time off. You still have until Sunday night here, right?" he asked quietly.

"I do."

"Maybe we can head down to Boston for the weekend. Or if you wish, I can even go back to New York with you so you don't have to feel so rushed on Sunday morning."

"We'll talk."

After a minute, they ended the call. Kylie and Devin would drive into town shortly and they'd all meet up for lunch somewhere.

Anywhere but the Cauldron. They'd been glad to be there,

helping Matt segue into his role as hero rather than villain, but now, they needed something new.

Jon hung up and drummed his fingers on his desk, wondering why he felt so disturbed. They'd taken down Westerly and Sandra. But Jon had come to Salem because of the murders of three other women. Deanna Clark, Willow Cannon, and Cecily Bryant.

The difference in victimology was the factor that mattered—even if Westerly had committed a nearly perfect imitation of the other murders with his wife's help. How did they know all the details of those crimes?

The other victims had been down-and-out, all dabbling with drugs or alcohol and prostitution. It was the matchbox from the Cauldron that had led him here. And he'd found another one, too.

"What is it?" Jackson asked.

Jon looked over at him. "The serial killer is still out there."

"Yes," Rocky agreed. "And we still know nothing about him. Or her. Unless... Do you think Sandra was the murderer? We know where Westerly was. We don't know where she was during the other murders."

Jackson was studying Jon. "No," he said quietly. "Sandra had an agenda. She wanted to be the wife of a powerful man. Kylie threatened that, so Sandra wanted to rip her to pieces. But his political future was Sandra's fight. We can check the video we have of Westerly's speeches, but I think we'll find she's always nearby."

"She was with him at the time of one of the murders, at least," Jon said. "I watched those tapes several times to see if I could fathom anything at all from them. So the serial killer is out there."

"He could have moved on. He could be in Maine for all we know," Rocky said.

Jackson shook his head. "There is a connection here."

"The matchboxes," Jon reminded Rocky. "It was a match-box that brought me here from the start. The killer has been here, is probably from here. And he's either thrilled to see Westerly in jail and blamed for the crimes—"

"Or he's furious that another man is 'taking credit' for his work," Jackson finished.

Jon nodded. "Back to the drawing board." He picked up the notes he'd received from Angela: dossiers on Carl Fisher, Matt Hudson, and others they'd come to know who spent time at the Cauldron. Notes on those who ran history and ghost tours, notes on—

He stood suddenly. "There's someone out there I need to see. Now."

"Done!" Devin said. She stood from her computer, folding her hands together and stretching them over her head. She looked at Kylie, who had just finished talking to Corrine— for the third time that morning. "Sorry, just sent a manuscript off—under deadline! Were you able to have a decent night?"

"I had a great night," Kylie said, "and came out earlier to find coffee brewed and a breakfast bar. Talked to friends, showered forever. It was really good. You have an amazing water heater for being out here. And… I feel great."

"It's a good feeling when a case comes to a close," Devin agreed. "Well, part of this case came to a close. But you know you've done something that was important, that brings justice and might save other lives, and it feels as if something has been lifted. Anyway, we're supposed to meet in town for lunch."

"I know…" Kylie patted her shoulder bag. "And I'm all set."

Devin reached for her own bag, and Poe let out a squawk of protest. "Oh, we'll be back!" Devin told the bird. "Auntie Mina is here somewhere. You'll be fine!"

"Bye, Poe," Kylie said, touching the bird's cage. The raven

did seem to be a great pet—truly quite a character. She followed Devin as she set the alarm and they headed out the door.

"I hear you'll be heading back to New York, starting a new job on Monday," Devin said.

"It's a great job," Kylie said. "I love New York City. Of course, I love this place, too, and Boston and all. But I've always loved what I do." She hesitated. "Heading back into that job was the most important thing in the world to me until last Friday."

"You can't give up what you love. That's giving up yourself," Devin told her.

They slid into the car, and Kylie sighed. "I know."

"And I know Jon would never ask you to."

"I know that, too. And I would never ask him not to do what he does."

"Also, this case isn't really over."

"Because Westerly isn't the killer Jon came here to find," Kylie said.

Devin glanced at Kylie and smiled. "But I believe Jon plans on taking the weekend to go into New York with you. Rocky and I will stay here, Jackson will head back to headquarters for now, and…we'll keep at it. This man—or woman—will kill again."

"I could call Dr. Sayers," Kylie said.

"Pardon?"

"He's got some kind of talent. I saw a murder occurring, and then Jackson saw the cemetery where I'd be attacked. He either saw it as a suggestion or…saw into the future? I don't know how but—"

"You don't go anywhere alone."

"Oh, no, I wouldn't think of it. I'll bring Jon. He came with me when we went back to Dr. Sayers before."

"Good," Devin said determinedly. She fell silent until they pulled into the municipal lot on Essex Street and parked. Then she looked at Kylie and said, "I know your job is important to you, but for the time being, well, don't hang around alone at night. Be with people."

"My building has a doorman. You have to show ID to enter," Kylie assured her. "And I will leave work with other employees, I promise. I won't be alone." She smiled. "It's really not all that easy to be alone with millions of people."

Devin cast her head to the side doubtfully, arching a brow.

"I guess we can be alone anywhere," Kylie said. "But I promise you, I will be alert and aware and pay grave attention to everything around me."

"Sounds good. Let's head to Jon's office."

The streets were busy—tourists itching to get started on a long weekend had arrived. Some of the snatches of conversation Kylie and Devin heard had to do with how appalling it was that a man like Michael Westerly could have proven to be such a wretched monster.

Nearby, a mother grabbed her child's hand, begging her husband to head to the green so that he could just run for a bit.

They were almost at the door of Jon's office when Kylie's phone rang. She stopped walking, and Devin looked back at her.

"It's Dr. Sayers," Kylie said. "I'll be right in. I'm going to try to set something up, and yes, I swear I'll make Jon come, I'll make you all come to his office with me."

Devin nodded and stepped into the office.

"Dr. Sayers," Kylie said. "It's good to hear from you. I want to come in for another regression."

"That's great. I'm surprised, though. I heard they arrested Michael Westerly yesterday, that he and his wife were killers. I was calling to say goodbye and to see if you planned on being at the Cauldron any time before you left," he went on. "I was in late last night and Matt was telling me something about a letter and a grave he found that you might want to hear about. But if you want a regression, that's great—absolutely great."

"I was wondering if I could set up a time with you. Possibly tomorrow morning?"

"Oh, Kylie. You won't be able to make that."

As he spoke, she felt the knife, pressing hard into her back, nearly enough to pierce her flesh. She heard his voice, over the phone and at her ear.

At first, she was in disbelief.

But of course. She'd been with him when Annie had been killed, and he had been the one to hypnotize Jackson as well. Jackson hadn't given away a place, he had just said *green* and *blue*, but that didn't matter because they'd been trapping Westerly...

Not the serial killer.

Dr. Sayers pressed the knife closer. One little move on his part...

She was right in front of the office where Jon, Jackson, and Rocky were working; they'd be looking for her any second. "If you're going to stab me, you should do it right here, in front of witnesses."

"That wouldn't be right. You're going to walk to the cemetery."

"Why would I do that?"

"Because you see that cute little kid there? He must be about four. I'll slice his throat right in front of his parents. That child could die."

She saw the little boy the mom had wanted to take to run around Salem Common, a large grassy area nearby. They hadn't left yet, and the mom was being hard-pressed to keep up with the boy.

"It will be on you," Dr. Sayers whispered.

"No, it will be on you."

"But will you risk it?"

Only idiots walked away with a killer. But he would kill her here—or worse, kill her and the boy.

"Start walking, Kylie. It's really so beautiful, so poetic, so historic," Dr. Sayers said. "And think, it's you. You could live a dozen lives, more beautiful lives… I could even speak with you again, from the other side, of course."

Such a little distance. A few blocks. The little boy would be far enough away, and there might be a way to get far enough from Dr. Sayers. He wasn't wielding a gun; he had a knife.

They started to walk.

She swore inwardly. The kid and his parents were right beside them. It seemed they were heading to the wax museum. They'd be with them all the way past the cemetery.

"I'm walking," Kylie said, aware that Dr. Sayers laughed softly, watching the little boy. "And I'm so curious… I mean, you could get away with all this. Maybe they'll find doubt about Michael Westerly. He was an amazing copycat."

"He has power. And his wife has a mouth."

"Meaning?"

"I could always learn anything I wanted from her, just hanging out at the Cauldron. I made a point of us getting friendly and even inwardly laughed myself through a few therapy sessions with her. Socially, professionally, she talked only about her husband. She talked about her husband's hard stance on crime and how he had access to many police reports. I have to say, though, you did absolutely astound me. I have never seen anyone like you. And that will make this extra special."

"Because I'm not an easy victim, like those other poor women?" Kylie asked.

They passed the Peabody Essex Museum. They were so close to the cemetery.

"You're special. I may get some of that special from you!"

"You'll be caught. It's a busy day. People will see you."

"Oh, I judge my moment and my place. I'll just walk away, right down the street and around the corner to my office. Thank you for worrying about me, though."

They'd reached the cemetery. Others even came through the gate with them. People were milling about, but Sayers urged her toward the back of the cemetery while others were busy looking at the *Mayflower* grave or others of historic note.

"You're going to get caught," Kylie told him again.

"Like I told you, thank you for worrying. And you're right, I might get caught. But then, Westerly won't be able to steal the credit for what I did. This is all his fault, you know. He had the bloody nerve to kill here—in Salem! Oh, those foolish idiots. Sandra, so mean and jealous at heart. I saw enough of her, you know. She had a stone-cold heart. She couldn't have cared less if he slept with any woman out there, she just couldn't see her future ruined.

"Anyway, I'm losing myself here. I'm sorry to make you pay, but you must. Everything turned upside down here because of you. You just had to see that murder as it was happening. I'm still amazed how that happened. That bloody copycat. How dare he? How dare he imitate me, and in my own town? Atrocious. I'd rid the world of him, if I had half a chance. Pity I can't stab him to death! I would have done it if I got a chance—"

They were moving farther and farther back through the graveyard. She could scream…get cut to ribbons, but possibly survive. The little boy was at long last gone.

She jerked from Dr. Sayers, spinning to face him, just as they neared the far wall. Right where she had been with Matt, just days ago.

She smelled the earth of the cemetery, saw the blue of the sky. Saw the man before her, lifting the knife, ready to slit her throat.

And then, something like a sledgehammer slammed into

him. He let out a shocked croak, and the knife went flying, its razor-honed edge glinting as it soared away. In that second, time seemed to stand still, and the world was in slow motion.

Then she heard the thud near her; Dr. Sayers was on the ground.

Jon was on top of him and Rocky and Jackson were rushing up, ready to grab the doctor. Then Jon got up quickly, reaching for Kylie and pulling her close.

For a moment, he just held her. They were both aware of Dr. Sayers screaming they'd ruined history; how poetic and wonderfully brilliant it would have been for his last kill to have been in this cemetery. Kylie, the witness against one killer, bleeding into the grave of another.

She didn't know how long she and Jon stood there; she was trembling in his arms. It was a while.

Then he lifted her chin.

"I don't think we should go back for that regression I heard you were suggesting," he said.

She smiled and shook her head. "No. No more regressions," she agreed.

EPILOGUE

Corrine's wedding reception was on a rooftop in midtown, and the weather had held perfectly for it. Kylie, Jenny, and Nancy made gorgeous bridesmaids.

Jenny was the one to catch the bouquet, but Jon knew Kylie hadn't really tried. It was rather funny, he thought, that neither of them had tried. Corrine's new husband had managed to throw her garter over his head, where it landed directly on Jon.

The wedding was a good occasion. At one point in the evening, he found himself alone at the table with Corrine, Nancy, and Jenny. They were staring at him, as if demanding his intentions. It felt like an interrogation.

"Kylie told us she's moving," Corrine said.

"To be with you," Jenny added.

"And you're fine—a lovely man, truly," Nancy added quickly. "But..."

He leaned back, smiling. "Yes, we talked it through. Apparently, there was a young man who was neck and neck with Kylie for her job, and he still wanted it. All is copacetic there."

"But what will she do? Kylie's not the type to just sit home and grow daisies," Corrine said, a beautiful bride—a perfect mother hen.

"Well, here's the thing," Jon began. "Our boss is an amazing human being. He's already opened a historic theater. Now he's doing a museum on the history of Washington and the United States. None of us even knew about it until a week or so ago, and he might have been waiting to find someone like Kylie. She will not be growing daisies or cleaning house— well, she will be cleaning house, but so will I, we're both pretty good at it—but she'll be doing what she loves. She'll be very busy. She's also decided she wants to take self-defense classes and I don't even know what all else yet. I promise you, Kylie will remain her own woman."

Across the patio, he saw that Kylie had paused while chatting with Corrine's father and was watching them. A bit worriedly, perhaps. She excused herself and walked back toward the table.

"Well, all right, then," Corrine said. "You have our blessing!"

The girls rose as Kylie reached them.

They nodded to her and walked right on by. Kylie arched her brows at her friends, then sat next to Jon, taking his hand. "And that was…?"

He laughed. "A blessing!"

She smiled and slipped into his arms. "I've made my decision, you know."

He nodded and absently fingered the white garter that lay on the table. "Think this means something?" he asked her.

"If that's a proposal, it's lame."

"Oh, I thought this meant you had to ask me."

"Really?"

"We could ask each other," he suggested.

She smiled, stroking his chin. "I'm not a diamond girl—I

don't like expensive gifts. I like little gestures. Or maybe an incredible antique book."

"Is that a yes?"

"Did you ask?"

"I did."

"Then we need to decide how and when, what kind of a wedding... Maybe just a charming little chapel somewhere. But until then..."

Her voice trailed. He saw her eyes and the laughter in them. And the love and commitment.

"Until then?" he prompted.

"The reception is dying down. I think we should run away and enjoy our last days of living in wickedly wonderful sin."

"Are you asking me?"

"I am."

He stood and drew her to her feet and into his arms. "Then we need to see just how quickly we can say our goodbyes."

It was amazing just how quickly they could.

★ ★ ★ ★ ★